KILL FOR YOU

SYN BLACKROSE

KILL FOR YOU

THE KOSLOV BROTHERS
BOOK 2

SYN BLACKROSE

ISBN: 9798867244170

Book Cover by Hannah at HC Graphics

Edited by Christy Erasmus

Proofread by Jen Sharon Fiction Editing

Formatted by Unalive Promotions

Interior Art by Saralyn Everhart with Crafted Chaos

CONTENTS

BLURB

LEV

I don't do relationships. I don't do feelings. I don't do what's considered the norm.
I love hurting people. I love their screams. I love their begging. I live for it.
Until him. Aaron. He has his own version of crazy.
His crazy mixed with mine? That's a recipe for disaster.

AARON

My life is not my own. My stepbrother won't let me go. I have to end him.
I'm not normal. I fantasize about things I shouldn't and it's his fault. Lev.
Lev has been my obsession since we started working for the Kozlov brothers.
I need him. I want to be owned by him. I want to drown in his crazy until we are one.

To all those who need to escape real life for a few hours. I hope this unconventional love story helps.

"Believe nothing you hear, and only one half that you see."
— Edgar Allan Poe

TRIGGER WARNINGS

This book is only for mature readers only 18+

This is a dark romance, and whilst I'm aware peoples definition of dark varies, my stories will be on the high end of that scale. Main triggers are:

- TORTURE (GRAPHIC)
- SEXUAL ASSAULT (NO MINORS / NON BLOOD RELATIVE)
- HOMOPHOBIC LANGUAGE
- UNALIVING
- KIDNAPPING
- SOMNOPHILIA
- PHYSICAL ABUSE
- MENTAL ABUSE AND MANIPULATION
- COMPLEX MENTAL HEALTH ISSUES
- DEATH OF PARENT WHEN MC A CHILD
- VIOLENCE KINK
- CONTROLLING BEHAVIOR

Please remember this story is fiction, and not a guide to sex and lifestyle or morals. It is pure fantasy. Please do not read if that is something that upsets you. I do not condone any of the behavior in this book, again, it is purely fiction.

PLAYLIST

Spotify Link: https://sptfy.com/P4o9
Deftones - "Bored"
Slipknot - "Killpop"
Marilyn Manson - "Killing Strangers"
Korn - "Freak On a Leash"
Muse - "Save Me"
Alice In Chains - "Black Gives Way to blue (Piano Mix)"
Plaza - "Touch and Go"
The World Alive & Bad Omens - "One of Us"
Maneskin - "Honey (Are You Coming?)"
Placebo - "Every You Every Me"
Royal Blood - "Little Monster"
Royal Blood - "Triggers"
Alice In Chains - "Check My Brain"
Our Last Night & Sam Tinnesz - "Hell To Have You"
Sleep Token - "The Summoning"
Pearl Jam - "Alive"

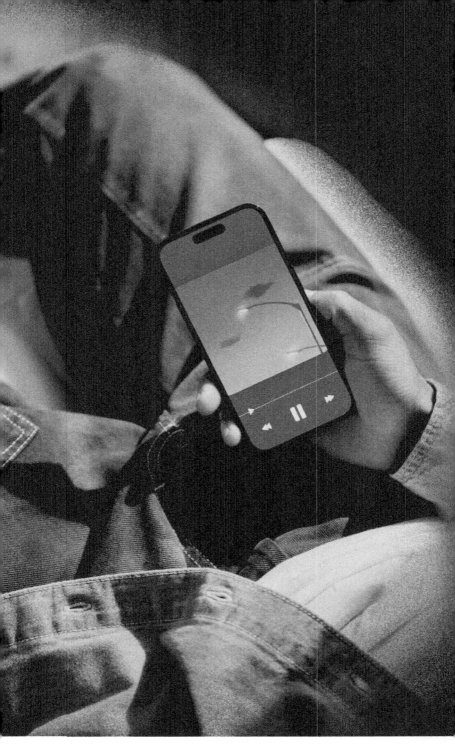

PROLOGUE
AARON

AARON - 12 YEARS OLD

"Throw it long, Aaron, like I taught you," Jake hollers to me. We are at our local park throwing ball after his school football practice. I love spending time with my big brother like this. My mom is not well, she is in the hospital with cancer. My dad said she will be going to heaven soon, but I don't want her to leave.

Jake keeps telling me everything will be fine, though, and I believe him. He is the best big brother. Well, technically, he's my stepbrother. My mom married his dad when I was six years old. I don't know my real daddy but Jake's dad is the best too. They both look out for me, take me to football games, and teach me how to be a man.

"Ready?" I shout to Jake.

He claps his hands. "Yeah, throw it."

I pull my right arm back like Jake taught me and throw the football as hard as I can towards him. It glides perfectly into the air as it curves its way towards him where he catches it easily.

"Yes! You did it, Aaron. Awesome!" he shouts and runs over to me with a big smile on his face. I think Jake is proud of me. He rubs my dark hair roughly. I giggle. "We'll make a football player of you yet," he says right when his cell phone rings. He looks at the screen before answering.

"Hey, Dad," he says. I can't hear what Daddy is saying, but Jake has gone still, frowning as he gazes at me. I frown in sync with him.

"Okay, see you soon," he says and ends the call. He crouches in front of me and even though he's only fifteen years old, he is a lot bigger than me.

"Dad is coming to pick us up. Mom needs to see us, she's not feeling great," he says softly, gripping my shoulder and gently squeezing it.

I relax and comfort blankets me. "We're going to the hospital?" I ask.

He nods. "Yeah. Come on, let's go wait for Dad in the parking lot."

He keeps his hand on my shoulder as we walk quietly to wait for Dad. A few minutes pass before his car turns up, and we both hop in quickly. Dad doesn't say anything, doesn't even say hello to me as we drive to the hospital. The silence in the car is so thick you could bite into it. Jake occasionally looks back at me from the passenger seat with a reassuring smile. All I do is focus on the streets that pass us by. Families outside enjoying the final hours of sunshine, smiles on their faces, and I hate them. I hate that they are living their lives, full of happiness while we are beginning to mourn the loss of ours. My hands fidget in my lap, unable to contain the need to move as I rub them together over and over until they are sore. The soreness distracts me from the heavy feeling in my stomach. Mom might be leaving me.

We arrive at the hospital, and after parking the car, we head to see my mom. As we ride the elevator, Jake grips my shoulder again. "It's going to be okay. I'll always look out for you, Aaron," he whispers.

I believe he'll look after me, but it doesn't stop my stomach from feeling nauseous like I've eaten too much candy on Halloween. Every year Mom would stop me as I shoveled gobs of candy into my mouth after trick-or-treating.

"Aaron," she'd said. "Any more candy and you will be sick, save some for later."

She always said it in a sweet teasing voice. Halloween was always our thing, eating candy on my bed while watching the neighborhood fireworks from my bedroom. I was always too scared to watch them outside, so instead she would cuddle up with me under a blanket and we'd enjoy them together.

Will we ever get to do that again? Will she help me make good decisions? Soothe me when I'm scared? She will get better, right? She has to get better.

We get off the elevator and head to my mom's room. I hate it here. I don't like the antiseptic smell, and I don't like how poorly she looks in her bed. She would feel better at home.

"My little boy," she says when she sees me. She doesn't look like Mom. She's thinner and paler than she was four days ago and her voice sounds weird, all hoarse and rough like she has a cold. I run to her side and she holds me in a hug.

"Mom, when are you coming home?" I ask and I can

feel tears in my eyes. Boys don't cry, my daddy says, but I can't help it.

"Aaron, don't fuss, she's not well," Daddy says.

"Leave him, Ron. He's fine," my mom says to my dad, who sits on the chair in the corner of the room. Jake is standing a little behind me. I can feel him, always there for me.

Aaron, you need to listen," Mom says, gasping. Then she gasps again as her breathing fails her, clamoring for the oxygen mask. She's able to fit it over her mouth in time to take a few slow breaths. I wait patiently for her words. I want every last one of her words.

"Aaron, I am going to be leaving for Heaven soon, do you remember?" she asks. I nod. "You have to promise to be a good boy, make Mom proud, keep going to school, and make the most of your life," she says, succumbing to another coughing fit.

"Always remember," she says once she catches her breath. "I love you so much and I will always be by your side, my beautiful little boy." A few tears leave her eyes along with a small choked sob. The dark circles under her exhausted eyes are as dark as bruises.

"I don't want you to go, I want to go with you." My stomach gets tighter, and the tears pour down my face. She's going to die, I don't want her to die.

"No, you have to stay here. Live a long, beautiful life, Aaron, and I will be waiting for you at the end. Be happy and that will make me happy," she whispers and grabs me in a tight hug. We are both crying, and I don't want to move. I sniff her neck and hair. She smells like my mom, flowers and hugs.

"I love you so much, my boy," she gasps.

"I love you too, Mom."

She gently pushes me back and strokes my cheek, before kissing my forehead.

"Jake, can you take Aaron outside for a while? I need to speak to your daddy," she says.

"Sure, come on, Aaron," Jake says, and he guides me by my shoulder away from my mom.

I end up crying all night, begging for my mom to come home. Daddy ignores me, but Jake crawls into bed behind me, stroking my hair.

"It's okay, I've got you now, baby brother," he says softly as I drift off, dreaming of Mom, hoping she feels better now that she is in Heaven.

CHAPTER 1
AARON

He's up to something, that dickhead brother of mine. Jake is the stupidest, most reckless person I know. He's a whirlwind of destruction when he wants what he wants. Like making me follow in his dumbass footsteps and be part of this hell.

Jake heads up a crew, dealing in drugs on a small scale for the Kozlov Brothers. These brothers are not just any brothers. They're sadistic. They're the "likes to remove parts of your body and drown you in acid" kind of psycho brothers. And I'm a little worried we may be on the receiving end of their reputation. Jake and the other guys are being shady as fuck. They don't really talk in front of me, and the group has become more disjointed, leaving me on the outside. I'm hardly even taking on deals anymore. Whatever they're doing, they're hiding it from me.

Currently, I am standing in the doorway to our living room, watching Shay huddled in the corner, whispering with Jake, who seems to be giving him instructions by the way his hands are aggressively gesticulating. Shay is another member of our crew and an okay guy. As usual, I walk in and the talking stops. Fuck this. I want answers.

"What do you want, Aaron?" Jake asks in the usual pissed off way he talks to me.

To think that once upon a time he was my wonderful big brother who was the focus of my world. That guy's nowhere to be found these days. In his place is a creepy and controlling asshole, who's just like his fuckhead father.

"Sorry, am I not allowed in our apartment?" I ask. I shouldn't push him, but I can't help it. Being left in the dark is fucking agitating. I put my hands in my pockets and play with the switchblade that I always keep on me. I tend to fidget with it a lot when I become anxious or nervous. Or when I get the urge to want to push it through Jake's dead heart.

"You wanna say that again?" he says as he moves closer to me. But I don't respond, which immediately defuses the situation.

"Didn't think so. You need to stay here tonight. Tommy and I have business across town and Shay has to go on a deal," he says.

"Should Shay be going on his own?" I ask. We never go solo.

"Did I ask for your fucking opinion?" Jake shouts. Wow, defensive. Another red flag that something is going on.

Given, I'm not the brightest person in the world with my screwed-up brain, I get why Jake might not see fit to tell me. I can't concentrate for shit, and with how many voices vie for my attention, I'm definitely unhinged.

"Whatever," I say, heading back to my room with the

decision made. Today, it's Crazy's turn. That voice has come up with the grand idea to follow Shay.

Later that evening, Jake and Tommy leave to do whatever their business is, which means I am here alone with Shay. I remain in my room to avoid being obvious. Shay's bedroom is next to mine and the walls are thin, so it will be easy to tell when he leaves.

I sit on my bed, dressed head to toe in black. That's what you wear when you stalk, right?

I play with my switchblade and I get lost in thought, imagining the blade cutting skin as I rub the tip up and down my palm. I don't necessarily like hurting people myself, but I do enjoy watching. I think it stems from childhood, when Jake used to stick up for me against bullies in high school. I'd be completely mesmerized while he either beat them to a pulp or threatened them to within an inch of their lives. It gave me a thrill, especially knowing I was the cause of it. The fear and begging in their voices made my dick hard. I loved seeing them so helpless. As time has gone on, though, and my relationship with my stepbrother and stepfather is in tatters, my tastes have gotten more hardcore.

After spending years being verbally and physically hurt by my supposed family after Mom died, my desire for violence increased. I feel like I'm in control. A control I never had over my own decisions or body as I grew up. It's definitely screwed up, but it's there, and my god is it there imagining Jake being on the end of that violence. I could groan at the intoxicating thoughts of watching Jake be cut open, bled out, watching the pain etched on his face twist and writhe.

Out of everyone in my life, Jake is the only one that

holds any power over me. The only one who summons the young boy who I try to keep locked in my head. His voice overpowers the other's when Jake is around. I fucking hate it.

"You better fucking hide, you little cunt. I told you I didn't want you hanging with Sam after school. You should've come home when I told you to."

The young boy in my head runs with fear-laced adrenaline pumping through his body, knowing that running's all he can do. He can't hide.

We could never hide. Only submit.

"P-Please, Jake. Please, I'm sorry."

"Not yet, but you're gonna be. What did I tell you about running from me? You obey me and you fucking come when I call you."

That's the problem. That young boy comes when he's called, powerless to do anything against Jake, too paralyzed with fear. Meanwhile, I want to stab Jake in his cold dark heart. If he still has one.

I hear Shay's bedroom door open and softly close. He's trying to be discreet, but you can hear everything in this apartment. I lean against the door, listening closely for the familiar sound of the front door shutting. Putting my blade and phone in my pocket, it's time to go.

Luckily it's winter, the dark of night appears sooner, enabling me to stick to the shadows. I'm freezing my ass off, but I follow Shay two blocks away from our suburban part of town to a more risky area. Shit, this is Santini turf. Their bar "The Limes" is lit up at the end of the next street. I have a bad feeling about this.

Because I have been focusing on my surroundings, I've lost sight of Shay. *Shit Aaron, not the best time to get distracted.* I hastily walk down the street. There are a few people milling around and I scan the area, hoping to get sight of Shay.

As I come to the end of the street, out of the corner of my eye, I notice Shay standing at the end of an alleyway with two other guys, but I can't see what they are doing. Is he dealing on Santini turf?

"Hey! Hey you!" a guy shouts from behind me. As I look over my shoulder, I recognize one of the guys as a Santini grunt. Fuck. The guy and his friend run towards me, and I think I'm about to die, but then a hand grabs my arm.

"What the fuck are you doing here, Aaron?" Shay hisses at me.

"We need to go," I say. "We're about to have company."

But I'm too late.

One of them grabs Shay, and I don't know what to do.

"Now this is a fucking surprise. Just wait until the boss sees this. Kozlov pussies out to start a war." The large brown-haired muscle man laughs with the equally large blond next to him. Shit.

"Look, we are just leaving," Shay says, trying to calm the situation.

The brown-haired guy punches him across the face. I jump forward, clawing at him, trying to get him off Shay but the blond one pulls me back and backhands me across the face. I fall to the ground, disoriented. I try to stand, only to hear the grunts and painful cries from Shay. The two guys are beating the shit out of him, I need to act fast otherwise they're gonna kill him.

Instinct has me grabbing my switchblade and heading

towards the brown-haired guy who sees me approach. I duck as he takes a swing at me, and jab my blade upwards above his ribcage. Time stops as a lightning sensation runs up my arm at the feel of my blade cutting into skin and flesh. It's magical. I'm the one with the power, and it makes my chest fill with confidence, pushed out and proud like a peacock. I want to revel in the feeling. Show off the fact that I owned this fucker. He staggers back as I pull my blade from his torso.

Blood gushes out, and he collapses to the ground, going pale and wheezing. His warm blood coats my hand and I can't stop staring at it. A smile spreads across my face. Fuck, I'm dizzy with the electrical surge that has bolted through me, making me feel like I'm levitating above the asshole who is bleeding like a burst pipe. I quietly hope the bastard dies.

Blond guy is now distracted, having run to check on his friend. I bend down and lift Shay who's not in a good way. Dammit. I force him up, but he can hardly stand straight. I don't have a choice, we need to get out of here before more guys turn up. I try to multitask by getting out my phone and calling Jake while pulling along a half conscious Shay in my arms, who is trying so hard to move as quick as he can.

"What?" Jake answers.

"Help. Shay and I have been jumped by some of Santini's guys. We are a block away from Grinston patch where The Limes Bar is. Not sure we can make it," I puff out, succumbing to the weight of Shay. We're not going to make it.

"You fucking idiots. On our way, we were nearly home," he says.

Thank god, that means he's not far away. My eyes are frantic as I keep checking around us for any signs of the Santinis approaching, but no more than five minutes later, Jake's truck approaches and rolls to a stop. He gets out and grabs Shay from the other side, helping him into the back of his truck.

Hearing a commotion of shouts down the street, we see the Santini crew members heading our way.

"Fuck! Tommy, get us out of here," Jake shouts as he jumps back into the truck.

I get in next to Shay as Tommy pulls away. Shit that was close. But is it wrong to admit it was fun too?

We speed off down the dark streets, heading towards the hospital. Shay is drifting in and out of consciousness, bleeding around his mouth and gripping onto his ribs tightly. His eyes are beginning to swell.

"What the fuck were you doing, Aaron?" Jake shouts at me. He turns his head to face me in the backseat, eyes full of hate and accusations. At first I don't answer, his rage is palpable and I can feel myself pulling back, wanting to avoid his attention.

Don't let him get us. Do what he wants. It'll be okay.

The young boy is grappling with anxiety in my head, wanting to protect us. I'm too distracted by the voice to answer.

"Do I need to break you in again, baby brother?" Jake asks with a predatory snarl in his voice. With those words, the young boy in me succumbs. I can't resist it. I become submissive to Jake's demand and fold in on myself.

The car is quiet but charged with an aggressive energy that you could reach out and touch. I'm fixed to the spot, I can't respond or move.

Jake's victorious chuckle fills the car. "Thought as much, now keep your mouth shut until I say otherwise. We will talk about this later," he says, turning back to face the front of the car. I remain silent for the rest of the journey.

CHAPTER 2
LEV

Removing the used condom from my dick, I stand from the bed and tie it off, throwing it into the trashcan that's on the floor. Movement behind me has me turning around, looking at the hot as fuck couple sprawled out on top of the white sheets, both their tight bodies covered in sweat, their deliciously naked skin glowing under the dim night light. It was a good time.

"You not gonna stay, Lev?" the woman purrs at me, her long red hair clinging to her skin and her blue eyes hazed over in lustful exhaustion. Not sure of her name or her boyfriend's name, but it's of no consequence. I don't do repeats.

"Nah, got shit to do. But thanks for the fun." I smile and walk over giving her a chaste kiss on the lips. I then lean over her hot as fuck boyfriend who is laying on his stomach. He has the perfect plump ass and a thick mop of curly brown hair. He grabs the back of my head, drawing me into a kiss that quickly becomes heated, and his arms link around my neck, trying to pull me back down into bed. Such a greedy hole.

I smack his ass and pull away. He lets out a sigh of disappointment, but I continue putting my clothes on as quickly as possible so I can get out of here. This always happens. As soon as I fuck, I'm immediately disinterested and turn off mentally, wanting to find that thrill in a new body. I've never had a preference, man or woman–couldn't give a shit–as long as it's a warm body that I can lose myself in for a while.

Giving one last lingering look over the couple who look like they are about to pass out, I turn and walk out of the door. I'm so tired right now and need my bed. I've been burning the midnight oil for too long now, working longer hours at the clubs, setting up new contracts for dealing, and I am starting to get burnout. Especially with my nearly daily sexcapades. I'm surprised I can cognitively function. I can't give up sex, though. It's the only thing that settles me and helps me sleep. Well, it's either sex or torturing someone, and I haven't done much of the latter recently.

I make my way down the apartment complex stairs and leave into the night. It's cold as fuck now that we are entering winter, but I have always preferred the cold. I love the raw edge of the icy chill that cuts across my skin like a sharp razor. It reminds me I am alive, keeping all my senses alert.

I get into my car and make my way home. I notice it's three am so at least I'll avoid the questions from Seb. Since he and my big brother Dima have been together, I have become somewhat tolerant of Seb. It helps us being close in age, him twenty-six and me twenty-seven. I don't want to kill him so that's a positive for him, and he makes my big brother happy, which is a fucking miracle in itself. But Seb loves to stick his beak into my business, especially when it comes to who I'm screwing. He tries to hide his interest but he is a nosy asshole who loves gossip.

On the drive home, I keep the window slightly open, hoping the ice-cold air will keep me awake long enough to get home. It seems to take forever to drive fifteen minutes, but I finally start to relax as I turn into our long driveway. I can hear my bed scream for me. Christ, when did I become such an old man?

Making my way into our palatial home which is on the far edge of town, I drag my ass down the lavish hallways. I'm not very bothered by "things", but Dima did a great job decorating here. It's all black and white marble with hints of red painted on any bare walls. It suits us. The only part I had any involvement in was the building of our "holding pen" down in the basement. Let's just say it's not a place you want to be taken when visiting. I head down a corridor, straight toward my room, which is on the ground floor to keep away from the loud fuckers upstairs. Seb is noisy as hell, and the longer he has lived here, the less he hides it. It doesn't bother me, quite the opposite, I always get a hard on when hearing them screwing, but I want to keep my head on my shoulders. D would fuck me up if he knew how I reacted. Well, he would try.

Sticky and gross, I put my phone on charge beside my bed and head straight for the shower. It takes a lot of energy to screw two eager lovers at the same time, but it's a great way to get in that cardio and burn off that energy. I'm a big guy, all muscle and harsh edges. I'm often told how sadistic I look with my cruel-looking hawk green eyes, body inked with tattoos, close-cut beard, sharp military haircut, and constant pissed off expression, but it always seems to work to get me laid. That and putting the fear of god in any of the assholes I play with. Taking people apart and making them beg for mercy is the biggest high I get in my life. The power is addictive, and it feeds the bloodthirst I have developed since my first kill as a teenager. Dima and I got into the drug trade young, our parents were not exactly caring, so we made our own way in life. Might not be the best way, but we have created a great life for ourselves.

Stepping under the hot stream of water, I let out a long exhale, feeling my muscles relax and the call of sleep taking over my body. Sex and death are my vices, and if I could have both together that would be pretty fucking perfect. Most people want to be traditional, settle down, maybe have kids and pets. Whereas I sometimes wonder what it would be like to have someone who enjoys playing too, killing and fucking happily ever after. That's not in the cards for me though, I'm not built that way like Dima is. I don't desire love or normalcy and that one special person in my life. I would like to share my two passions, but I never want my life to be about someone else. That sounds horrific. Dima has that spot of my devotion and that's challenging enough as it is, there isn't more to go around.

I get out of the shower, quickly towel dry myself off, and walk into my attached bedroom, sliding my naked ass under the bed covers. It's a large bedroom, but again, it's basic. I'm not interested in materialistic things. I just have my ridiculously large bed covered in black sheets, a couple of basic side tables, and two chairs with a table in the corner because Dima insisted I had to fill the space.

My phone that's been charging on my bedside table goes off, and I check to see who it could be at this time of morning. Lifting the phone, I see Jules' name. Jules is our right-hand guy. We run a small cartel, dealing with the drug trade in our city, using the two clubs my brother and I own, Starlight, a burlesque slash cabaret club, and Desire, our strip joint, to push the money through until it comes out clean. Grinston is a decent-sized city on the East Coast and we tend to be left alone with plenty of cops in our pockets to make our lives more than comfortable.

"This better be important, Jules," I growl into the phone as I sit upright and try to focus. I'm on the verge of passing out now, the struggle to keep my eyes open is real. It feels like heavy weights have been attached to my eyelids.

"Well I wouldn't call if it wasn't, dickhead. We gotta problem. One of our guys was caught in another territory, dealing, and is in the hospital after being fucked up. I got the police handled, but it was on the Santini turf, and they weren't happy. They want to meet tomorrow, actually that's this morning now, with you and Dima, otherwise they are threatening a war," he says. I can hear traffic and sirens in the background, he must be at the hospital.

With frustration filling my body, I collapse back onto the bed. Closing my eyes and rubbing my hand roughly over my face, the urge to hurt something or someone is building. This is the last thing we need right now.

"Fine. What time and where?"

"Nine-thirty am at The Lounge on the outskirts of town, they want it neutral. Also, I should mention, one of our boys stabbed one of their guys in the exchange."

Fucking hell, that's only six hours away, and I haven't slept yet. I grind my jaw. It's like babysitting fucking toddlers.

"Did he kill him?" I ask as an afterthought.

"No, but he punctured his lung. He will be in the hospital for a while."

Well that's something at least. "Okay, be ready to go with us in the morning. I want whoever the fucker is from Jake's men that got all stabby, brought to Desire tonight." My eyes start to close as I lose the battle to stay conscious. Christ, I've gotta be up again in four hours.

Jules' chuckle echoes down the phone. "You got it Lev, now get some sleep and I'll see you in a few hours."

He disconnects the call before I drift off, dreaming of all the ways I can teach a lesson to whoever this stabby prick is who has made more work for me.

CHAPTER 3
AARON

"Always the fuck up, Aaron, I don't know why I keep your sorry ass around, you little cunt," Jake scolds me.

Tommy, another crew member and kiss ass to my stepbrother stands off to the side, smug as hell smile on his face as Jake lays into me.

We only got home from the hospital five minutes ago after being there all last night and most of today with Shay. I barely got through the door before Jake started in on me.

My cheek is on fire after the punch Jake just landed on my face. The bastard is strong and cruel, but I'm used to his hits. It's been happening for years. I'm only twenty-four, and I lost count at eighteen. I can't describe in words how much I hate him, how much I hate everything about him, his crew, and my useless as fuck stepfather who made us this way. My head hurts from the battle between which voice in my head will win as I sit here on my knees, being berated by the person I detest most in life. Jake took away any chance of normalcy I could have had and used his manipulative ways to keep me around.

"I was only trying to help, Jake. They were going to kill Shay," I argue.

Shay's the only one in the group I would consider close to a friend, even though that word is a stretch. He's the only one who tolerates my weird ways and is nice to me. I don't regret stabbing the asshole who was beating on him, in fact, I enjoyed it, but that's a piece of information I keep to myself. I know I would enjoy it even more if it was my dearest stepbrother on the end of the blade.

A shadow casts over the top of me, and I look up to see an angry Jake looking down on me like I'm a bug on his shoe, an irritant. We are such a contrast to each other, mirror images of our biological parents. While I have black shaggy hair, tan skin, and brown eyes like my mom, he has golden blond hair that's always in a messy man bun with blue eyes and fair skin like his evil father. We only match on height at six feet a piece but where he is muscular, I'm more like a lean baseball player. I'm still strong and well-defined.

He continues to stare down at me, and while I know he hates me, there has always been another feeling lurking beneath the surface. It's the way he looks at me, the way I catch his gaze when it lingers on me for too long, and it sets my body cringing. My insides curl in disgust. I was sixteen when things changed between us. He was too interested in me, and it didn't help that Jake's dad encouraged him to mold me to be like them, unfeeling and living a shitty dead-end life of drug dealing and fucking up anyone who got in our way. I've lived in hell. Old memories from years ago try to replay like a horrific movie.

"It's about time you started fucking around with girls, boy. Don't want folk thinking you're a fag. You need to start being

like Jake, acting like a real man instead of a pussy. Your mom was always too soft on ya."

Shut up! Shut up!

I manage to ward off the memories of my useless step-dad. Now just to deal with his younger carbon copy of a dickhead son.

"You shouldn't have even been there. Shay can handle himself, and now because of you we have to meet with the Kozlovs tonight."

He crouches in front of me, grabbing onto my hair so tightly I wince, pulling my head back so he can look me in the face.

"You will take the blame for this, baby brother. You will tell them you didn't know you were on their turf and that it was a mistake. I will not have this crew torn apart and end up buried underground because of you and your curiosity. Do you understand?"

I hate it when he calls me baby brother. It's a trigger that puts me in a trance. It flicks a switch in my head, and I'm that eighteen year old again, afraid. It sounds fucking tragic, never failing to send me into a frenzied panic as I fight to regain control of my mind. But he's asking me to take the blame and of course I understand that it falls to me. Always falls to me. I have a strong suspicion the dick-head is up to something that will get him into deep trouble with the Kozlovs. I'm not sure what the actual plan is, he doesn't share much with me, but I've seen the signs. He's more on edge nowadays, having secret conversations with other crew members that I'm never part of. To be honest, that's part of the reason I followed Shay, to see what the hell is going on. I'm involved whether I know the plan or not, and I would be guilty by association.

Deciding that I need to be compliant to diffuse this

situation, I agree. It goes against every part of me to submit to my stepbrother, but for me to end him, I need to remain close. I want him dead. I've been planning it in my mind for years but with everything going on right now, this might just be the right time. There are so many other factors his death could be blamed on. Mainly the Kozlovs taking him out.

"Yes, Jake. I understand," I whisper, cowing under his sharp gaze. Vulnerability is the only thing that pacifies him, and it's not hard to conjure when I'm under the influence of his commanding tone. Certain words and phrases revert me back to the scared young man who wished someone would save me. They push the crazed part of me that wants to take him apart to the back of my mind.

He knows it, too. It took him years to turn me into the fucked up mess that I am. I war with the conflicting voices daily and exhaustion wears me down, overwhelming me. In those moments, I wish he'd just end me.

Pulling away from me, Jake stands to walk away. My hand twitches with the urge to pull out my switchblade and stab him in the back. Or even better, to cut his throat slowly and listen as he gurgles his last wet breaths while looking at me, realizing it was me that ended him, that I'll live on without his suffocating presence. My cock jolts, excited at the thought. My cock is as fucked up as my head.

"Good, now get yourself cleaned up. Lev has asked to see you. I am warning you, do not fuck this up. You won't like the consequences," he says, and off out the door he goes, not even looking back.

Wait, did he say Lev?

The last few threat-filled minutes dissipate as that one

name sends my stomach aflutter. Lev. Hot, sexy, and murdering psychotic Lev.

I've been fantasizing over him since I first laid eyes on him months ago. That guy ticks all my boxes, and I don't know if I can contain myself. What will he do? I love the idea of him threatening me, but, to be honest, I don't want him to hurt me. Not my thing. But I would enjoy watching him hurt others.

Last month I saw him remove a guy's teeth with pliers, and it was the hottest thing I've ever seen. I came hard that night after replaying the scene over in my head.

My brain shifts so rapidly from one feeling to another, it gives me whiplash. Sometimes, I can't keep up. I was diagnosed with ADHD when Mom was still around.

"All that kid needs is a firm hand, Marie," my stepdad argued, thinking it was a bullshit diagnosis. And boy was he determined to give it to me. "I'll teach him how to focus."

After my mom died, that's when things really turned to shit. At first I thought it was grief, but the hurtful sting of rejection dominated the interactions I had with my stepdad until it was undeniable. I'd looked up to my step-dad–who I'd considered my dad–and Jake, but that worship died along with Mom.

Poor Mom. Bet he was shit to her too. No, I know he was shit to her. I was too young to understand her tired eyes or why her fierce spirit faded until it was a timid ghost of what it once was, but I get it now. I wish I'd looked harder. Maybe I could have done something. Convinced her to leave that fucking bastard who never should have had kids.

At least he's been mentally castrated. A stroke from too much booze and drugs left him unable to care for himself and he's holed up in a care home, thankfully in another state. That's called karma, motherfucker. After years of verbal and physical abuse, I'm happy for him to rot there.

Realizing I am still kneeling on this shitty floor, I pull myself onto my feet. I share this apartment with Jake and two other guys from the crew, one being Shay and the other Tommy. Speaking of Tommy, I'd forgotten he was in the room.

"He's too soft on ya, fuckface. It's about time he gave ya a proper beatin' after fuckin' this up for us," he sneers, walking over and getting into my face.

This asshole has no idea about the beatings I've endured, but he can think what he thinks. I'll destroy him too and enjoy every second of it.

"Fuck off, Tommy. Jake isn't here to see you kiss ass," I clap back at him, ramming into his shoulder as I pass by. He doesn't intimidate me at all.

Unfortunately, I don't get far. It doesn't take much to piss him off. He grips me by the arm, pulling me towards him.

"Who do ya think you are talking to like that, you little freak?" Spittle flies from his mouth. "You're nothin' and no one. Not even your brother or daddy care about you. Hell, Jake is even making you take the blame and deal with the wrath of Lev, clear sign you mean nothin' to him." He smiles like it's a victory, as if he's telling me something I don't already know, but he's in denial. He is such a prick. I want to laugh hysterically at the fucking stupidity. He hates me because he knows my stepbrother has a fucking weird and disgusting obsession with me and he's jealous. It's so fucking obvious that Tommy wants him, but Jake isn't interested. Jake might be different with me, but he's a homophobic asshole who would probably shoot Tommy in the head if he knew that Tommy wanted him. I remember the homophobic comments and slurs when I was younger that Jake and his dad used to use, thinking it made them tough. At least I knew how they felt. After realizing I was gay, I knew my sexuality had to be locked in a steel closet.

I push him back with both hands, and that takes him by surprise. I get great pleasure in knowing how to get him where it hurts.

"And how does it feel knowing that Jake would rather fuck his own brother than you? Hmm? Now I'd say that's a bigger blow. Even his family is a more attractive option than a run through piece of shit like you."

Jake's cruel possessiveness of me is obvious and in these close confines, the underlying tone of it is clear as day. Instead of it repelling Tommy, he's still set on my stepbrother. Tommy is all mouth and only preys on those he thinks he can overpower. With his bald head, heavily pierced ears, and tattoos of fake tears on his face, he tries to convey hardass, but really he's just the standard shit-head bully.

His face pales. I beam. I've said those secret words out loud and it feels amazing. I don't normally answer back or defend myself, but I've reached my breaking point with this asshole. I have to keep strong. The boy without hope or the strength to fight needs to stay buried.

"Open up, baby brother."

The nausea builds. *Not now, Aaron.*

I force my mind to block out that time of my life. Fuck, I wish I could burn the parts of my brain that store that shit. I want it forever locked away, but sometimes those memories force their way to the surface like a tsunami.

Tommy squints those dull and lifeless brown eyes at me. I know he's trying to think of a retort, but I'm bored with this.

31

"Now, if you don't mind, I have to go meet Lev, unless you want to tell Jake you stopped me from going because of your pussy jealous ways?"

He says nothing as I walk away. My overactive brain yet again takes a leap and shifts a gear. I can't focus too long on one thing and anger has quickly been replaced with excitement. It builds like a tidal wave. I'm going to have all of Lev's attention.

I can't help the smile on my face as I shower and daydream. What will it be like to be face to face with the man of my darkest fantasies?

After I am all clean, I stand in front of my closet, trying to decide what to wear like this is some kind of date. Fucking ridiculous. Making my choice, I change into my ripped black jeans and a plain black tee. I look in the mirror and put my fingers through my thick shaggy black hair and decide I'm good to go. Grabbing my thick winter coat, I head out the door.

CHAPTER 4
LEV

W hat a shitshow of a day and it's still not
fucking ended. This morning's meeting with
the Santinis was tense at best. Luckily with
Dima's charm, he convinced them that this situation
hadn't been given the go ahead and would be dealt with in
house. He added a little compensation on the side to
sweeten the deal. Hopefully this will be the last we hear
from them.

Something isn't sitting right with me. Call it gut
instinct, but I think this crew intentionally sold in their
territory. Jake's a slimy fuck, but he has always just done
his job, and we haven't had issues before since he keeps
his crew in check. However, my spidey senses are telling
me I may need to cut the fucker open to find out his
secrets. There is only one punishment for betrayal in this
family and it's death…a very slow and painful one, which
I am only too happy to be part of.

Hopefully, after I deal with his dickface brother who is
coming here tonight, I can get a drink, find a hot body for
an hour, then pass the fuck out. I want this day over with.

After hardly any sleep last night, I am running on empty and this mess with the Santinis has made it fucking worse.

I'm sitting in my office here at Desire waiting for...I think his name is Aaron? Andy? I don't fucking know. I know he exists, but I don't remember all the guys in each crew. We only deal with the heads. Maybe I should break him apart too, find out what his brother is planning, or maybe he is a part of it?

As I mull over my options, the door opens and in walks Jules, followed by who I presume to be Aaron or Andy. Huh. How have I not noticed this guy before? He is the kind of sexy ass man that would take my interest in any other setting. He has that rock band look going on but his eyes make him look innocent. Now I'm wide awake, watching this hot fucker stride in. It is also disappointing. Under different circumstances, I would definitely like to have him panting my name, but work is work.

"Lev, this is Aaron, the dick that stabbed one of Santini's guys," Jules states, pushing Aaron into the chair across from me. Interesting. He isn't scared or even intimidated by me. He actually looks like he has met his hero with how bright his eyes look, that one celebrity you'd kill to meet, which is weird as hell but arousing at the same time. He has shaggy black hair, smooth skin as if he hasn't gone past puberty yet and can't grow any facial hair, large brown Bambi-like doe eyes, and a cute little eyebrow piercing above his left eye. I don't think he has blinked yet, and I am dumbfounded. I'm used to fear or panic when anyone is brought to me like this. Maybe he's unaware of my reputation?

"Uh, boss, do you need me for anything?"

Jules' question snaps me out of the trance I have going on with the hottie, I must have zoned out.

"No, Jules, I got this. Just wait outside."

He nods in return and leaves, closing the door behind him.

I lean back in my leather chair, creating the atmosphere of "relax and no one will hurt you." This one is different or maybe from another planet with how eager he is to be here. He is all but bouncing in his seat.

"So, you wanna tell me what the fuck happened last night?"

I am surprised by the big smile that crosses his face. What the fuck is this guy smiling at? Have I unintentionally invited the Joker into my office? His manic smile is giving me those creepy ass vibes and he still hasn't answered.

"What the fuck you smiling about?" I bark as I stand and move around to the front of my desk, leaning against it directly in front of where Aaron is sitting. He's forced to crane his neck back and look at me. His smile disappears and I realize he may not have intended to have done it in the first place. Okay, this guy is weird as hell.

"Sorry, I didn't mean to do it, it's just, sitting here talking to you feels like a dream."

I am so damn confused now. Has this guy lost his mind? What the hell is he talking about? Jesus Christ, I must be tired, this conversation is the most bizarre moment I have ever been in.

"I don't know what the fuck you mean by that, but can you answer the damn question? Tell me what happened last night, and it would be wise not to lie to me."

"Sorry, okay, well, Shay and I went to meet a contact, but one of the Santini crew pulled up on the street to stop us. That's when shit got outta hand. Shay was being attacked, so I stabbed the guy. It was only a scratch."

He speaks so quickly that it takes a second for my head to compute what he said. I raise my eyebrow. "Only a scratch? You punctured his lung, you dumb shit. What is wrong with you?"

He shrugs and smiles coyly. This is getting stranger the longer this meeting goes on, and I have reached my limit of human interaction for the day. Not even getting laid is gonna help now. He is still staring at me, smiling, and it's pissing me off.

My patience snaps. I grab the collar of his T-shirt and pull him upright. We are about the same height, but I am much much bigger. Christ, he's pliant, which only increases my confusion.

"Was it on your brother's orders?" I snarl, our noses nearly touching. His eyes have gone all shiny and hooded. Is he high?

"*Step* brother, and no, it was my idea. Shay came to protect me. I wanted to prove to Jake that I can deal on my own, but I didn't realize where the boundary of our turf was until it was too late and Shay jumped in, that's when it all kicked off."

I push him back down into his seat and walk back around the desk to sit across from him. I place my hands on the flat surface and stare into those doe eyes of his.

"We both know that's bullshit. I've been doing this long enough to know when I'm being lied to, but I'll play along. Here's the deal. You get me proof of what Jake is up to and who else is involved, and you are off the hook. I want to know who he is in contact with outside our guys."

"But what if I don't do it?" he asks.

So naive.

"I will cut your fucking tongue out and kill everything you love." I mean every word.

His eyes widen. He knows I ain't playing. Slowly, he nods with a hesitant, "Okay," coming from those biteable lips. Has he got a multiple personality disorder? He has gone from a weird smiley guy who isn't affected by anything, to timid and shy. The shift is so sudden that it's jarring. I get up and move to the door and as I open it, Jules walks in. Okay, meeting is over.

"Take him home and make sure he has a burner with my number on it. Don't mention this to anyone else," I tell Jules.

"Got it. Come on, shithead, let's get you home," Jules says, walking towards the door.

Aaron stands to follow but stops in front of me, nibbling at his lower lip as if he is trying to control himself from speaking. Shocker, it doesn't work.

"It was great meeting you, Lev." My name is a rumbling purr, an octave deeper than his usual voice and intense arousal rolls over my skin. Then off he goes after Jules, severing the moment and leaving my brain in the confused fog he pulled it into.

What the fuck is going on today? Have I slipped into another timeline, or did that interaction actually happen?

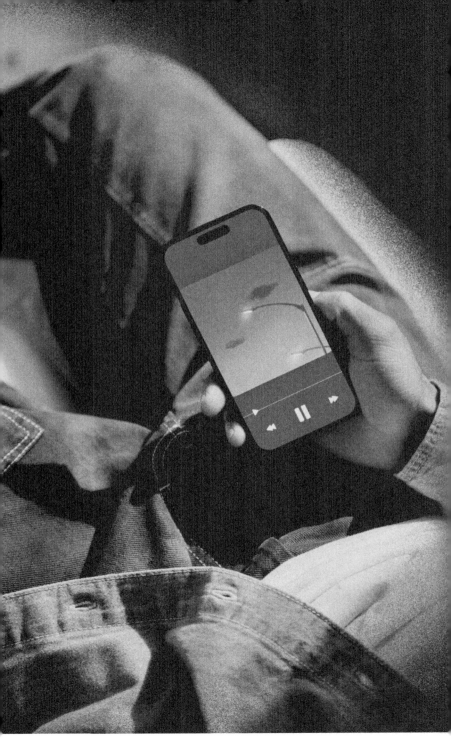

CHAPTER 5
AARON

L eaving Desire, we step into the cold dark night and Jules guides me to his car. After I strap myself into the front passenger seat, he starts to drive. We sit in silence for a few moments until I feel something hard thrown into my lap. It's a phone.

"Here's your burner with Lev's number on it. Do not share it if you want to live, Aaron. Don't cross him, trust me...whatever you think your brother is capable of, Lev is so much worse."

"Got it. Is Lev single?"

Jules side-eyes me as he continues to drive with a frown etched onto his forehead as if he's trying to figure out if I'm some kind of alien that has dropped out of the sky. To be honest, most people in my life look at me that way, but I can't help it. Maybe that's why my stepbrother and stepfather treat me the way they do.

"Is something wrong with your brain, Aaron? After all that's been discussed, that's your question?"

"Uhhh, yeah?"

Jules shakes his head. "Lev is forever single. Doesn't do

relationships or seconds so get that idea out of your head if you know what's good for you."

Yeah, I doubt that will happen. "Okay, but he is hot, though." I continue to stare out the window, watching the dark streets pass by one after the other.

The car ride remains silent until Jules pulls up at the end of my street, out of view from my apartment building. He turns to face me. He's a beast of a guy and nearly takes up the entire front of the car. His ice-blue eyes pin me to the spot.

"Get the fuck out of the car, Aaron."

I sigh. I fucked up again, I shouldn't be allowed to talk to people, clearly. I slam the car door, and Jules speeds off into the night. It's fucking freezing. I hug myself as I slowly jog towards my building, dreading what kind of welcome party I'll get from Jake. I pray he isn't home.

My prayers didn't work, Jake's sitting in the living room waiting for me with narrowed eyes as if he knows what I've been asked to do.

"You do what I told ya?"

Putting my mask of indifference in place, I respond back as cool as I can.

"Yep. Thinks it was all me. Just scolded and threatened me. No biggie."

"Good, and keep it that way. I'm keeping you off deals for the next month until you learn how to fucking behave. I won't have you ruin this for us."

Ruin what, though? I want to ask, but it's not worth the hassle. I really need to work out how to handle this. I've been struggling to see what he's planning. You'd think living with him full time, I would at least have some knowledge, but he's too clever to slip up in front of me and it's not like the other two will volunteer the information.

He walks past me to grab his coat before heading towards the door.

"Where are you going?" I ask.

"Going back to see Shay. He called and they're discharging him hopefully tomorrow, no thanks to you."

There is nothing I can say to that. The door slams as he leaves, putting a violent ending to that conversation. It's my fault, I suppose. I shouldn't have followed Shay, but I did it with the right intentions.

It was a good thing too, or I wouldn't have had this opportunity to find out what my stepbrother's true intentions are. He would have left me out of this mystery plan, one that would drag me down with them if the Kozlovs found out. Well, not if but when they find out.

This is my chance to have an ally behind me, so that I can end my stepbrother for good. If I prove myself to Lev by doing his bidding and acting as his informant, I'll have the best ally I can have.

The possibility of getting rid of Jake makes my entire soul drift off into a land of tranquility and freedom. The iron chains he has around me will be cut free. I've dreamed of this moment since I was sixteen, when he first started his reign of terror on me, all the while his dad encouraged it.

The visions of Jake's torment from my youth overpower me when he gets in my face, it's just like when I was a kid. Repulsion twists my insides until I gag. But his all-consuming power is there and it's not going anywhere any time soon. It's like having too many people walking into the front door of my brain, a stampede, railing me over again and again. I can't get up, and I can't kick them out, helpless to stop any of it. It's all triggered by one emotion leftover from that scared kid in my mind. But I'm not him anymore. He's a fucking cowardly shadow, and I wanna wipe him out of existence, but he is also a comfort when Jake takes it too far. It's so damn confusing.

A hot shower to warm my freezing body is the solace I need before I turn in from this hellish night. The rush of water from the showerhead combined with the rising steam seeps into my bones, and I'm almost lulled into something akin to bliss until a bang on the bathroom door has me nearly jumping out of my skin.

"Aaron, you in there?" Tommy shouts through the door. I choose not to open it. I don't want to deal with him and his rages tonight.

"Yeah, what do you want?"

"No need to be a princess, fuckface. Where's Jake?"

"He went to see Shay about fifteen minutes ago."

There's a grunt before footsteps walk away and what I assume is the apartment door slamming shut. He is so damn hormonal when it comes to Jake. Pathetic.

Focusing back on the heavy spray of hot water, it almost burns my skin, but I love how the heat clears my foggy mind, locking all the monsters in my thoughts away and allowing the happy pleasures to rise to the forefront.

The main focus of my daily pleasure currently is Lev. Just looking at him is like watching my favorite porn. He doesn't need to really do anything, just him standing there and smelling so good makes me want to melt into the floor. I could literally just watch Lev go about his day and jack off to it non-stop.

As I lather the body wash and rub it over my body, I take in a deep breath and think about how commanding Lev is. Everything from his body, to his evil eyes and raspy voice has me shudder to the core. His savagery wraps around me like a safety blanket and I want more of it, more of his attention. After months of watching him I finally have his focus on me. His anger and scowling only make me want to bathe in it, to lick it off his skin and to never stop drowning in him.

A soft sigh escapes my lips as I slowly rub my cock up and down, picturing Lev over me, threatening me with all the bad things he could do and then brutally kissing me while rubbing my dick. My hand picks up speed, trying to mimic what I think Lev would be like. I guarantee he wouldn't be gentle; he would be crude, aggressive, and passionate—everything my body yearns to receive from him.

"Ahhhh, f-fuck, Lev!"

My release spurts out against my stomach as I try to control the trembles of orgasmic pleasure that skitter like tiny pebbles of ecstasy all over my body.

I lean back under the now tepid water, trying to regulate my breathing, and calm my racing heart. Another smile, one that I control this time, stretches across my face. Weightlessness buoys me until peace settles into my bones. I dare say I feel "normal" for the first time in I don't know how long.

Y'know? I think two crazy lovers could make one normal couple. Calm each other's madness. Well, maybe not normal but more controlled.

Maybe.

CHAPTER 6
LEV

Hmm, that's better. Inhaling my cigar while I watch the girls work the stage at Desire, I start to feel myself unwind and the knots in my shoulders loosen. I blame Seb for all the shit going on. We had a peaceful life until he showed up with his demented ex. Now, it's like we are cursed with problems.

Bonnie, our club manager, walks over to me with my drink, only a soda. I need to keep my wits about myself. I've been drinking too much lately and it slows me down.

"Thanks, Bonnie. All good?"

She slowly grins and tosses her long brown hair over her shoulder, hand perched on her curvy hip, tits pushed out. Ever the professional and she knows how to market her goods.

"All good here, handsome? Do you want some company?"

Do I? I'm all pent up, but it's not sex I am craving, I'm craving pain and I don't mean my own. This situation with Jake's crew has got me all wound up and unsettled. I hate having to wait, I'd prefer to get on with forcing out the truth, but I know I need to be patient. As Dima has reminded me. Daily.

"Nah, I'll be heading out soon, maybe some other time."

"Okay, you let me know if you need anything, Lev." She sends me a dazzling smile, which honestly, does nothing for me. I'm not into foreplay and flirting so it has zero effect.

Leaning back, I take a sip of my drink. It refreshes my throat from the cigar smoke that tickles it, and I try to empty my mind of any thoughts. Fuck, this isn't doing anything, not even the tits and ass on stage are helping.

Jules approaches my table. Obviously he got the little shit home. He sits down across from me, and I take another drag from my cigar, inhaling it deeply, enjoying the effects of the tobacco. It's like a mini massage for my blood, keeping the tension at bay.

"He any bother?" I ask, blowing the smoke away.

"Nah, he is weird as fuck though. Was asking if you were single and saying how hot you are. The kid is insane."

My eyebrows raise. This Aaron is full of surprises. It's rare that anyone shocks me, but either it's his confidence or lack of awareness that has my interest. The guy is unstable.

"Oh, he is more than that, he is a maniac. I could tell by his eyes that his crazy is on another level, even though he tries to hide it."

"More crazy than you?"

"Ha! Fuck you. Not more crazy, he is just a different kind. But seriously, I don't trust the Santinis, and I definitely don't trust Jake. That guy is up to something."

And it's bugging the shit out of me.

"Why not just bring him in? Treat him to the holding pen experience. You'll get your answers. Besides, I'm sure Aaron would be thankful to get that sick fuck away from him."

The holding pen is what Dima and I call our basement. It's more like a torture chamber with all the bells and whistles. It's my playroom and not many make it out of there alive. But that Aaron comment has me curious.

"What do you mean?"

"Well, everyone knows how weird Jake is about Aaron, and I mean weirdly obsessed like he is his boyfriend or some shit."

"You saying he wants his brother?" Well, stepbrother, but still, that has my eyebrows climbing off my forehead.

Jules nods. "Yep. Something is not right with that family. So, you gonna bring them in?"

"Not this time. I need to see how far this betrayal extends and if any of our other boys are involved. Just feels off, and I need to be smart on this one. I can have my fun later."

"True. You told Dima?"

"Yeah he knows my plan, Simon too. Dima is onboard but it's only the four of us. Don't want to risk it getting out to any of our other crews."

He sets his hands on the table as he rises out of his seat. "No worries. Well, if you don't need me for anything else, I'm heading out. See ya tomorrow."

"Yeah, see ya tomorrow."

After Jules leaves, I try to relax, try to encourage myself to want to fuck one of the dancers but it's hopeless. Screw it. Time to go home and maybe going a few rounds with the punching bag will help, otherwise it's another night of unrelenting insomnia.

Punching the gym bag, a mild relief washes over me. I have been at this for an hour and my arms are screaming under the burn, my hands are aching, and I can see little flashes in my vision from the exertion. Sweat runs down my face and body, making puddles on the floor, but it feels good. The door behind me opens, and I know it's Dima. We have a weird sixth sense when the other is around.

"You're down here late, brother, everything okay?" he asks on a yawn.

D walks towards me. He is wearing sweats and his hair looks like he has been dragged through a hedge, so I must have disturbed him. "Did I wake you?"

"No, I came down for some water and Simon was out front. He mentioned you were in here, just wanted to check in."

"I'm fine, just pent up."

"Uh huh. Is that code for you getting impatient for some blood?" He smirks, knowing me too damn well.

"I'm just frustrated. Sex ain't working, but this will do for now. We need to make some headway on this, D. If Aaron doesn't come back with anything soon, I think we should just bring them all in. I don't like fucking traitors in our family." All the frustration that I have managed to push back in the last hour has returned in full force.

"I know, I'm pissed too, but there is no point unless we have all the info of who is involved. They may still continue with whatever they are planning without Jake's crew. We need to be smart. Take the head off the snake, not just the tail."

"Yeah, yeah. Just fuck off back to bed, D." I know he is right but I won't give him the satisfaction.

"We will get them, Lev. I promise. I have always promised that this family comes first, yeah?"

Loyalty is the heart of our family. Without it we have nothing. Dima has never steered us wrong before. I know his words are full of sincerity.

"Got it, now get out, D."

He smiles. "See you tomorrow, fucker."

I head back to my room and begin to wash off all the sweat and frustration. Fuck. I need to break some bones or cut some skin. I am going insane. Aaron needs to come through, and soon, before I take the doe-eyed little shit down to the pen instead. Although I have a feeling the sick fuck would enjoy it.

As soon as my thoughts turn to the little shit, all I see are those big brown eyes. *Doe*. Such a shame. I would love to ruin him, to have him crying and begging at my feet for my dick. Christ, I could cum just thinking about it, my cock is hard enough. Nope, not going there, he is a distraction and an absolute nightmare that I just know is going to cause problems.

Ignoring my dick for the first time in my life, I dry off and walk towards my bed, thinking of anything to calm me down.

Fucking doe.

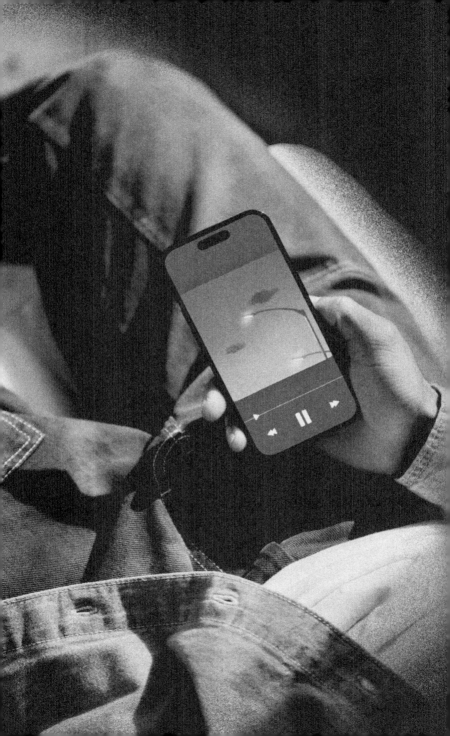

CHAPTER 7
AARON

After picking up some beer and food from our local store, I head back home desperate for warmth. I've nearly lost all feeling in my fingers. When I walk in, Jake and Tommy are in the kitchen talking, so I ignore them as I start to put stuff away in the cabinets.

"You've been gone over an hour," Jake says.

Typical statement from Jake. I'm always out too long, on the phone too long, basically everything I do is wrong and he's always suspicious. It's fucking suffocating.

"Well, it was busy. I got back as soon as I could." I move to put the beers and milk in the fridge.

"Shay is back. He's resting so don't bother him. We need him better as soon as possible. You listening?" Jake says.

"Yeah, that's great he's home."

Tommy scoffs. "No thanks to you."

He walks out of the apartment, and I silently pray he gets hit by a car. I think the mere fact that I exist annoys

Tommy. How we've all lived together this long and haven't killed each other yet is beyond my comprehension.

Moving around the kitchen, there is an uneasy shift in the air. Jake's watching me. The familiar sensation of acid rises up my throat. I have to get away. Being on my own with him is torture.

I swiftly finish up and hurry down the corridor to my room. My room is next door to Shay's, so I quickly look over my shoulder–no sign of Jake–and softly knock on Shay's door before pushing down the handle.

Shay looks up from where he's lying in bed. The bruises on his face are starting to turn yellow and green, and his eyes are slightly swollen. He winces as he tries to move himself up the bed, so I rest my hands on his arms to stop him.

"Hey, how are you feeling?" I whisper.

"Sore, but I'll be okay."

A beat of awkward silence stretches between us. I don't know what to say.

"Why did you follow me, Aaron? It wasn't safe. We could have been killed."

"Because I was curious about what you were doing, and we never go on deals without backup. I thought you may need it. Which you did. Why were you there Shay? Did you know you were on Santini turf?"

He turns his head, purposefully not looking me in the eye, which gives me the answer that he did know. I sigh.

"What's Jake doing, Shay? Why were you there? I'm part of this group too, and deserve to know what's happening."

"Look, just keep your nose out of it Aaron. It's safer that way. I don't have a choice but you do. Be smart for once and just fucking run."

Shay looks so tired. I always thought he was good looking with his dark hair, hazel eyes, and typical Irish fair skin along with the temper to match. But he looks older than his thirty years, too young to have witnessed and experienced so much that his body is weathered by the toll it's taken.

He's at the end of his tolerance. Shay is an okay guy, which has me wondering what Jake holds over him to keep him here, and to make him do his risky bidding. It doesn't sit right with me.

"Why would I run?" I ask.

"I'm not blind, Aaron. Your brother–"

"Stepbrother," I correct.

"Whatever, your stepbrother is not just unstable. Don't think I haven't noticed his disgusting obsession with you. You need to leave before this whole mess blows up. What happened to me is nothing compared to what will happen if this whole thing of Jake's comes to light. The Kozlovs will kill us. All of us, and it won't be quick."

I gently rub my fingers over my mouth. I'm smiling. *Shit.* That name has created a new emotional response for me. I turn into a needy, smiling horndog.

What would it be like to see Lev hurt Jake? It would be epic. I can't stop myself from getting turned on and have forgotten for a moment that I'm in Shay's room.

"It isn't funny Aaron," he says, his angry voice bringing me back to reality. "This isn't a fucking joke. Stop being stupid and get with what's going on here."

It's the most angry he's ever been with me. And fuck, I'm the reason he's hurt.

"Sorry." And I really am. My stupid brain.

He exhales a disappointed sigh. "Can you just leave, Aaron? I'm not in the mood for this right now. I want to sleep. My head is killing me." He closes his eyes and pushes himself further into his pillow.

"Sure, let me know if you need anything," I say as I get up and leave the room.

As I walk back into the kitchen to grab a bottle of water from the fridge, Jake appears in front of me again, looking like he wants to rip my head off, his eyes narrowed, his lips pursed in annoyance.

"What were you doing in Shay's room?" He crowds me into the fridge door, and I feel myself becoming smaller.

I hate myself for being so weak. It's like he knows what tone to use to unbalance me and throw my mind into turmoil and chaos. Like a lock he turns that only he has the key for, and I don't know how to turn it off again.

We are okay. It will be over soon.

Not now!

"I was just checking on him," I say, avoiding eye contact, and staring at the floor.

"Yeah, well stay the fuck away. It's your fault he's hurt," he says. He's close enough to me that his hot breath fans over my face.

That does it, I'm so sick of his shit. A flare of anger ignites erasing all thought, and I look up, pinning him with a glare.

"It would have been worse if I hadn't followed him. Why was he on his own, Jake?"

The confidence is short lived. A blow from his fist into my stomach has me on my knees, gasping for breath as Jake grabs me by the scruff of my hoodie, yanking me back up.

"Watch your fucking mouth and stop asking shit that ain't nothing to do with you. Always said you were missing a few brain cells in that fucked up head of yours," he sneers as he pokes the temple of my head with his finger.

He doesn't move or let me go. We're suspended in time, engulfed in dark silence while I squirm under his intense gaze. My ears buzz, and the horrible feeling in my gut builds until I'm near to vomiting.

It's coming. He's going to do it soon. Cross that line that I never want to cross.

Please don't touch me. Please don't. The boy in my head chants his pleas over and over, making me want to scratch the voice out.

The past floods to the surface. Every heavily implied innuendo, every lust-filled story of what he would do to me, the way he used to push his body against mine, lingering for too long.

"Open wide baby brother…"

No! I won't go there.

Get out of my head, get out of my head, I beg, hoping the boy listens. Fuck. I just know Jake is thinking about the same thing.

Come on Aaron, get your shit together.

Breathe in…breathe out.

Too busy focusing on my breathing to prevent a panic attack, I jolt against Jake's hold as the front door slams followed by Tommy's heavy footfalls. I spy Tommy from the corner of my eye and he stands still, staring between us. Jake takes a moment before he composes himself, moving back and releasing me.

"Get the fuck away from me, Aaron, before I end you." The low harsh whisper of his voice holds all the promises of cruelty. I've heard it before, but I know this time there is more meaning in his words. The fact that others see it and he doesn't try to hide it like he did at home when we were younger makes it worse.

I walk briskly to my room, feeling the glare of Tommy on my back as I walk away like this is all my fault. Nobody speaks, they don't have to, the atmosphere in here is enough to narrate what is going on as the tension builds daily. The pressure cooker of emotions is going to explode and I'm the sole cause of it all. I don't want to be here.

Maybe it would be better to take Shay's advice, forget about Jake, and just leave, but that's hopeless. Jake would make it his mission to find me and ensure that I never attempt to leave him again.

When I get to my room, I close the door behind me. I need a minute to process this. Pushing the threats from Jake away allows me to focus. Jake was angry at me for talking to Shay. It's clear he wants to compete with the Kozlovs with dealing and potentially taking over other territories. He's trying to keep me away from Shay because I think he knows deep down, if I push Shay enough, he'll tell me what's going on in order to protect me. I still don't understand how or why Jake is even thinking of doing something like this, unless the reward is huge, but then again, his arrogance is what will end him one day, a day I am hoping is imminent. We are only a crew of four, so how does he plan to do it? He must be working with someone else on this, he has to be.

Putting my ear to the door, I listen for any movement or signs that Jake is going to follow me, but all I can hear is the mumbling of chatter between him and Tommy before the sound of the TV being turned on. I should be safe from being disturbed for a while, so I go to my closet and pull up the carpet at the bottom corner. Gently, I pull it back, revealing the loose floorboard that I lift to display the burner phone Lev gave me. I need to tell him and in all honesty, I need the protection because as much as I would love to tear the flesh from my stepbrother, I'm secretly scared he will get me first.

With shaky fingers I send a text.

ME:
Need to see you.

I check the sound is turned off and the light is low on the screen. I am about to put it back when I get a response.

LEV:
Why? You have info?

ME:
Yes.

LEV:
Fine, meet me at Desire tonight at 7.
Come through the back, Jules will meet you there, doe.

Doe? Why is he calling me doe? Never mind.

ME:
Okay.

Like an electric shock, the shift in my head is instant as the involuntary smile on my face spreads. It seems to happen when I think of the hunky killer, which is becoming a frequent thing. My whole mood alters, erasing anything else that's happened, it's like some kind of amnesia. My stomach bubbles like it's a washer on rinse spin. I get to be near him again tonight. I need to compose myself and try to be normal around him. But I also need him on my side to take down my shithead stepbrother.

Deciding on my faithful ripped black jeans, my Alice In Chains retro T-shirt with my leather jacket, I quickly look in the mirror and style my messy hair. Which means I just run my hands through it to make it look acceptable. I change my eyebrow piercing to a black barbell, which I keep for special occasions, and use my burner phone to book an Uber to collect me at the end of the street.

The noise from Tommy and Jake died down a while ago. Luckily when I left my room, the guys had gone, probably out on some dealing or secret shady meeting, and Shay is still holed up in his room fast asleep. It makes leaving a lot less difficult. Making my way outside and down the apartment steps, my phone pings informing me of the Uber arrival in two minutes, so I speed walk to the end of the street. It feels like Christmas. I can't wait to inhale Lev and listen to that devilish sexy voice berate me.

ARRIVING AT THE CLUB, I head to the back entrance as per instructions. I'm right on time. I knock two short thumps against the heavy door. Within seconds the door opens, and I'm greeted by Jules who looks me up and down before raising a brow at me. I must look hot.

"Come with me, Aaron," he orders. Jules looks like he belongs in the WWE with how large he is. He's hot and looks like he could throw you around, but he seems to dislike me and I can't get a good read on him. Plus blonds aren't really my type.

I follow Jules through the back corridors of the club, the heavy thrum of the music from the main floor vibrates beneath my feet. The fluttering in my stomach builds with the anticipation of seeing Lev. Warmth spreads over my skin and I'm at risk of breaking out into a sweat. I clench my hands at my sides in order to stop my fidgeting.

We finally come to a stop outside Lev's office and Jules quickly knocks before opening the door. I'm hit with the smell of cigars and an undertone of what I can only describe as exotic and earthy aftershave. It's Lev's scent. The smells combine and give me a comfort that I have never felt before. It's an unusual feeling of safety, which is on repeat in my head.

You are safe here… you are safe here…

I give myself a mental slap to push away the voices trying to break through my thoughts as I walk in and see Lev sitting in his huge brown leather chair. He looks so dangerous, living up to his reputation. I take in his short black hair that's sharply cut at the edges. He's dressed head to toe in black, the tattoos on his neck looking sharper than I have ever seen them on his tanned skin. I almost come to a stop when his gaze lands on me.

He's like a damn lion who's about to kill its prey. He slowly inhales the large cigar that's currently between those sexy-ass lips. It's such a sultry look, I almost drool, watching those large manly hands remove it from his mouth. Those green eyes of his, vibrant and zoned in on me like the hawk he is. I have an overwhelming need to go over to him and straddle his thighs, to feel those huge arms around my body, cocooning me in a bubble of safety that I crave from him even though I hardly know him. That would then be followed by a hard fucking.

"You just gonna just stand there? Sit down."

My balls tingle at his command as I take a seat. It's gonna take a miracle not to get a boner right now.

He frowns at me and stubs out his cigar in the ashtray

that's sitting on his large mahogany desk as he continues to study me.

"Do you know what a creepy fuck you are? You are smiling again," he says.

I quickly put my hands to my mouth. Great. I have been told most of my life that I smile at the wrong things. It's a reflex reaction to a feeling, and normally I don't know what that feeling is that makes it happen. But recently, I know it's because of him. Being around him I'm like an eager puppy intent on pleasing its owner.

I try to relax my face. "Sorry, it just happens," I say followed by a shrug. I can't explain it any better.

"Uh huh. As fascinating as this is, what you got?" He leans back into his chair and links his hands together behind his head.

What I would give to rub my hands over his short hair and over that dusting of beard-stubble on his face. He is so fucking hot. The material of his shirt stretches over his chest and biceps, and he's like a king in his lair, relaxed, in control, deadly as sin. Screw that, he is a demon king.

"Earth to fucking Aaron!" he shouts, which wakes me from my lustful thoughts.

"You are grating on my fucking nerves, you know that? Now unless you want me to bleed the answer out of you, you wanna tell me what you have on your shithead step-brother?" He quirks his brow, which is more threatening than it should be.

"Err yeah, sorry. Jake is planning something." My brain is short circuiting and unsure of what to focus on, so I sound like an idiot.

I think if Lev wanted to kill me, this would be the moment. The look of death and impatience on his face makes the room feel colder than the sub zero temperatures outside. I should be scared, and I am, sort of, but my brain computes it differently. I just don't care how his attention is on me as long as it is.

"No shit. Now, you have thirty seconds to give me a proper fucking answer before I get Jules here to pin you down, and I'll get to work forcing you to talk," he threatens and a hint of excitement takes over his eyes.

I don't mean to do it, but the groan is out of my mouth before I can stop it and heat creeps over my face. I never blush. I glance at Lev and a look of shock crosses his face before he puts his pissed-off mask back in place.

"Did you just fucking groan?" he asks as I force myself to remain quiet and fidget with my hands on my lap.

"My god, you are bat shit crazy, aren't you, doe?" It's a rhetorical question but I don't miss that term "doe" again.

"Jules, leave us."

I don't look at Jules, but I hear him leave by the opening and soft closing of the door. As soon as it clicks shut, the walls close in. Lev's presence dominates the room. He's still staring at me and my breath hitches. The attention is thrilling but also unbearable. My skin itches all over so badly, I want to remove my clothes. My reaction to this man is not like anything I've ever experienced. I really do think I'd let him do anything to me, and I would do anything for him to keep his eyes on me. I never knew what an attention whore I was.

"Now, why don't we start again. Tell me what Jake is planning." I don't miss how the tone of his voice has altered. It's huskier, affected by the cigar with the deep growl that carries it. It's like a beacon of light has shone on me, and I want to follow it.

"Jake had sent Shay on his own. I was never supposed to be there, but Shay has told me to leave the crew and not get involved. Jake's more anxious than usual, not letting me work. I think he intended to do what he did, but I think he's working with someone else. I just know it."

"Is Shay home now?"

"Yes, why?" My voice shakes. I don't want Shay hurt any more than he already is.

"Worried for him?" He smirks at me, toying with me.

"Please don't hurt him," I say.

He slams his fist on the desk, making me flinch, and my eyes widen at the pure rage on his face. This is the true Lev in all his glory and what a sight it is.

"And why the fuck not? I should take your entire crew out for what they are doing, so don't think you get to give me orders. I make the rules, you follow them, understand?" he roars.

I nod. I can't force any words out of my mouth. Holy shit. He's stunning. Once again I've completely forgotten the trail of this conversation. His mere presence beguiles me.

He snorts and shakes his head at me with a slight hint of a smile.

"You certainly are fascinating, doe. Now get the fuck out of here and keep me updated. Remember, they are only alive because I need to find out who is involved. As soon as I do, you won't be able to save them."

I know this already, but Lev leaves no doubt in my mind that he means what he says. After a brief moment of me memorizing his features to store for later, I catch his eyes. He's scowling at me like I belong on a psych ward. Before I push him over the edge, I walk out of the room, and am greeted by Jules.

"You certainly have a death wish," he says.

"Why do you say that?" I ask. And here I thought I was pretty chill. Wasn't I?

"No sane person would look at someone like Lev, or any of us, as heroes, Aaron. You all but had hearts in your eyes in there. Just reel it in, Lev doesn't do relationships and he has no patience, so be careful."

Huh. Here I thought I'd hidden it well.

He walks past me and I follow him to the rear exit, leaving silently as he opens and closes the door behind me.

For a moment, I relish in the cold air. It cools my warm cheeks, and as the grin stretches on my face, my feet nearly lift off the ground. I could fly away right now.

Lev is the perfect drug for me and I want more.

CHAPTER 8
LEV

W alking through the front door at home, the smell of pizza lures me to the kitchen. I'm starving. Making my way in, I see Dima, Seb, and Simon opening four boxes of pizza.

Dima nods in my direction. "Wasn't sure if you wanted any, but got extra," he says, pointing over to the food.

I hum in response as I uncuff my long sleeves and roll them up to my elbows, opening the first few buttons of my shirt with the need to relax and unwind. Seb's staring at my chest. I smirk.

"Hungry, Seb?" I wink at him, and he rolls his eyes. Gotcha, brat.

"Shut the fuck up, Lev, I'm warning you," Dima admonishes, pulling Seb into his lap like some child. It's ridiculous looking at two large men sitting like that. Seb pretends he hates it, but he loves it really.

"Well you should tell your boy to stop staring, it's rude." I love pushing them both, it amuses me when my brother gets feral over him.

"Lev," Dima growls. He really does sound like an

animal when he gets possessive.

"Ignore him, baby, he's just being an ass," Seb says, coddling my big brother. Dima presses a hard kiss on Seb before aiming his warning look at me, like it ever works. Simon comes to sit next to me, and I await whatever tirade of questions that's about to come from D.

"So, any news on Jake and his boys?" Dima asks. "Jules mentioned Aaron had been to the club."

"Only suspicions at this point. He is trying to find more. Although it appears Jake seems to have taken a liking to his brother." I bite into my pizza, enjoying the cheesy greasiness of it.

All eyes freeze on me. "What the fuck are you looking at?"

"What do you mean a liking...? Are you telling me Jake wants to screw his brother?" Dima says with the same level of disgust in his tone as I feel in my throat thinking about it.

"Well, technically stepbrother, but yeah. He's gonna try and get more info, but Jake has restricted Aaron. He has less access to the crew's information." I drop the pizza down and sigh. "Let me bring him in. I'll get the fucker to sing," I say, clenching my fists on the table. The need to hurt and destroy this fucker is taking over my life. The craving for blood is becoming as important as my need for oxygen.

"Soon, brother. Let's give Aaron another week first, we need names," Dima says.

My appetite now gone, I lean back and turn toward Simon.

"Keep a listen out, actually, I want you to do some subtle digging into the other crews. They like to gossip... just see if anyone stands out." I glance back at Dima. "We need to move this along somehow; we can't just rely on Aaron." Dima reads between the lines. I'm on my last nerve and he knows it, so he nods.

"Okay, but be careful, Si. I don't want anyone being tipped off, thinking we are asking questions," he says.

"No problem. I'll start tonight, we have to collect payments anyway. We can put the feelers out and let you know tomorrow," Simon says.

That gives me a little reassurance, enough not to completely run psycho across town.

Hearing heavy footsteps approaching, I turn to the door and in walks Jules.

"Any pizza left?" he asks, walking over to the open boxes on the counter.

"Help yourself," Dima mutters while nibbling at Seb's throat.

For fucks sake, do they ever stop? I'm surprised Seb has the ability to walk with how much they fuck. And the sappy side of them, which they seem to only display here–*lucky me*–is nauseating.

"What'd I miss"? Jules asks with a mouthful of pizza, 'cuz he is classy as fuck.

"Just updating them on Aaron and his fuckhead brother."

Jules chuckles. "Don't you mean doe?" He smiles at me. Bastard.

"Shut the hell up, Jules. I'm feeling pretty stabby today so don't piss me off," I warn.

He doesn't respond but keeps that smug smile on his face. I can tell he is about to shit stir, and I can't decide whether to slit his throat or smash his head against the kitchen island.

"Doe? Who is doe?" Seb asks. Nosy fucker.

Before I can respond, Jules the dickhead decides to answer. "Aaron. It's Lev's pet name for him. You should see this guy. He is fucking crazy as shit, but he looks at Lev like he is a god. It's weird and hilarious at the same time."

I actually think smashing his head against the wall appeals more.

"Well, well, got yourself a fan, brother?" Dima says.

"Yes I have, and he isn't sane. And before you ask, no I haven't fucked him, and no I don't plan to. He has a weird-ass smile, and I think he would bite my dick off and enjoy it."

I snap back, hating this attention on me. Luckily nobody comments on the doe reference, and I am glad of it. Do I want to fuck Aaron? Yes. But he displays all kinds of stage-five clinging and so many red flags it makes me look normal. Well, maybe that's a stretch.

"Hey, we ain't judging, we all know your dick has been through the whole city." Dima laughs along with everyone else.

"You done?" I snarl at my brother.

He huffs a smile and nods.

Seb gets off Dima's knee, gives him a quick peck on the cheek, and turns to leave. "Right, I'm going for a run, see ya later."

I can't help but admire that ass of his as he walks away. I have never seen such a juicy one like Seb's.

"I will tear your fucking eyes out, Lev. Knock it off!" my predictable brother barks at me and I grin at him.

"Love to see you try, brother."

Dima glares, itching to jump across the table and choke the life out of me. Riling up Dima suddenly makes my appetite return, so I continue eating as the low chuckles from Simon and Jules alleviate the tension in the room.

CHAPTER 9
AARON

"Where the fuck have you been?" Jake's murderous voice barks as I walk into the apartment.

He storms toward me, anger etched on his face. Shay stands in the corner, wincing and body recoiling. His exhausted eyes say a lot. He's still healing, but his concern for me keeps him in the room.

"Jake, I'm twenty-four. I don't have to answer to you," I say. Making my body rigid, and keeping my head held high, I try to stand up to him, but as he walks closer towards me, I can feel myself shutting down. Desperate for something to keep me grounded, I think of Lev and try to channel the strength that fills me when I've been with him. Our interactions aren't even friendly, business-like at best, but his confidence and fearlessness bleed into me, giving me a strength I have rarely been able to show.

My brother's laugh is vicious, and I know nothing good will happen tonight. He won't allow it.

"Because I'm the head of this crew and need to know

where you are. I fucking own you, baby brother, remember?" he challenges.

His manipulative words hit where he wants them to, and I'm spinning.

I try to stop the images from showing themselves, but they come anyway.

"You are mine now, baby brother. I own you," he'd said. "You only have me to rely on."

He repeated that to me so often that eventually it became true. I believed it.

His voice is like an army of ants biting my skin, and a strong urge to hit my head against something to stop the thoughts it conjures is overpowering. I want to peel myself out of my own body so that I don't have to share my mind with the boy trying to overpower my thoughts. Jake can control him, but I won't let him have any piece of me.

With every last piece of strength I have, I manage to compose myself enough to answer. I come up with the only lie I can think of. "I was out having a drink. It's not fair I get singled out. I don't see Tommy around ... you gonna call him out too?"

Frustration overtakes all reasoning just as the first punch hits my face, knocking me into the wall behind me. Before I can sink to the floor, my jaw burning from the impact, Jake pulls me back up and slams me into the hard surface of the wall where I can already feel the tenderness of bruises forming on my back from the force. The last beating was over a month ago. At least I've had time to heal.

"It's about time you remember who's boss here. You are mine, and I will make sure you remember," he threatens, pushing his forehead into mine. His breathing is coming in fast from all the adrenaline that must be pumping through his veins. He gets a twisted thrill from treating me this way, and before I know it, he punches me again in the stomach. I fall to the ground, and then the impact of his booted foot into my ribs takes my breath away. There's another kick to my back and I try to roll away from the onslaught of punches.

Shit, this one's going to be bad. I can't breathe, it's like my stomach has pushed my lungs into my throat. Tears build behind my eyes, but he won't have them.

It's okay. It's okay. It'll all be over soon.

That chant repeats over and over as the young boy tries to soothe me. Another fist lands on my face, dizziness and a wave of sickness hit me like a freight train. I'm on the verge of passing out. I wish he would just kill me.

We just need to keep quiet. It'll be okay. It'll be over soon. Just hold on.

"Jake! Leave him alone man, that's enough. He knows now," Shay shouts from a distance. Everything is starting to sound far away, like they are at the end of a tunnel, and my ears are ringing.

Jake's above me, panting, watching me. My body screams with pain, my face feels like it has been lit on fire.

Curled up, broken on the floor, my resolve strengthens. I'm not going to be able to kill Jake myself, but he's going to die. It'll be like fucking Christmas for Lev. And me.

"Get him up and take him to his room," Jake says.

I see his feet move away from where they were in front of my face as Shay approaches, squatting in front of me. My vision is a little blurry and my body is shutting down, trying to protect myself while also trying to contain the anger that is nearly at the surface. It's an extreme contradiction, feeling weak but also crazed with the thirst of violence. It's hard to know which force is stronger, but that's what Jake does to me. He took all the sanity from me years ago, chipping away parts of my mind until I turned into this mess.

"I told you this would happen, you need to leave Aaron, please," Shay whispers.

It's the first time he's spoken to me with emotion that gives the impression he actually may give a shit about me after all. He places his arms under my back to encourage me to stand up.

As I move, the cry of pain bursts from my mouth of its own accord. The room spins and my ribs and face hurt like a bitch, but once I'm on my feet, I'm able to scuffle along with Shay's help, to my room. He sits me on my bed before he disappears.

He returns with a first aid kit and cleans up the cut on my face, which I hadn't realized was bleeding, and then heads off again, returning with a couple of ice packs for me to rest on my cheek and ribs. Fuck!

"Why don't you lie down, Aaron, try to rest. Do you need anything?"

"Yeah, can you pass me my earbuds and phone please?" My voice trembles. I'm drifting away, struggling to keep a hold of my emotions. I need my music to calm shattered nerves. It's what I used to use and haven't needed for a while.

He passes them to me, with an attempt at a comforting smile and he leaves, closing the door behind him. The sound of the closing door is like permission to let myself give in.

My hands shake as I place the earbuds in my ears and press play on the one track that always helped as a kid when this happened at home. The song *Black Gives Way to Blue* by Alice in Chains filters through the earpieces, and I curl up on my side until I'm comfortable, letting the tears stream freely down my face. My younger self reappears, the scared young boy in my head, baring his soul, begging me to hide away.

Come with me, he scares me. Please come with me and we will be safe together. If you hide with me, he won't find us.

No, I have to stay here. I have to kill him. For us.

He will hurt us, please, don't let him hurt us, he begs.

I have to do this, I say. I have to abandon the boy in my head so I can finish Jake, it's the only way.

No, please. Don't leave me.

As I pull away from his voice, the fear intensifies, leaving me cold and terrified. I can't do it. I can't leave him. The very notion brings me feelings of extreme anxiety. I can't catch a breath at the idea of him not being there. He is the only one who understands and helps me cope.

I cave, giving into his pleas. *I'm sorry, I will stay.*

It's going to be okay, we will be okay. Just rest. Hold onto us, the boy in my head whispers, reassuring me. I let myself take comfort in his voice rather than fight it. Just like that he has taken over, I can't stop him. He is my weakness, a part of me I can't let go of. I am as controlled by him and the coping mechanism I have developed as I am by Jake. He makes me feel less alone in this prison that has been built around me.

I listen to the song on repeat until darkness takes me to rest in a place where nobody can hurt me. I'll never allow anyone to see me like this. As the lyrics play over and over, I slowly relax, my breathing evens out, the tears are less, and just as my eyes begin to close, Lev is the last thing on my mind.

AARON - 8 YEARS AGO - 16 YEARS OLD

"I won't do it," I say to my piece of shit stepdad.

"Yes you will, boy. You'll earn your keep here. I'm too old to do it myself, and it's about time you man up and take responsibility like your brother does," he scolds me.

He isn't my brother, I want to yell back but hold it in. He's an imposing figure, even though he's useless, barely moves all day, and does nothing but drink, fuck whores, smoke weed, and pop pills.

"Well, let him do it, I want to make something of myself, not be a drug dealer living in this shithole the rest of my life," I say. I don't understand why they are pushing this on me.

I sense a presence behind me before I'm pushed to the floor. It knocks the wind from my lungs and a heavy body holds me down. It's Jake who always sticks up for his dad, and ever since I turned sixteen, he always finds an excuse to put his hands on me.

"Don't talk back, you little cunt." Jake sneers, pushing my face hard into the dirty carpet. He has me in a grip I can't get out of. He's only three years older than me, but is a lot bigger than I am from all the football he's played. That stopped soon after high school when he redirected his life, which is now being the hard man of the streets, taking pleasure in controlling me, hurting me. Realizing that the older stepbrother you once looked up to is a sick fuck, fucking sucks.

"Now, get your shit together so we can go."

He moves off me as I scramble to my feet, glaring at him. He grabs my wrist, pulling me with him, away from my stepdad's laughter.

"That's right, you little pussy. Your brother will straighten that attitude out," he shouts as we head out the door to Jake's car. He still has a firm grip on my wrist as he manhandles me into the passenger side, locking me in.

As he gets into the driver's seat, he starts with his tirade of verbal abuse that's becoming a daily thing, and it's breaking away a part of me each time. Long gone are the days as kids where he played ball with me, took me to watch his football practices, kept the bullies away, and helped me settle in when me and my mom moved in.

"You know, you only make it harder on yourself and you won't get out of this. You will do as you're told, willing or not."

Same shit, different day.

"Fuck off, Jake," I bite out, grasping for some control.

In a snap movement, he swerves the car down a side street and comes to a stop.

"Jake, what the—"

Grabbing my neck to hold me steady, he backhands me across the face, and pushes me into the seat so that he can lean over my body. With the shock of the sting still echoing across my face, it takes a moment for me to realize how close his face is to mine. He's never hit me before.

"Don't you ever think you can talk to me like that, you ungrateful little bitch. I am the one protecting you from what dad really wants to do with you, so you will obey me."

He's changed so much. All I see is hate in those blue eyes. He never smiles anymore, he's an emotional desert.

I manage to scoff. "Protect? You call this protection? I call it abuse!" I shout.

He clings to my throat harder, restricting my breathing, making a swell of panic rise in my chest. This is more than his *new usual. I'd gotten used to the insults, and the threats, but I never thought he would put his hands on me.*

"Dear old daddy wanted to offer you out for other services, you know, put that mouth of yours to good use, but I convinced him not to, that you could deal instead."

Icy repulsion and shock dump over me like a bucket of water. I know my stepdad and stepbrother detest me. Since my mom died, I have become an easy target, who do I have on my side? Knowing it sounds naive, I never thought this would be how far my stepdad would take it.

"You're lying!" My voice cracks in disbelief, and my throat closes, suffocating my air supply until I'm panicked for breath.

"I'm not, but I ain't sharing you. You're mine now, baby brother. I own you. You only have me to rely on now."

Cold fear filters through my blood. Only him? Is he really all I've got? I notice a hardness against my leg. Holy fuck, he's hard and he's staring at me. His grip on my throat relaxes, but the queasiness in my stomach rises, leaving a bitter taste on my tongue. Disgust and shame run rampant in my mind. I'm frozen in time, unsure of what to say or do.

He pulls away.

"One day, Aaron," he mutters under his breath. Those three words alone send a fear through me that I haven't even felt from his evil dad. I remain silent for the rest of the journey and do as I'm told.

It'll be okay, it will all be okay.

I repeat this on loop in my head, reassuring myself that I can deal with this, because it will be okay, won't it?

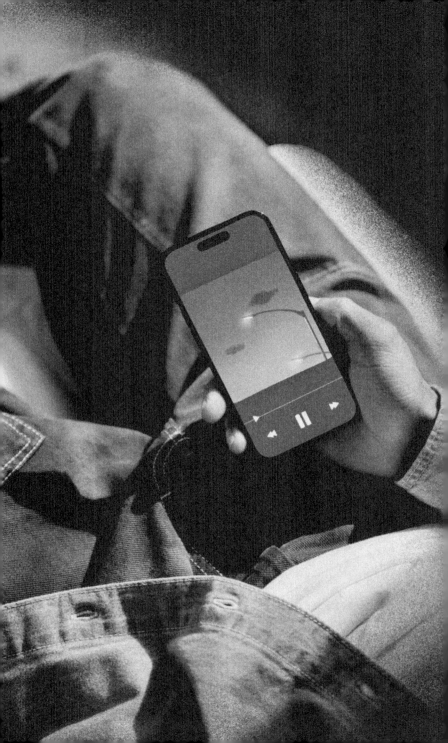

CHAPTER 10
AARON

Waking up, I move onto my back and immediately regret it as a dull pain radiates from my sides. My jaw is tight and achy. Reruns of last night play out in front of me, remembering Jake's fists and feet laying into me.

First, I take out my air pods, then, slowly and gently, I get myself into an upright position to stand from the bed. I take deep breaths before I push myself up to prepare for the pain. I feel dirty and bruised, and what I wouldn't give for a hot bath right now. But I don't have that luxury so a shower will have to suffice. If I can make it to the bathroom, that is, I need to piss.

As I gingerly move toward the bathroom, the door opens and Jake fills the space in front of me. His face is indifferent as if he didn't beat the shit out of me yesterday. He remains eerily quiet, raking his eyes over the bruises that must be on my face, the way I grip my stomach, highlighting the damage he's done. He barges past me without speaking as I make my way inside the bathroom. I hear a vibration as I go to close the door and notice that Jake has left his phone on the countertop.

Without thinking, I scan the message that has just appeared on the lock screen. It mentions a time and place from an unknown number.

Friday. Nine pm. Huh, that's five days from now.

Just as the screen goes black, the door swings open nearly hitting me in the back, and I stumble. Jake strides in, grabs the phone off the counter, and looks at me.

His fiery gaze says, *"Did you look?"*

But I ignore him, turning to switch the shower on. As I try to take my top off, which isn't easy, I realize he hasn't left the bathroom.

He's staring at my back. I want to comment about his staring, but before anything can come out of my mouth, he leaves without a word, slamming the door behind him. Hobbling over as fast as I can in my state, I lock it. This is all getting too much, but now I have a lead. I can follow them and see who they're meeting. Or should I contact Lev and let him deal with it? I continue to ponder that question as I quickly wash myself, scrubbing away Jake's touch like a stain on my body.

The warm water makes me feel a lot better. Having more movement in my joints is a relief, but I definitely need some pain meds to get through today. Thinking it over, I decide that it's best I go alone. I make the excuse that it's so I don't disturb Lev, but the truth is, the thought of praise if I get any info to give to him outweighs the sane option.

So far, Lev has found me annoying, weird, and has berated me like a brat. I want to experience some praise, see which I prefer best. For the first time in twenty-four hours, yep, my smile is back. Stepping out of the shower, I check over my face in the mirror, Jake got me good. My jaw is slightly tender and bruised. It hurts to open my mouth to brush my teeth, at least he didn't get me around my eyes–that would've been worse. My ribs are tender, but from experience, I know they are not broken so another small mercy. I just need to look after myself and rest plenty before Friday.

FOR THE NEXT few days I keep myself mainly to my room, trying to stay out of the way, only leaving for food, drink, and bathroom breaks. It's now Friday and I feel a lot better. I can move without much pain and the bruising is starting to fade, only slightly tender to the touch. It looks worse than it is and I'm thankful. I need to be ready for tonight. Laying on my bed, I grab my switchblade and play with it in my hands as I try to plan out in my mind how to do this.

Jake is meeting whoever this other person is at an abandoned factory building on the outskirts of town. I recognized the address. I've been there before on larger dealings in the past. I can drive but Jake has never allowed me to have a car, another restriction. With no other choice, I book another Uber that can drop me off about a quarter of a mile away from the location. It's all country back roads around the old factory site, and not a lot of cars use those roads, so I'll need to walk it so I don't get noticed.

Ideally, I should arrive five minutes or so late so I don't come across whoever Jake is meeting when they arrive, and god forbid if Jake sees me.

After I make the booking, I put the phone in my back

pocket. I dress in all black and as I attempt to pull my hoodie over my head, there is a small knock on my bedroom door.

It's Shay. Great.

He leans against the doorframe, scanning the room before analyzing what I am wearing. It's obvious I'm going out.

"Where are you going, Aaron?"

It's really starting to piss me off how everyone talks to me like a young teen who's going out after curfew.

I choose not to answer. I'm tired of the cryptic messages. He could just tell me the truth, then I wouldn't have to risk stalking Jake and getting caught. He takes in a deep breath like he is preparing himself and walks further into my room.

"Jake and Tommy have left. Please tell me you're not planning on following them? If Jake comes home to find you gone, he will hurt you, Aaron."

Yeah, no shit.

"You already know the answer to that, Shay. I saw Jake has a meeting tonight and I want answers. *No.* I deserve answers."

"I can't let you do that. It's dangerous."

"Well, then tell me what's going on!" I beg, having reached the end of my patience with him.

"I can't do that. I have more at risk in this than you know, Aaron."

I nod, knowing he'll stay firm on his decision so that leaves me with no choice. I turn on him and punch him in the face, which sends him into a heap on the ground. Fuck. I shake out my hand. His face is hard.

"I'm sorry, Shay, but I have to do this. I will be back

before them, so it's up to you if you want to warn them or not."

He groans on the floor. Yeah, I'm a dick. He's only just recovered since being out of the hospital, but I actually don't give a fuck anymore. I'm in this alone and I'll do whatever it takes to end my stepbrother. He tries and fails to grab my leg as I pass him by. Getting onto his knees, holding his jaw in his hand, he looks broken and conflicted, but I'm done.

"Aaron, please don't," he pleads. Fuck him.

"See ya later, Shay." And I leave without looking back. I don't want to see Shay get hurt, but I have to start putting myself first, just as he has.

The car arrives on time, and the driver looks a little bewildered as to why I want to be dropped off on a mostly abandoned road. Especially when I'm dressed like I'm about to either murder someone or commit a robbery, but I can't worry about that right now.

I know this factory area well. We've done a few dealings here before when it's impossible to do them in town, so I make my way through the sparse forest, keeping to the complete darkness of a clear sky. I regret not wearing a coat over my hoodie and there's a chance I may freeze to death, but it could be a good thing. The bite of cold will keep me alert and help me focus.

Making my way through the trees and woodland terrain, I approach the edge of where the old factory lies. It's a huge building, almost completely covered in windows. It's certainly old and I notice that there are two large SUVs, plus my stepbrother's truck, and a light that's coming from the building where the main overhang doors are wide open. There are some old shipping containers scattered around the yard, which probably is the best cover for me to get as close as possible and at least take some pictures.

I crouch low and scuffle quickly in between the containers. I can't get too close, but all I need is a clear view. I moan when I crouch down, fucking achy ribs, but the adrenaline starts to kick in, making each waddled step easier. At the opening there are two armed guards, which I find interesting. They don't look local and with the guns they have, I would say whoever Jake is meeting with is a bigger deal than I first thought.

Managing to sneak behind a container that is directly in front of the open doors, I can see Tommy and Jake, shaking hands with two other men I don't recognize. I can't hear what they're saying, but they're having an intense conversation from the way they're all standing. Backs straight, shoulders rigid, all of them trying to give off vibes that my dick is bigger than yours. Tommy looks on edge though, his eyes shifting constantly between Jake and whoever the guys are he is talking to.

I get out the burner phone Jules gave me, zoom in on the men, and start to record, making sure to get as much of a visual on these strangers as possible, including the two guards.

Paying more attention to the phone than what is going on in front of me, I see one of the guards start to stroll towards where I'm standing. Shit. I startle, resting my back against the container wall and try to steady my breathing, which is harder than it sounds. Especially when your heart pounds like it will burst through your chest.

What the fuck do I do if he comes around here? I don't have any weapons, I want to beat my own ass for not bringing at least my switchblade. A couple of minutes pass and I don't hear any footsteps. I take the plunge and peer my head around the corner of the container, where I notice the guard has walked back and is chatting with the other guy. Jake is now shaking hands again with this stranger, appearing to be coming to the end of the meeting, so I quickly take a picture of them, not remembering my phone has the flash on.

Shit!

"Did you see that?" one of the guards says, and I make a run for it, still crouching, over to the other containers on the edge of the woodland. Luckily the only light visible is within the factory, so I think I can go unnoticed if I'm quick. Pain ignored, I run as fast as I can until I'm shrouded in the darkness under the trees. I stop and look back and see they are just milling around. Hopefully they think they imagined something. Goddamn it. How do I get out of here? I can hardly call another Uber. I really need to plan more before making stupid decisions. I don't even register what I am doing until I am calling Lev.

"What do you want, doe?" he answers, and I can hear music in the background.

"Help me, I'm stuck here and I don't want them to find me," I whisper yell, hoping he can hear me.

There is a beat of silence, and the music in the background becomes distant. He must be walking to somewhere more quiet.

"Are you high? What do you mean stuck?"

"I followed Jake tonight and got you more info, but I can't get home. I'm in the middle of fucking nowhere. But I have proof now."

I swear to god the rumble that comes through the phone is like a lion's purr. "You followed him on your own? You are insane, doe. Pin me your location and Jules or Simon will pick you up. Stay covered for now, okay?

They will message you when nearby. Keep your phone on silent."

"Okay. Thanks."

He grunts back like the caveman he is and ends the call. I really hope they take me back to see Lev so I can show him what I have. I'm craving his attention already. If I wasn't at risk of drawing attention, I would be jumping up and down.

CHAPTER 11
LEV

What the fuck was Aaron thinking following his stepbrother tonight?

Well, it is obvious the guy doesn't seem to think at all from what I have witnessed. But I can't think about that too much. A rush of excitement pounds through my system–Aaron might have information, and I'll get to have my fun, finally. I'll find out all their secrets and get my dose of blood before I completely lose it and end up hurting someone else for no reason.

I call Dima and let him know what's happening. He is making his way back to the house to be here for Aaron's arrival. I pace my brother's office, itching to get started on this. If I get what I want, I may even entertain the idea of fucking doe as a job well done. I might actually get some sleep tonight for the first time in over a month.

I'm not sure how much time passes, but finally, Dima walks into the office and pats me on the shoulder.

"Finally got something to go on then, brother?" he asks as he sits in his ridiculously over the top office chair. Such a snob.

"I hope so. I only know the stupid idiot followed Jake to a meeting on his own, got some footage then realized he couldn't get home." I roll my eyes at the foolishness of the situation. Not that I would ever say it out loud, but I respect Aaron for it. He went in without fear. Reckless, but fucking hot.

We remain in silence, awaiting the return of Jules with Aaron. I can't sit still, so I return to pacing the length of Dima's office, while he is on his phone, no doubt texting Seb like they are ever apart for more than ten minutes. Just as I am about to goad Dima about Seb, the door flies open. Aaron walks in, flanked by Simon and Jules. I notice straight away the light bruises on his face, which look like they are at the end of healing. What the fuck happened? An anger stirs in me that's foreign in its intensity. It's protective in nature and I immediately rebel against it. I only look out for my brother and that's as far as I go.

Dima takes over the conversation, which I am grateful for. I want to know who touched Aaron, more than I care about the information he came to bring me.

"You good, Aaron? Your face is a little bruised," Dima says.

That fucking freaky smile of Aaron's appears as he answers, but his eyes remain on me as he speaks.

"Oh that wasn't tonight. I got into a fight a few days ago. I'm good now."

Well that smells like bullshit to me, but it's not my business. *But it is.*

"Alright, what you got, Aaron?" Dima gets straight down to business.

He smiles at me one last time, then takes a seat in front of my brother and starts to explain the events of tonight, from finding the text on his brother's phone and then what happened at the abandoned factory site.

Dima's questioning eyes flick to me now and then as Aaron explains tonight in detail with such excitement, it might as well be show and tell at pre-school. I have never met someone with such varied personas, and I wonder if there are more sides to him yet to uncover.

Just another reason I need to stay away from him, his quirks and odd behavior thrill me and I need to shut that shit away. After he has finished his story of his never-ending list of stupid decisions tonight, I walk over to him. I wouldn't be surprised if he wanted a sticker saying "star pupil" on it with how eager he is.

"Gimme the phone," I order, hand stretched out to him. He passes it over and gently places it in my palm. He touches the tips of my fingers with his, keeping those doe eyes of his fixed on mine. I don't think I am imagining the look of adoration he is aiming my way, and I have no fucking idea why, but I like it.

I scroll through the phone until I find the video footage and the one picture of Jake shaking hands with some guy. I zoom in, and I am surprised the phone has not burst into flames with the fury I am aiming at the picture. Steam must be leaving my ears, because I am about to fucking blow.

"Those motherfuckers!" I flip the screen around to show Dima. "It's Carlos Silva's men, D. I thought you said we could trust him. That son of a bitch."

Dima made a deal months ago for Carlos to be our new distributor, but looks like we are getting fucked over big time. Dima stares at the picture, confusion on his face, lips pursed. He looks up at Jules and Simon and turns the phone to face them.

"Do either of you know their names?" he asks.

Jules takes the phone and looks at the screen, with Simon looking at it over his shoulder. Simon and Jules both nod.

"Yeah, that's Hugo and Mario," Simon says. "They are normally at the container handovers, a couple of Carlos' grunts."

"I doubt he knows," Dima says as he looks up at me. "I know Carlos, Lev. If this was him he would have been there or at least his right hand man. These guys are lower members. From the look of it, I'd guess Jake's crew has formed an alliance with Carlos' guys to start their own trade, that's my thought."

"So, what now, D?" Jules asks.

"I'm gonna call Carlos," Dima says, knowing what I want. "Jules, Si, find out where these guys are since you know where they hang out, and bring them in. Use force if you have to. I will let Carlos know what happened and we will deal with it ourselves. I'll ask him to get his boys to stand down when you are on their turf. Then, we can bring Jake and his boys in."

I nod in relief. Finally, we are getting somewhere. After Jules and Simon leave, Dima stands to leave too, with phone in hand already calling Carlos.

"I'm going to find my husband before they bring them in. I'll see you in the pen later, brother." He then looks to Aaron who is still sitting obediently, grinning. I would love to get inside his head to see what goes on, the pull of intrigue is becoming stronger and it needs to fucking stop. "Good job, Aaron. You were stupid for following them on your own, but well done."

Dima smirks at me before leaving with his phone to his

ear and no doubt on his way to fuck his husband for probably the hundredth time today.

I look back to Aaron who gets to his feet and walks over to me, no smile this time. He looks different, stoic, cold and intense as he watches me. It's like another person has entered the room. Looking at him now, this is the Aaron I knew was there amongst all his other traits. This is personal for him, and he also must be wondering what it all means for him now.

"I want to watch," he states. It doesn't feel like a question, and I am a little surprised by the ice in his voice. Hmm, I like this cold Aaron, this could be fun.

"You wanna watch me play? Why?"

"I love watching you work."

Again, that surprises me. I would have remembered him had I seen him before, and most of the work I do is here in the holding pen.

"When have you ever seen me work?" I am not sure how we have gotten closer, but we are so close that I could take that sexy ass mouth for a kiss that I really want. That cold look in his brown eyes does something to me, triggers the need to fuck him while hurting others at the same time.

"I saw a couple of months ago when you removed the snitch's teeth from Mark's crew. I watched through the window," he says with a soft lilt to his voice like he is recollecting a happy memory.

I think back and, ahhh yes, I remember. That little bastard had been gloating around town about our business and talking up his involvement. He needed to be put in his place. It worked and he is an obedient dog for us now, with a nice set of dental implants.

Thinking of that day, I get warm all over. The image of

being watched while I play ... I never thought about it before.

Judging by the smile that's back on Aaron's face, I think the little doe gets off on the violence, and that in turn makes me want to strip him bare right now and rut into him until he can't move.

I let out a husky chuckle. I can't let that little comment go, so I push against him and grab the back of his neck firmly, fisting the hair at the nape, making him look at me.

The way those big brown eyes dilate and how his body relaxes into my hold, I think I have met my match for crazy.

"Does it get you off, doe?"

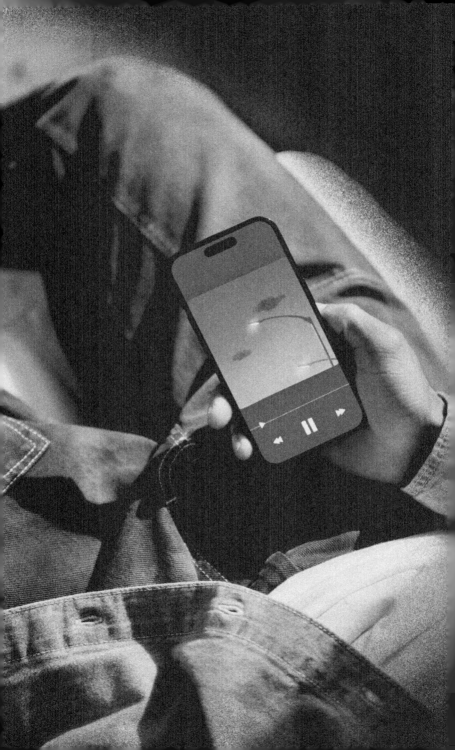

CHAPTER 12
AARON

What a stupid question, but the way he holds me so firmly around my neck and bores those evil green eyes into mine, I bet he can read all my secrets and desires. My body quakes. For a brief moment, I fantasize about Lev tying up Jake and Tommy. His large naked torso covered in their blood, hurting them so badly that their cries sound like tortured animals in the night. Lev watching me as he works while I jerk myself off, bathing in his savage presence. Oh hell, yeah.

"Yes, when it's you."

His painful grip on the back of my head shoots pain down my neck, but I don't care. I'll take it if it means having him this close to me.

His other hand grips my throat and tightens. His eyes glint with excitement. I have no idea how to flirt, and it's hard to date when you're someone like me with a psycho stepbrother keeping tabs on you, but I don't have an issue telling the truth.

I want to say more, but the longer he holds me, the

more malleable I become. You would think my heart would be racing with anticipation, but it steadies its rhythm. Lev calms my storm while creating a tornado of need. I've always dreamed of being owned by someone like Lev.

"You are trouble, aren't you? Are you that desperate for me, doe? Desperate for a dicking … is that it?" He chuckles.

I love the sound. It promises depravity, it promises passion, and it promises the darkest depth of hidden hungers that I want to inhale quickly before they disappear. It's so fucking freeing not to pretend.

He leans in and bites the lobe of my ear followed by a lick. Oh shit, I think I might die. All other feelings have been overridden by his sensual touch. That lick sends hums of electricity across my sensitive flesh, prickling my ear when he moves away. My dick is so hard and eager to leave my pants right now, if only it had a mind of its own and could pull my zipper down itself.

He pulls back, settling his hard eyes on me. "You want me to fuck you hard? Because I will, and it will hurt. Can you take it?" He rubs his nose up and down my neck, inhaling me, igniting thousands of goosebumps over my skin all the way down to my balls.

My head is in a lustful daze. It's everything I wanted. I give an eager nod. "Yes, whatever you want."

"You give yourself too easily, doe, but I'll take it and I won't stop."

"I don't want you to stop."

Lev freezes, and I'm not sure why I said it out loud. It's true but something passes over Lev's face, and I'm not sure what it is. Have I made him uncomfortable? I want to take it back for fear that he might pull away.

"Let's be clear, Aaron, I will stop. I don't fuck twice, and I don't do relationships or feelings. If you are looking for that you should leave and forget about this."

My mind is warring between getting what I crave, which is Lev over the top of me, or not getting the full package of what I want, which is for Lev to own all of me. But I can't say no. I need to feel it, if only once.

"Okay," I mutter before he pushes me down to my knees.

"I haven't got time to fuck, but you can hold me over until later. I'm all riled up. Open that sexy mouth as wide as you can, doe," he demands.

I make a mental note to ask him later why he calls me doe. Not that I have an issue with it, I love that he has a name for me, but I wanna know why.

I stare up at him as he undoes his belt and I'm so hyper with need, it's hard to keep still. He pulls his pants down enough to reveal the most monster-sized cock I have ever seen. Oh shit, a pierced monster cock. I admire the shiny barbell that glints in the light. I'm not sure half of his dick will fit in my mouth, and that's just the length, it's girthy too, but his scent is all masculine and heady, making me float like a drugged up needy whore.

It's slightly musky too with hints of his body wash. Fuck would I love to coat myself in that body wash. I open my mouth wide and eager as he taps the head of his dick onto my tongue several times. Fuck me, it's heavy and each tap leaves a salty taste from where he's dripping. Dripping for me.

I want to laugh so hard right now, but I don't want to weird him out with any more of my odd behaviors.

I refocus and stop overthinking, giving my full attention to the delicious piece of meat that I'm about to enjoy.

He has a prominent vein running up the side of his shaft, and I want to trace it with my tongue. It's dick perfection.

"Get ready," he says, and shoves his cock in and out of my mouth with such force, I wretch loudly, gagging. No build up, he just takes what he wants. He's holding my head steady with both hands as he fucks my mouth viciously, the piercing smashes into the back of my throat. I'm sure it will leave a nice imprint that I'll enjoy looking for later. I can't wait to have a mark of Lev carved into me.

I am so lost in another world and enjoying this face fuck that I startle when I feel a sharp slap on my cheek.

"Eyes on me, little doe. Show me how much you love my dick. I wanna see tears."

Fuck, yes, I can do that.

Saliva is now free flowing down my chin as he thrusts rapidly in and out of my mouth. He groans on every thrust as I try not to gag as much as my body wants to. The tears are streaming down my face, but I find myself relaxing and opening up more to his cock.

My mind drifts off to erotic heaven. I move my hands up his thick muscular thighs, relishing in the feel of soft hairs before I move them around and grab the firm, smooth, and meaty globes of his ass, forcing him deeper.

An animalistic growl rumbles from his chest. If I could choose to die in any way I wanted, it would be like this. Death by cock-choking. Lev's cock.

"Fuck yeah, I knew you were a cock slut. That's it, you gonna take my load? Swallow it like a good cum guzzler."

I try to nod as I mewl, my own erection becoming unbearable. His grunts become more rapid and his control slips. His speed increases, which takes my breath completely away as I struggle to hold onto my own orgasm and take air in through my nose at the same time. I remove my hands from his ass and attempt to touch my own dick, but Lev slaps me again across the face. *Hard.*

"Uh-uh, you won't be coming until you are on my dick. Shit, I'm close." His grunting turns into heavy panting, and his movements falter before thick ropes of warm cum hit the back of my throat, making me swallow on instinct.

"Fuck yes," he hisses. When he's finished spurting, he pulls out as I fall forward to the floor, trying to catch my breath. I think that was my best BJ ever.

Sitting back on my knees, too shaky to stand, Lev is already zipping up his pants. He looks so composed, even though I can see he's trying to relax his breathing. My dick is aching so much right now, but I know pleasing him and following his instructions will make it so much better for me. Anything to keep his eyes on me.

For some reason, I briefly think of others he might do this with, and I start to vibrate with an abnormal amount of anger, jealousy, and possessiveness. This isn't good. I'm already territorial. But the thought of seeing someone else touch him builds a fire in me, the urge to hurt someone. As far back as I remember, when I fixate on something it's almost impossible for me to shift that focus. It's almost like an "I licked it so it's mine" situation. It got worse after my mom died. The feeling of being unwanted, along with my grief, made me cling harder to anything that would grab my attention and provide security and comfort. Lev is my new focus, and his cock.

"You certainly know how to give head," Lev says.

Lev gazes down at me and grabs my jaw, using his thumb to rub his cum–which has escaped my mouth–over my lips. He then lifts his thumb into his mouth, savoring his own release, his pupils flaring as he enjoys the taste of himself on his tongue.

And he should, it's the best thing I've ever eaten.

A text message alert breaks the moment, and he pulls his phone from his pocket, scrolling through it. "Get yourself fixed up. The boys are on their way, and then you are with me tonight. I don't plan on letting you sleep. I'm extra horny after I play."

I have never heard someone demand sex like Lev does in such a serious and authoritative way. There's no flirting, eye winking, or teasing in it. He's matter of fact, but on him, it only makes him more fucking sexy.

If that's possible.

"Fine by me," I say. My ass clenches at the thought that his monster dick may actually break me, and my dick feels even harder at the images of what he will do to me.

A whole night. I have every intention of making sure his cock leaves a permanent marker in my ass, and that I'll feel him inside me for days. I hope the ache will take away all the other shit I know I'll have to endure after tonight from Jake. Thinking about Jake raises another question.

"What about Jake? He'll want to know where I am."

Lev looks at me, brows furrowed, and the question is obvious. Why do I, an adult, need to let my stepbrother know where I am as if I'm some child with a protective parent? I scoff to myself at the ridiculousness of it.

"Why? You are twenty-four, Aaron, a fucking adult. Tell him to fuck off or that you are getting laid."

"That will make it worse."

"Why would it make it worse?" he asks.

I start to feel uncomfortable. How do I explain this without it sounding … well, like it is.

"He has a weird obsession with me. He doesn't like me hooking up with anyone or staying out for the night."

Lev is silent as he stares at me. "Are you telling me your brother wants to fuck you?"

Trust Lev to be blunt. "Stepbrother and yes. He has always been too engrossed by me, he has gotten more controlling. He will kill me Lev, I know it. I want out of the crew, but I can't do it without help." I pause. "I ... I want him dead, Lev. I want it over, but I can't do it with all the support he has, it's impossible."

The cogs in Lev's mind turn, thinking my words over.

"Yeah, Jules mentioned he seemed to have an odd obsession with you. Well, he will be dead soon after I'm done with him, but if you like, when we have him, you can do the deed. My gift to you for being a rat."

That comment about being a rat should sting, but it doesn't. Ridding the world of a sick and twisted fuck like Jake is a service to the community. Then Lev shocks the shit out of me with a smile. It's not a nice smile, it's an evil and maybe slightly deranged smile, but I love it none-theless. He's enjoying this.

"But if he finds out about me ratting him out before then, I'll be finished for good, Lev."

He shrugs. "You will be fine, Aaron. Just keep acting and it will all be over soon enough. Hopefully we will get the info tonight to put an end to it."

"But what do I tell Jake about tonight?" I'm whining now.

"For fucks sake, do you want me to do everything? Christ, can nobody think for themselves anymore?" he complains as he walks to the door. He stops, looks back to me, and sighs. "Tell him Jules called you with a job to make up for the Santini shitshow and if he has questions, tell him to call me if he wants to meet his maker sooner."

He pauses for a breath. "Jake's the one that did that to your face, isn't he?"

Lev's nostrils flare. But … but I thought he didn't give a shit about anything or anyone other than his brother?

"Yeah, he was angry when I came back from our meeting. Asking where I'd been. I lied but it made no difference."

"I'm going to enjoy taking him apart, doe, and you will have a front row seat," he says before leaving the room.

As expected, the smile on my face is instant. This is turning out to be the best fucking day ever. I'm aware of how insane that sounds. Does he actually care about what happens to me?

Leaving the office to follow Lev down to the holding pen, I try to coach myself mentally–I will not get turned on as he works. I am about to witness my version of the hottest porn I've ever seen, and it hasn't even begun yet. The prospect of what he'll do to those guys is enough to keep me on that euphoric edge.

This is going to provide me with some serious jerk-off fantasies, and they already start playing like a record, spinning in my brain. Fuck, oh god, how am I going to do this?

As we walk down to the holding pen, I pull out my phone and text Jake.

ME:

> I won't be home tonight. Jules has me doing some work for him to make up for the Santini fuck up. I will text you tomorrow before I get back home.

J:

> What the fuck you mean you won't be home? What's he got you doing?

ME:

> They just want me to sit in on some interrogation and clean up. I think it's just to keep me in line. I'm not sure how long they will be keeping me here. It's not like I can help it, Jake. Gotta go.

J:

> Fine, but you better get your ass back here tomorrow, and I want details.

Well, that's better than it could've turned out. I put my phone on silent and slip it into my back pocket. At least he'll be off my ass for the rest of the night so I can enjoy watching Lev play.

Speaking of Lev, I head down towards the door that leads to the holding pen. It's a huge shiny black door like you would see in a maximum security prison. As I walk in, I'm straight away blinded by how white the walls are in here. It's so clinical and creepy, the kind of thing you would see in a horror film. There are drains scattered all over the black tiled floor, tools lining the wall at the back of the room, a bed in the corner that looks like it belongs in a morgue, complete with straps in all the four corners, and two industrial-looking fridges. It's clear what happens down here, and I can't help but be equally as excited as I am turned on to see what will happen tonight.

Noticing Lev on the other side of the room, I realize this will be a test of restraint. Lev's looking over his tools, wearing nothing but a pair of sweatpants, and I swear to god, I may cum at the sight.

His chest is so muscular and broad, tattoos cover his arms, hands, chest, and his neck. I'm so drawn to them that I want to lick them all over. The thought of seeing that body covering mine tonight makes me want to submit to him, kneel at his feet like I'm confessing at church. Let him do anything he wants. *Fuuuck*.

I think I'd even let him tie me up in here. He looks so at home in this room of horrors. My king Lev is in his element in this room, and he commands it. This man, this beast, who is in total control, powerful, and clearly blood-thirsty. It is the most erotic sight I have ever seen. There's no turning back from this feeling for me.

"Are you just gonna stand there, doe? Make yourself comfortable," Lev says. "This is going to be a long one."

He smirks and heads over to the corner of the room where he grabs two metal chairs and brings them to the center of the room, positioning them to face each other. I stroll over to one of the countertops at the side of the room and jump my ass on top of the stainless-steel surface. A cigarette would be perfect right now. I quit years ago, but being around the cigar scent that lingers on Lev mixed with the dangerous atmosphere, I could kill for one right now. No pun intended.

A few minutes pass by before the door opens and Jules and Simon strut in with two guys who have their hands tied behind their back. They walk them over to the two chairs and sit them down facing each other.

Fear flashes in their eyes as they tentatively scan the room and look back at each other. They are definitely trying to keep hold of the panic they must be feeling. But it's a sight I welcome. I can't help the smile on my face, knowing what pain faces them. Guys like them are no better than Jake.

My blood simmers under my skin, warming my body. The thought of being able to have Jake down here and do what I want to him stirs those parts of me that never rise when I am engulfed in his presence. The need to make him suffer as he has made me suffer all these years takes over me. I wonder for a moment why this part of me has forced its way past the carefully constructed walls I built in my mind.

It must be this room. This space blankets me in security, while at the same time giving me the freedom to just be me. I also think the sex god who is currently pacing back and forth between his victims has a lot to do with how I'm feeling. His openness shatters my barriers piece by piece and he takes away the loudness that exists in my head.

As Jules and Simon secure the men to the chairs with zip-ties, Dima appears at the door and marches over to his brother, where they have a hushed conversation. I've never seen Lev look as relaxed as he does right now, probably because that constant pissy scowl he wears is nowhere to be seen.

My body is on high alert, watching him. It's slightly unnerving the way I react to him. I just want to stand behind him and cling to him while he works. I'd love to feed off the high he gets from his victims as he hurts them.

He's so fucking intoxicating that I want to climb him and not let go. This crush is not a good thing. Lev is opening up all those parts of my brain that I have kept a lock on for so long, the sexual desire for violence, being dominated, and feeling safe enough to allow the voices to come out to play. There's nothing I can do to stop these feelings from coming to the surface. Lev would surely kill me if he knew what a besotted little bitch I've become, and I know after he has his way with me, it will get worse. A lot worse. I attach easily, searching for that anchor to balance me.

Jules and Simon take their place behind each man tied

to the chairs. Lev walks into the center of the room like he's on stage about to perform for an audience. He's wearing his signature demonic grin, which makes those intense hawk-shaped eyes even more savage.

Am I drooling right now?

"Shall we start?" he says.

Let playtime begin.

CHAPTER 13
LEV

Fuck me, have I needed this. It feels like forever since I was last down here. While part of me wants to rush through so I can get that high as quickly as possible, the other part of me wants to savor every second, every cry, every scream, and every drop of blood I am about to serve on these two cunts.

Luckily Carlos was on board. Dima just informed me that he wanted this filmed for proof and let's just say he was less than happy with the footage of their meeting with Jake. He had noticed some issues with shipping and some inconsistencies on amounts delivered, but they had not been able to work out what was happening. Now the cards have all fallen into place. He was angry, but considering how he has only been our distributor for a few months, as a kindness so to speak, he was fine with us dealing with his boys. Maybe Carlos isn't the dick I thought after all.

"Remove their shirts," I order Jules and Simon, who are both standing behind each of the men currently strapped into their seats.

Of course one of them starts shouting and complaining,

trying hard to wiggle out of his restraints. It's amazing how the human mind works, even though they know deep down this is the end, that they can't escape. They still hold onto the hope of breaking free and surviving. But I enjoy this part. Dima hates it when they get all noisy, but I enjoy them crying, trying to find a way out. It amuses me. The guys tear their shirts open with the knives they have retrieved from the wall to reveal their bare chests.

Hugo is the more controlled one. Going by the scars on his face, he has been through a lot in life that's probably made him stronger, as opposed to the hysterical Mario who is putting up a decent fight. His black curly hair is sticking to his sweaty forehead.

I can almost taste the salty panic. Mario will be the best one to start with. I have found they are more likely to give answers when the desperation to live takes hold with the fear of the pain that is coming. I stand in front of Mario with my special knife that's normally used for skinning animals, but over the years I have used it for flaying human skin. Works just as good for that.

"Mario, tell me, what were you meeting Jake and Tommy about the other night?" I ask as I gently glide the side of the knife down his face, not cutting the skin, but building the tension, hoping to raise his anxiety.

"I didn't want to be there … it wasn't my idea, I swear!" he shouts, shaking against the chair so hard the metal is rattling around the base as his jittery movements cause it to rock.

"That wasn't what I asked, maybe you need an incentive. Here is what I'll do. For everything I do to your friend Hugo here, I will do the same to you if you don't give me a straight answer, got it?" I ask, moving over to Hugo who is sitting in a more rigid manner. It's a lie, though. His rapid breathing and heavy sweating give him away. He's not as bad as Mario, but the signs are there in the subtle glisten above his mouth and along his hairline. I walk behind him, wanting Mario to have the full view of what I am doing to Hugo. Mario's eyes follow the knife as I slowly drag it down Hugo's chest before I stop above his left nipple.

Holding him by the shoulder, I swiftly flick the knife down in a slicing motion, removing his nipple, it's like cutting butter. Trying to hold in his scream, the little grunts of pain that come from him are low and guttural. Snot and spit drip down his face as he grips his lips in between his teeth, trying so hard to control himself. I smile and pick up the severed nipple with my fingers and take it over to Mario. Oh dear, Mario does not look good. His olive skin is so pale, tinged with green. It looks like he is about to vomit, so I wiggle the nipple close to his face.

"Now, shall I make it a pair? I took his left, maybe I should remove your right one." I laugh, having the best time.

"Please don't...please, Lev. I will tell you anything," he pleads.

They always do.

I drop the nasty piece of flesh onto the ground and look over at Hugo who is bleeding quite a lot from the wound, but he is still holding strong, refusing to show weakness. I can respect that. I happen to glance over to where Aaron is sitting on the countertop, and I'm not sure if my eyes may be deceiving me. He looks like he is on the verge of cumming. His eyes are hooded, his tongue repeatedly licking his lower lip. As I trail my eyes down his body, I see him subtly rub his hand over his crotch. Fucking hell that's hot. My dick starts to rise to the occasion. This is fucking perfect. I am quickly brought back to the room when Dima clears his throat and looks at Aaron, his face scrunched in disbelief.

"Are you fucking kidding me, Aaron? This is an inter-rogation, not a jerk-off session. Stop rubbing your dick," Dima says.

"Shut up, D. Let him do what he wants. You seem to have forgotten what you and Seb did down here in front of everyone a few months ago," I remind him.

"That was different," Dima says, and I swear there is a sulkiness in his voice.

I roll my eyes. "No, it wasn't. You don't like it, you can leave." I walk over to Aaron and stand in between his legs where they are parted against the countertop.

He flinches when he realizes that I'm in front of him. He must have been in his own world. That weird-ass smile lights up his face. I lean in towards him. "Enjoying the show, doe?"

He legit moans in an airy way, his mouth hovering over my lips. "Yes," he whispers.

I swear you could touch the sexual energy between us right now.

I grin at him and hold the back of his neck. "You can have your fun, doe, but remember you are not to cum. You can only do that sitting on my dick." I lick the side of his face, needing to taste him, and his body trembles under my touch, which forces his thighs to grip around my hips harder.

"I promise," he whimpers, so obedient.

Tearing myself away from him, I walk back to the toys I am about to play with. It is no joke how hard my dick is, but it makes this scenario feel more empowering. I have always wanted to mix my two addictions at once, and it looks like that is about to happen, courtesy of my little weirdo in the corner. *My little weirdo? Where the fuck did that come from?* He isn't mine. It's the dick lust making me think that.

Moving away from those thoughts, I get back to work.

"So, Mario, I will ask again, why were you meeting Jake and Tommy?"

CHAPTER 14
AARON

Holy shitballs. I knew it would be hard to control myself while watching Lev play, but fuck, I didn't think my restraint would falter so fast. He is like a deadly panther with the way he prowls around this room. He controls everything in it, and it fills the air with a thrum of power and strength that I want to overdose on. When he cut that nipple off, I nearly came. I had to grip my dick to stop myself, but then I couldn't help rubbing it, especially when his attention shifted back to me again.

That muscular broad chest, which now has flecks of blood on it, and the way his face has contorted into this demonic king, I can't look away. I don't give a shit about the others around us.

But I'll keep my promise; I won't cum until he's fucking me later.

While I'm enjoying the show, part of me wants him to hurry the fuck up so I can ride him like an eager cowboy. Gripping myself hard again and clenching my ass, I try to hold down the longing to get off.

Feeling eyes on me, I turn to the side and see Dima watching me. His mouth curls up in the corner, before he looks back onto Lev. Getting control of myself, I follow his gaze back to the show as it plays out in front of us. They should do a subscription service for this.

"They were just discussing how they were going to start distributing to other turfs and what the shares would be. I wasn't involved in any of the negotiations, I was just there as muscle," Mario blurts out, evidently afraid he will join the one-nipple club too.

Much to my joy, Lev leans over him, placing the tip of the knife over his small brown bud.

"See, was that so hard?"

The loudest scream I have ever heard ricochets around the room. Lev has sliced off the nipple in question, and Mario fights against his restraints, in pain and shock.

It's a glorious sound.

I know that the smile has not left my face and I try but fail to stop my hand rubbing my hard dick through my jeans again. I let out a small murmur of pleasure that I don't think anyone could hear until the focus of my attention looks over to me, watching what I am doing. Lev looks like he wants to pounce on me right now and, fuck, I'd let him. I need him so fucking bad that if it doesn't happen soon, I may go into a frenzy and kill the bastards myself. Cutting our connection, he focuses back on the crying mess that is Mario. Snot and tears mixed together are not a hot look.

Is it wrong that I am jealous that the one-nipple man has Lev's attention and not me?

"You...you said you wouldn't if I told you," Mario cries.

"I lied," Lev says. "Now, next question."

He walks back over to Hugo who is so much more controlled in this situation, but I'm bouncing with eagerness to see what Lev will do next. I want to rub up against him while he plays so I can feel what he feels. Am I deranged? Probably, but this is, like, the best foreplay I have ever experienced.

"Jules, hold his hand out," Lev orders.

Jules unties his left hand from the chair with ease because Jules is a fucking machine. He grabs Hugo's hand in a tight grip, forcing his palm to face upward and spread his fingers.

Huh, I have no idea what's happening right now but me and my cock are all for it. I stop rubbing myself so I can zero in on what is happening.

"Don't look away, Mario, you wanted to be with the big boys. Now stop being a pussy and endure it like a man. Simon, hold his head," Lev says.

Simon uses both his hands to grip Mario's head in a firm lock so he can't move, forced to witness what's about to happen.

"You see this knife, Mario? It's a skinning knife, and what's amazing about it is that it cuts through human skin like butter. I don't even have to try. Watch."

Lev glides the knife over the skin of Hugo's little finger starting at the tip, and this time he can't hold in the scream. The knife flays off the skin so smoothly, it's like watching an apple getting peeled, leaving the raw meat of his flesh exposed. Lev continues peeling his entire finger at a slow and tortuous pace. The agony of it bleeds out of Hugo, trying to pull away, crying, screaming. He's in the middle of a panic attack, breathing too fast and shaking.

After Lev has finished removing the skin from the whole finger and only the nail remains, he holds it up. It looks like a translucent piece of wax paper. Hugo sobs as Lev does his show and tell by dangling the piece of skin in front of Mario. He is quiet. I think the reality has hit home for him and he is going into some kind of shock. I have no idea.

"Do they have to be so fucking loud," I hear Dima mumble from beside me as he rubs his temples, trying to stave off a headache. I smile. The brothers are so similar yet so different.

"Give me the names of all involved, and I may let you go."

That's a fucking lie, but the little flash of hope in Mario's eyes shows how naive the guy is. Lev has already lied once.

He's a killer, but he gets off on the taunting. This fuels a blood hunger in him, gives him a high like no other. This is the most animated, relaxed, and happiest I have seen Lev since I met him. I want to see more.

"It's only Jake's crew on your side, but…"

"Shut the fuck up, Mario, they will kill us anyway," Hugo barks.

Someone is loyal, except to the wrong person. A sudden awareness shoots through me. It angers me that someone has betrayed the Kozlovs, Lev in particular of course. Makes me want to do things. Bad things. From the short time I have spent in their presence, I have felt secure. Sure, it's a gut feeling, but I feel like these are the family members I should have had.

"Fuck off, Hugo, I want to live," Mario says. He's nearly hyperventilating. "Alex and Dom are running the show, they work for Carlos."

Dima scoffs and walks towards Mario. "No shit they work for Carlos, Alex is his right-hand guy. You fuckers don't understand the word loyalty," he says.

Lev crouches in front of a now sniffling Mario and gently holds his face, making me irrationally angry. Why is he touching him like that? I jump off the countertop and the movement alerts Lev. He frowns in my direction.

My smile vanishes, my nostrils flare, and my fists clench tight. I want to punch Lev in the fucking dick. I know he's not mine, but he is for tonight.

But Crazy, who has fought his way to the front of my mind, thinks it's more. Crazy doesn't get center stage often. He does help me feel powerful, though.

He is yours, you gonna let him touch another man? I don't fucking think so.

"Get your hands off him, Lev," I snarl at him, attracting the attention of the rest of the room. I can't stop the words coming out and I expect him to shout at me or even slap me, but he laughs instead. A genuine, beautiful laugh and I don't know what to do with that. Usually, he's pissed off. His laugh makes me more uncomfortable than him threatening to cut my tongue out.

"Calm down, doe. Save your jealous fit for later," he coos at me, and it actually works as Crazy retreats, reassured by Lev's words, but leaving me bemused as to how to get a grip on my overactive brain.

Feeling a hand on my shoulder guiding me back, I notice it's Dima. "Don't distract him, Aaron, just let him get on with it. Trust me, he isn't like that with anyone he brings down here, he is teasing them. It's his weird kink."

He rolls his eyes, but he's right. Try telling the other occupant in my brain that.

Lev holds Mario's face with his palm again, seemingly trying to comfort Mario, which is unnerving.

"Shush, it's okay now, nothing to worry about," Lev says. A yelp leaves Mario and his eyes widen, gurgling sounds come from his chest as blood starts to sputter out of his mouth. Lev stands, removing the knife from Mario's chest. Blood oozes from the fatal wound as Mario tries to gasp for air, which quickly turns into shallow wet gasps before his glazed over eyes remain open and he takes his last breath.

"Too trusting, that boy, but that's not you, is it Hugo?" Lev says.

"You're a piece of shit, Kozlov. I can't wait until they take you down," Hugo says.

Dima laughs out loud. "No fucker is taking us down, dickhead. We aren't the ones tied to a chair right now. You fucked up. You are the scum traitors to the family that looked after you. Carlos is so ashamed." He moves over to Hugo and bends down to face him. "You will die here the pathetic loser that you are with nobody coming to save you, no one to mourn you, and nobody to avenge you. Tomorrow you'll be nothing but pulp at the bottom of an acid drum," he says.

I have to give it to Hugo, he gives attitude until the end. "I couldn't give a fuck what you think of me, so just do what you gotta do," he says.

"Okay," Dima says, before standing to his full height. He removes his gun from the back of his trousers and fires a shot between Hugo's eyes. Brain matter covers the floor and Dima grins when he wipes his face, looking at his blood covered fingers. I'm shocked at his expression as he inspects the blood. It's like it's the most beautiful thing he has ever seen. Okay, someone has a blood kink.

"What a vain prick," Dima mumbles as he retrieves a tissue from his pocket to clean his hands.

I'm speechless after what I've witnessed today. I really hope it's a weekly thing that I can be part of. These brothers are stunning to watch in their bloody glory, but Lev, I am ready to submit to him in any way he chooses.

CHAPTER 15
LEV

"Simon, arrange the clean-up. Jules, make a copy of the recording, so we have something," I say.

"You got it," Jules replies, and they get on with their orders.

I am vibrating with the need to get my hands on Aaron, but we need to wrap this up first. I do not want to be disturbed tonight as I acquaint him with my mattress when he is face down being fucked like the little attention whore he has proven to be.

"D, what's the plan? You contacting Carlos?" I ask Dima.

"Yeah, I'll call him and let him know, then I'll arrange to meet him tomorrow and give him the footage. He's gonna be pissed," he says.

"Damn right he is. I can't believe Alex is heading this. You need to warn him about what Alex is up to so he can be a step ahead," I say.

"I will. Don't worry. Now I'm gonna call Carlos and then find my husband. You get some rest brother," he says.

"Oh, there will be no rest tonight. Better tell Princess Seb to have his earplugs in," I say with a leery grin.

Dima rolls his eyes. "Grow the fuck up, Lev." He walks out.

God, I feel high, just Jake and his boys left to go and it's done. I needed this tonight, to let go of the strain that was constricting me from functioning. But I still have another issue. I am still hard and need to fuck it out and I have zoned in on my chosen victim. Aaron hasn't moved from the corner. He is just staring at me, no smile, no fear; he has zero emotion on his face. I think he has reached his limit of being edged tonight because that is what this turned out to be. One long edging session, letting our dark wishes loose into the world before joining together and burning that energy.

Keeping my eyes on his as I quickly walk to him, I grab the back of his neck, and guide him out of the pen.

"Time to fuck, doe," I whisper into his ear. His body wavers, and he is slightly wobbly on his feet as I push him forward. I need him in my bed. Walking down the corridor towards my room, we see Seb, who looks like he is about to say something, but nothing, not even an atomic bomb is stopping me from getting into Aaron's ass tonight.

"Fuck off, Seb, we're busy." We march past him.

"Fucking dick," he grumbles, but I don't care to respond. I am on a mission and I will not deter from it. My cock is so hard right now. I can still smell the blood and death on me from the holding pen and it is making my state of arousal harder to contain. Mix it with the scent of Aaron who smells like the sea on a breezy day, and I am fucking feral. I want to roll my body over him so that he's stamped with my scent. I want my scent to linger on his skin for days so people will know that I've claimed his ass tonight. It sets off this new obsessive side to me, which makes more of an appearance in my life the longer Aaron is around me. Normally, I would bat that feeling away, but I am too far gone for that now. The barrier of my restraint has been breached, and Aaron is gonna feel it all tonight.

Pushing him into my room, he manages to remain balanced on his feet before he turns to face me. We stand, taking in one another, his gaze slowly wandering from my feet up towards my face, and I can't look away from those damn eyes. It's like we are waiting for someone to wave a flag to let us know that the race can now begin.

"Get naked, and do it slowly," I say.

"Oh, god," he whispers.

He is so loving this.

First, he removes his boots and socks. Then, he pulls his shirt over his head, revealing himself little by little. I feel like I am at a peep show. I nearly swallow my tongue. He has the hottest body. I knew he was in good shape, but the muscle definition is mouthwatering. The deep V at his groin makes the perfect cum gutters. All smooth and tanned, not a mark on him, no moles or birthmarks. There is some faint bruising on his left rib, but apart from that, he is a perfect blank canvas.

A few of my own bruises and bite marks will enhance his sexiness as well as remind him who rocked his world tonight. His small brown nipples are hard at the tip, and I lick my lips eager to eat them, bite them, and suck on them until they redden around the edges.

I watch as his hands move leisurely towards the top of his jeans, and I can already see how hard he is. When he undoes the top two buttons, the tip of his dick shows and I nearly cum from the fact that he has no fucking underwear on. Shit. My breathing is coming in at an alarming pace now. This striptease may send me into an early grave. Nobody has affected me like this little shit, and I'll be damned if I don't take my time enjoying the little freak.

Pulling his zipper down, he gently puts his hands into the side of his jeans and as slow as he can possibly go, pushes them down his thighs where they then pool around his ankles. He kicks the jeans free from his feet and here I am locked in place, admiring his perfect body in all its naked glory. Apart from the smallest amount of well-cropped black hair around his shaft, he is as smooth as a baby. His skin looks like honey. I want to lick every inch of it several times over and see if it tastes as sweet as it looks. His hard thick dick is bouncing, ready for me to make my move.

"Fuck, I'm going to rip you apart," I rasp. I don't recognize my own voice. Aaron affects me physically and mentally, the sensory overload of it all is shattering. It's a new experience for me.

Aaron unashamedly peruses my body, lingering on my chest where the blood and sweat still clings to my skin like it is a part of me. Biting his lower lip, he groans and gives his cock a couple of strokes.

"Just make sure you leave me in pieces, Lev," he says with that damn grin.

Game on, doe.

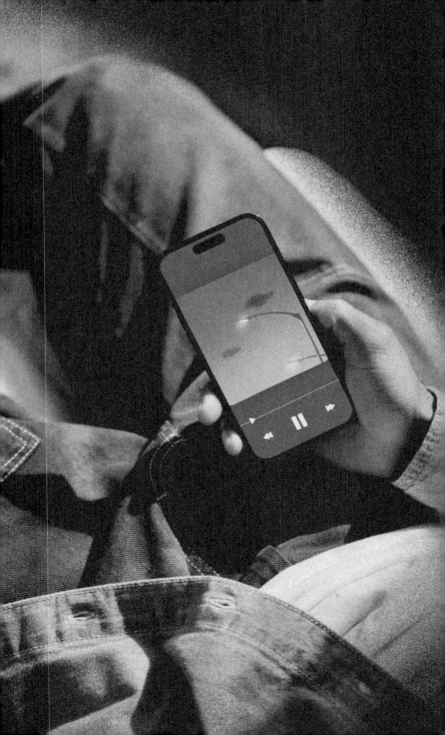

CHAPTER 16
AARON

A m I dreaming right now? I wish I had my switchblade so I could cut myself to prove this is actually happening. Imagining what your biggest fantasy would be like is one thing, but for it to be standing in front of you, offering everything you want, is a feeling I can't explain. It's like I am watching this from the outside. Never in my wildest dreams did I think I would get the full Lev experience. And for a whole night.

My ass tenses at the thought of that beast of a dick fucking me. It's been a long time since I've had anyone fuck me, and I am ready.

So fucking ready.

It's like being a virgin and a slutty whore at the same time. His attention on me is becoming an uncontrollable craving. When he watches me, it hushes the voices in my head. He's the only one who has ever managed to do that. I don't have fearful thoughts or feel weak around him, and it makes me want to grab on tighter to him so he doesn't leave.

Which he will. This is for one night.

I just don't want the craziness in my head to come back. Tonight I am settled. It's like a fucked up version of Cinderella. Instead of a carriage turning into a pumpkin, it will be my quiet head turning back to the madness after midnight.

I need to stop thinking about that right now and live in the moment.

Lev takes a small step closer to me and the room shrinks. The soft glow of the bedside light makes him appear larger and more potent somehow, surrounded in shadows and strength, like a demon that has come up to earth to corrupt and claim a soul.

Lev pushes down his sweatpants and underwear. Fuck me, he is absolutely breathtaking. Like a marble statue, if that statue had tattoos all over, specks of blood on his large, beautiful, glistening bare chest, and a tantalizing cock piercing that sparkles from the reflection of the light on the end of his hard as steel dick.

Finally, he moves towards me and we are nearly skin to skin. Wow. Honestly I think I will cum when he touches me. The band that feels like it is locked around my dick and balls is on the cusp of snapping and all he's done is undress.

"There are no safe words in here tonight, doe. So, if you don't want this, you need to leave now. I guarantee I will lose control as soon as I push into that gorgeous ass of yours," he says.

My eyes roll back as I whine. I need him to fucking touch me. *Now.* "Lev, just fuck me, please. Do what you want." I'm not beyond begging.

His smile is full of arrogance and promise. "As you wish."

Those manly hands grab a tight hold of my ass as our

mouths collide together in a brutal clash of tongues. Our full bodies press together, leaving barely any space between us, our cocks make contact, and the sensation creates a zapping of tiny volts around the tip of my dick. The barbell in his cock catches on the end of my slit as he rubs us together, hard, rolling his hips, creating a perfect friction. It feels so fucking good.

The kiss has taken our oxygen away, but we refuse to part. His hand moves to grab the back of my neck, which grounds me into the present. Tugging on my hair, he stops the kiss, forcing my head back, causing me to yelp in discomfort at the force of it as he starts to suck hard down my neck and aggressively bites the skin. The burn from his harsh stubble makes me want to rub it all over me. I arch my neck further towards his mouth. I never thought I would be into pain, but it seems as long as Lev is providing my pleasure, I will enjoy anything he does.

Before I can register what is happening, I am thrown on my back onto the bed with the heavy weight of Lev covering me, and it feels like the room has ignited into a place of burning euphoria. My hands claw at his back as I scrape my nails down his skin. He groans into my mouth, thrusting his hips forward into mine, and our bodies sliding together makes me dizzy and delirious as pure animal need takes over.

Pulling away, he grabs my throat and continues to grind his cock against mine. He isn't gentle, that damn piercing creates an extra sensation on my dick that makes it pulse in excitement. His hand tightens around my throat to the point where I now have to try and breathe through my nose. My head feels hazy with the lack of air, but it feels so fucking freeing. My eyes roll back at the sensation.

"You love that don't you, doe? You are such a needy

little whore for me." I moan at his words as he continues to rub his body over mine. "You got off on watching me play, didn't you? Watching me make those fuckers bleed."

I hum, trying to nod my head as he relaxes his hold on me enough for me to answer.

"Yes." It comes out as a raspy gasp from the lack of air in my lungs.

He pushes down on my dick harder. "I bet you would love me to fuck you in the pen wouldn't you, doe? Would you like that? Me to fuck you while they die in front of you, bleeding and begging."

The groan out of my mouth is deep and never-ending, "Fuck, yes, Lev, I'd love it."

He chuckles darkly. "My little monster," he mutters over my mouth before he rises onto his knees, and with scary strength flips me over onto my stomach. The room feels like it is spinning. Every part of my skin feels itchy, like the only thing that will soothe it is cumming and being stuffed full of that tasty slab of meat. Using his hand, he pushes my head into the mattress and sucks on the back of my neck, licking and nibbling slowly down my spine.

"Fuck, doe, you taste good, taste like fucking sin," he whispers as he moves further and further down my back until he is above my ass. I can't move right now. I am glued to the spot awaiting what torment he will put my body through next.

"Damn, you have a hot ass." He grips a cheek in each hand and squeezes hard before slapping both hands down hard on them, making them jiggle.

"Ah," I cry, the sting awakens all my senses. He pulls my ass cheeks apart. I thought I would feel embarrassment but instead it's all desperation for that part of my body to be owned. If I could move right now, I would sit on his face.

"Look at that pretty hole, begging for my dick."

All of a sudden, there is something wet prodding at my entrance. Realizing it's his tongue, I grip at the bed sheets with my hands spread to the sides, trying to hold on as he destroys my body and mind piece by piece. There is no gentleness in Lev's style, or slow build up, he drives that thick tongue inside of me, forcing it past my tight ring of muscle. In and out in quick succession, the sound of his saliva along with him grunting in pleasure and me wailing like a porn star are enough to make me cum.

Finding some strength, I arch my ass up into his face and start to bounce back on his tongue, but he stops and slaps his hand down hard on my ass. "I'm in control here, you get what I give you. Now stay fucking still," he commands.

I don't respond, just nod my sweaty head into the bed. The more he pushes into my ass with his tongue, the more the warmth of the sheets against my dick becomes unbearable. I need to move. Fuck, this is torture and also the most epic rimming ever to have happened.

Rivulets of sweat run down my back. It feels like the heating has been turned up in here, the sheets below us are starting to dampen from the moisture that's dripping off our bodies. After what feels like hours of him eating me out, he moves his mouth away and I can feel my wet, loosened hole on show. Before I have a chance to compose myself, two lubed fingers are pushed into me, and like a GPS, they find my P-spot on the first poke. I nearly fall off the bed. I can't stop the tremors that have taken control, the tickle and heat sensation on that nub inside me feels like he is massaging my dick at the same time.

"Please, Lev, *plleeeaassse*," I cry in frustration. I can't cope with the sensory overload. His body, his fingers, his scent … it's too much, but also not enough.

"Ready for me to tear this ass up? Does your empty hole need filling up?"

"Yes!" I cry out as he pushes harder onto my spot inside me. It's lucky I haven't cum. I feel like a limp noodle, loose, floppy, and at his mercy.

"I'm going in bare. I need to stuff you with my cum, I want to see you dripping with it. I plan on stuffing you all night, doe."

"Oh fuck, yes. Do it. Breed my ass." I put my hands behind me with the last piece of energy I can summon, and spread my cheeks apart, completely open for him.

"Fuck yeah." I can hear the squelching of the lube he is rubbing on his cock. This will be life changing, for me anyway, and while part of me is scared, I welcome it with open arms.

I feel his piercing at my rim, and he slides straight home with ease. His dick is so thick and long it feels like I'm going to tear in half. I swear the tip of his cock is poking my stomach. This fullness is like a sudden religious experience. The feeling of completeness in finding my missing piece and being right where I'm supposed to be. It really hurts, but the pressure is so good that I think after one push, I'll combust.

"Holy shit, you are squeezing me like a vice, so fucking tight, so damn greedy." And just as he promised, he lets go of his control and destroys my ass for anyone else. He lifts his hips up and down, setting a brutal and fast pace, holding himself above me by his hands like he's doing push-ups while fucking me through the bed.

"Ah, ah, ah, there, Lev. Right. Fucking. There," I

demand and he groans in response, doubling down on his efforts.

He pulls all the way out to his tip, then slams back in. Fuck! I think we are going to break the bed. The base of it is creaking so loudly, it sounds like it's on the brink of collapsing beneath us. I feel wet drips fall onto my skin. His sweat is like a shower all over me, his panting sounds like he has run for miles, and I just lay there taking it. It's violent, it's amazing, it's completely soul-destroying, and I don't ever want it to end.

"Oh shit, doe, I'm gonna cum, fuck, fuck!"

Just as I feel his cum fill me along with the loud filthy noises that leave him, I cum hands free. "Ahhhhh yesss."

I'm boneless, lying there with his cock still in my ass, his cum leaking out of my hole, his sweaty chest now lying flat against my back, and my own cum sticking between me and the bed. When this night ends, it will destroy me. I'm officially attached, and I don't want to leave.

We lie still for a few minutes, and I do think at one point he has fallen asleep, but then he moves and pulls out of my ass. The stream of his cum drips down my crack and I can't resist putting my finger around my hole, touching the now gaping entrance with his warm sticky release. I smile to myself before his big hands slap on my ass again. "Come on, doe, shower."

"I don't want to move," I complain. I don't think my legs work.

"Tough shit, we need to get clean so I can dirty you up again," he says.

While bitching at him, I force myself up. From the state of the bed and my stomach, yeah he's right, a shower is needed. I feel gross.

I follow him into his bathroom, admiring his thick juicy

ass that I wouldn't mind eating myself. Damn, the idea of suffocating between those muscular cheeks is more appealing than it should be.

He's staring at me over his shoulder. Dammit. Busted.

"Get a good look?"

"Not really, just thinking I wouldn't mind eating it."

He wets his lips with his tongue in a salacious manner and growls, grabbing me for a kiss. "You can have a bite if you want, but you ain't fucking me."

"I know. I prefer to be fucked anyway, but I still want a taste."

"Dirty little shit," he says and pushes me into his lavish shower that can fit at least three people in it. Of course, my overactive mind drifts to thinking of how many people he has had in here, but it makes me feel stabby so I reel it in. I'm here now and that's all that matters.

CHAPTER 17
LEV

The hot water on my skin washes away the blood, sweat, and cum off my body, making me feel satisfied and relaxed, more so than I have felt before. That may have something to do with the brown-eyed man in front of me who is taking his time running body wash over my body.

Aaron is in a trance as he glides his hands up and down my chest, teasing me as he goes further down my body, washing the soap around my groin but ignoring my dick. It feels good. I don't normally do this, but after tonight's activities and how hard he made me cum, I let it go. Aaron is the best fuck I have ever had. Not that I would say it out loud, but I have never had a connection with anyone like this before. It's like two wires that have joined together in perfect unison. He understands my needs and desires because he has them too. We are unhinged but aligned. The way he gives himself so easily to me to do as I want, and bends to my will. I find it more arousing than I should.

Aaron, however, is also a nightmare. He is unpredictable from what I have experienced so far. He has severe fluctuations in personality and mood, and is surprisingly possessive of me. I could tell when we got in the shower that he was thinking of past partners. His face looked like he was sucking on something sour. He is so damn easy to read. I want to laugh. He doesn't realize that I have never brought anyone back here. I always do my shit elsewhere. My business is private. It was only because of Hugo and Mario that it was easier to stay here. But I must admit, it was nice to break in my bed.

My head tilts back when arousal starts to rise in my dick again as Aaron lathers up my cock. Goddamn, his hands feel amazing. I open my eyes and stare into those big brown pools of innocence, which isn't true, but for a moment you could believe he is an innocent and sane person. However, these past few hours he has been with me is the most serene I have seen him. He has barely changed personalities and is more centered, but I won't read too much into that.

"Hands against the wall," I order and like a good boy, he obeys, beaming at me with that fucking creepy smile. "Ass out."

He arches his back and pushes out that plump bubble butt, which I fear will keep me hard for hours.

I rub my now fully hard dick up and down his crease. He tries to wiggle against it so I slap his right ass cheek.

"What did I tell you? You don't control this. Stay fucking still."

He is completely silent and is trying so hard to restrain himself. I hold his plump cheeks open and notice he is a little puffy from the fucking earlier, but not too bad. I rub the tip of my cock over his hole, intentionally making my piercing make contact with the wrinkled skin.

He shivers slightly against the touch but remains as still as he can.

Without warning him I push forward. He is still loose and lubricated from before and he cries out a high pitched wail. I love the sounds he makes for me.

"You like that, doe? Want another breeding from my dick?" I ask, rocking slowly in him.

"Yes, god yes," he whines, like he is far away in the land of cock.

"Stroke that dick of yours," I say as I start moving in and out of him, building to a tempo that has me a little breathless and warm all over. Christ. My cock is still sensitive. I only came a few minutes ago and I'm not gonna last.

"Ahhhhh, I'm gonna cum, *fuck*," he gasps.

"Cum for me, doe. Shit, cum. Ugggh." My feet twitch as I load up his destroyed hole at the same time Aaron shouts out his own release. I don't think I can move my body. Aaron is all but sliding down the shower wall, so I pull out of him, making him flinch, and hold him up by the waist. "Come on, bed. You need to rest before we fuck again."

He huffs out a small laugh, completely dopey in my arms. "Um, kay."

I turn the shower off and guide him out, offering him a towel. After drying off, we both go to the bed. I push the comforter on the floor. It's covered in our juices from our earlier activities. I bring over the blanket that's on my chair. As we bury ourselves under the blanket, I don't have the chance to speak or move before we both fall asleep.

Opening my eyes, it's still dark out, so I check my phone. I must have only had a couple of hours of sleep. I hear a soft snore next to me where I greedily take in Aaron laying sprawled out on his stomach.

I run my gaze over his strong back that glows from the hint of moonlight shining into the room from the gap in my curtains. My eyes lock onto that juicy bubble butt of his. The dip in his lower back makes the perfect curve, enhancing the roundness of his ass cheeks. Of course, after this short perusal, I'm hard, and I want back inside him. He told me to do anything I want, so I will.

I move onto my side and glide my fingers in between his crack. He has a little cum that has leaked out and his hole is still a little loose, but not enough to take me. I remove my fingers and he mumbles in his sleep, turning his head towards me. Eyes closed, lips parted, he looks so much younger like this. Life isn't wearing down that beautiful face of his. I scoff at myself. When do I ever use that word? *Beautiful.*

Looking back down at his body, I get distracted again by his peachy ass and grab the lube from my nightstand. I coat my fingers and dick, then as quietly as I can, I maneuver myself above him with my knees to either side of his thighs. Quickly, I check him and find that he is still sound asleep.

Using three of my now lube-coated fingers, I slowly press them into his tight heat and have to bite back the moan that wants to leave me. He is the tightest thing I have ever felt, so warm and snug. He moves beneath me, mumbling again as he wiggles his ass and falls back into restful sleep.

Removing my fingers, I aim the tip of my dick at his now sloppy hole, and push in slowly but firmly. Fuck. He feels so fucking good around my cock. Warm, tight, and wet. I start to move in long and slow thrusts, rolling my hips against him as I lean my body over him. That seems to do the trick.

Aaron jolts his head up on a loud gasp. "What the hell?" he says and with his half-closed eyes, still partly asleep, he looks over his shoulder at me and groans.

"Fuck, Lev," he sobs, pushing his ass back onto me. "You can fuck me harder than that."

He's a sassy thing. Pushing his face into my pillow, I place my hand on the back of his neck and move hard and fast. The only sounds in the room are panting and groaning, along with the slapping of my hips against his ass. The need to cum festers in my balls, so I stop and pull back.

"Hands and knees. Now."

He immediately does as I say, legs wide apart, ass in air and that gorgeous arc of his back, tempting me further as it highlights those round full globes. I line up my dick at his entrance and slam back into him, pulling his hips toward me on every thrust. Moving his hand underneath himself, he jerks his dick in quick hard strokes. "Lev, need to cum."

A growl comes up from my throat, the tingling sensation that was in my balls increases as I tilt my pelvis, on the edge of cumming. It builds into an overwhelming pressure, which is about to blow.

"Cum, doe, cum on my cock."

"Oh shit, yes...yesssss."

His hole tightens around my dick as he cums over his hand, which in turn triggers my tidal-wave of an orgasm, complete with mini shocks thrumming through my body. I feel lightheaded as I cum deep inside him. Fuck, that was intense.

We both collapse back into the bed, my eyes heavy as I start to drift off. "Never been fucked in my sleep before," he murmurs softly.

With my eyes barely open, I turn my head to face him. He is still on his stomach and looks like he is coming down from a drug-induced high.

"You're welcome." I lay back, letting my eyes close, ready for sleep to take me.

"Asshole," he mumbles under his breath, and I chuckle because it's true. He brings out that side of me more than usual. With that in mind, feeling a little more alert, I ask him something that has been on my mind.

"How long has Jake been beating on you and wanting to screw you?"

He sighs. "Tactful as ever."

"Would you prefer if I pussyfooted around it?"

He looks at me with a sad smile, and this smile is real. I don't like it.

"It started when I was sixteen. Jake and his dad used to beat on me a lot, forcing me to go on drug deals. Jake said that dad wanted to offer me out for 'other services' but he said he would look out for me if I dealt with him and did as he asked." He gets quiet, contemplating whether to continue.

"When I turned eighteen, he caught me with my boyfriend." He releases a long breath. "Let's just say it didn't end well. He blackmailed me, used it as a way to get me to fall in line so he didn't tell his dad. He manipulated me, he...he forced me..." Aaron trails off, struggling to finish that sentence.

I sit upright, fully fucking awake now. "Did he hurt you?"

His eyes widen, and I become aware of how in his face I am right now.

"I don't really want to talk about it, Lev. Things changed for the worse and as time went on, he became more controlling. More recently, all the secrecy and paranoia has made him more reckless. He's been getting closer to me. It feels like … I don't know how to explain it, but it feels like he is waiting to do something. To me. He's been more open about his interest in front of others and that worries me. Everyone knows, but they say nothing. He has control over everyone," he explains.

Those gorgeous doe eyes look up at me and I see tears glistening behind them. For the first time I sense genuine fear and hear the vulnerability in his voice. I have no fucking clue what to do.

"I know I'm weird, and I have a lot of triggers when it comes to Jake. When he calls me certain names, it puts me back in that mental space, and I'm that defenseless boy again. The boy who constantly talks to me in my head, drowning out all the other fuckers that live in my head too. It's like shards of glass, cutting away everything else, and it hurts. He scares me, Lev. I'm scared that I will never put that weak boy to rest."

I process everything he just said, and part of me does feel sorry for Aaron. He was dealt a shitty hand in life. Dima and I didn't have it easy growing up with an asshole abusive father and a mother who couldn't give a shit, but we had each other. Sex predators weren't an issue for us.

Gripping the back of his neck, I try my best to comfort him. "It will be over soon, Aaron. As soon as Jake is here, it will be over. He won't be leaving here alive," I promise him.

He smiles softly, but before he can speak, I cut him off. He is so damn predictable. "And yes, before you start your bitching again, I know you want to be in on it," I grumble.

A large genuine smile lights up his face and this one makes me more uncomfortable than the sad one. He is looking at me like he wants me, even maybe likes me, and I can't go there. Even though I have made my position clear to him, there is a flash of hope in his eyes and I need it gone. The demons he has, only he can fight them. Developing a co-dependency with me will only keep the voices silent for so long and I don't need that kind of pressure, for someone to *need* me.

Aaron jumps headfirst into whatever feels good, and I get that, especially since he clearly hasn't had a lot of good things happen in his life, but it can't be me. I'm not built that way and I don't want to be that person for him or anyone else. Maybe I need to end this now and kick him out, quick and painless.

Before I can say anything, he jumps up and climbs on top of me and my exhausted dick starts to twitch again, my self-talk forgotten. I don't think I have ever cum so many times in one night. As he straddles me his ass rubs up against my now hard again cock, and it's wet and inviting from the leftover lube and cum.

"Doesn't your asshole hurt?" I ask.

He smirks. "I'm taking what I can and that cock piercing is addictive." He puts his hands on my steel rod and guides it to his tight channel.

"Well, what are you waiting for? Ride me, doe. Make me cum."

With both hands, he pinches my nipples and leans forward, taking my mouth in a deep and sensual kiss. He pushes onto my dick, making us both moan in unison. He sits upright, looking like a hot cowboy about to ride his stallion. I grab him by the hips, and yet again, he fucks my brains out.

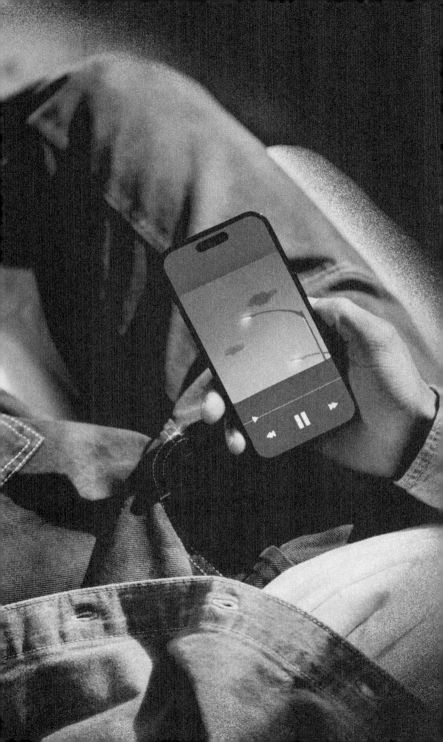

CHAPTER 18
AARON

The alarm goes off on my phone at six am. I try to pry my sleepy eyes open so that I can find my damn phone, but they're glued shut. Plus I don't want to wake Lev. I decided last night that it would be best if I leave before he wakes. I don't know if I can handle the rejection that I know is coming.

Resisting the clinginess that's pulling me to mold myself into those strong arms is like fighting to breathe underwater. I have never belonged somewhere more than I do right now. No masks. No pretending. No thinking of the past. Just mentally disturbed Aaron who enjoys getting off on his crush hurting others and wanting to be part of it.

Slowly and carefully, I get out of the bed, and I manage to dress myself. Giving one last look over at the bed, Lev is laying on his stomach, arms folded under the pillow, and I feel a pinch at my newly beating heart. He's stunning. His muscular tanned skin glows under the gentle hue of the nightlight in the corner of the room we forgot to turn off last night before we passed out. The temptation to lick his back forces me to physically restrain myself. I won't turn back. With a regretful sigh, I leave the room and already the anxiousness of returning to Jake is making me feel agitated. Remembering I said I would text him, I quickly fire off a message,

ME:

Just about to leave.

Short and concise, and he will still bitch about it.

Walking down the long corridor, I am greeted by who I guess must be Seb, which surprises me. I thought I would manage to dodge any interactions this early in the morning. He is standing in a doorway across the foyer to what looks like the kitchen or dining area. I'm not sure whether to speak to him, but luckily he makes that decision for me.

"Aaron, right?" he asks, and I can tell he is curious as he quickly scans me head to toe before a bright smile breaks out on his face. I must admit, he is hot. Dressed in gym gear, he has either finished a workout or is about to start. From the look of his tight body that appears to be a daily thing.

"Yeah, and I bet you are Seb."

He laughs. "Sure am, come on and have a coffee before you sneak out."

He turns, assuming that I will follow, which I hesitantly do.

Handing me a fresh cup of coffee, he points to the milk and cream on the counter. "Help yourself," he says as he sits at the table.

I join him. I'm not quite sure what to say, but Seb fills in the silence.

"Heard you got quite a lot from the boys last night?" he says.

I nod. "Yep, it was fun." I shrug and smile.

When I look up, Seb is just staring at me, probably because of my weird-ass smile or maybe what I just said. Who knows? Social cues are not my strong point.

"I see why he likes you, you are as screwed up as Lev is." He chuckles, taking a large gulp of his coffee.

"He doesn't like me, it was just fucking." I don't know why I tell him we are fucking, but he isn't stupid. He's probably had coffee in here with multiple men and women after Lev kicks them out.

Seb continues to watch me closely with his coffee mug lifted halfway to his mouth. I don't think he was expecting that response. "Hmm. Maybe, but I have never seen him with anyone before. He never spends the night here with a guy or girl," he says.

Now that's interesting information. Maybe he does like me? Ugh, fucking men. "Well, we didn't really sleep much," I say, proud of my Lev belt notch.

He snorts at that. "That's not surprising."

That comment gets my attention. Does he mean he knows him like that? I'm spiraling at the thought and Crazy has decided to join in the fun.

"Have you fucked him?" The question is out before I can stop it. Seb looks stunned, his eyes wide and mouth gaping. He's not looking at me, so I follow his line of sight and realize how hard I'm gripping the coffee cup. Crazy is back, and I need to put a leash on him ASAP.

He is mine!

Shit, don't lose it, Aaron.

"No, Aaron. I have only been with Dima and I will only ever be with Dima. Lev is more like an annoying brother," he says.

"Oh, sorry. I shouldn't have snapped." What the fuck am I doing?

"It's okay. You like him. Just be careful. Dima went for what he wanted with me whether I agreed or not, but Lev is more complicated. I don't think he'll ever admit he wants someone. His mind doesn't work like that. I mean, hurting others is a sport for him. It would take someone special to be good with that."

He doesn't say it in a way that's mean, it's more like a fact rolled into a question, asking if I am that special person. Hell yes is the answer. I would walk through fire to be Lev's main focus, especially now I've had a taste. I sound like a pussy, already clingy and moon-eyed after one fuck. Well, several fucks in one night, but still, I have to put a halt to becoming obsessive over him.

"What do you mean Dima wanted you whether you agreed or not?" That little point has me curious.

Seb's face takes on a look of fondness followed by a laugh of irony. "Oh yeah, he kidnapped me and tied me to the bed. I always thought I was straight, but who knew being taken against your will and shown what you had been missing would change my life like it did? And for the better."

"Lev mentioned last night that, er, you did stuff, down there, in the pen, in front of others." Christ, could I sound more awkward?

A blush tints his cheeks. "Fucking, Lev. Yes, I did, but it was a personal retribution for me. And yeah, I enjoyed it, and got off on it, but it's not something that appeals to me in the general sense. Sounds insane, but it freed me."

He raises his chin in defense, unblinking like he is challenging me to disagree, but there is no need. Who am I to judge? I get off on watching Lev torture others.

"Ha, if you're insane then what does that make me?" I swallow the remaining amount of my coffee.

"I don't know you well enough to know, but if you like Lev, I'd say you are beyond help." He grins.

I like him. "Yeah, anyway, I need to book a ride home before my stepbrother becomes suspicious."

"I can give you a ride home if you like? I was going to wash up but if you don't mind motorcycles, I can take you back."

"Thanks, but better not in case I'm seen. Anyway, isn't it a little early to have finished a workout?"

I need to get out of here. Standing, I put my hands in my pockets to stop the fidgeting and my feet cramp with the need to move, to fight the urge of wanting to return to Lev's bed.

"If I didn't then I'd never get to do it. Dima is always around me and he distracts me too much."

I chuckle. "I bet. Thanks for the coffee, Seb."

"You take care, Aaron." He waves.

I gently nod, walk out of the front door, and make my way down the long driveway to await my ride home. What a joke. Home. What kind of fucked up mess have I gotten myself into?

My car finally arrives and drops me in my usual spot. It's still dark out and fucking freezing, so I jog down the quiet streets until I reach my apartment. There is no way he will be awake at this time. Jake rarely rises before nine am, but recently his behavior is so erratic I'm not sure what to think anymore.

As I walk into the apartment, the light suddenly turns on in the corner of the room, and that's when I notice Jake sitting in the dark waiting for me. He looks a mess, hair disheveled, frazzled. His eyes are dark and I'm pretty sure he hasn't slept. Tentatively, I walk forward and try to be as casual as possible, but his severe gaze sends a quake of fear down my spine.

"Hey, I didn't expect you to be awake this early." I manage to keep my tone even, hoping he can't hear the underlying flurry of nerves.

"I just wanted to make sure you got home. So, what were you doing last night?" he says. Suspicion laces his tone, but he is always so damn paranoid when it comes to me.

"Jules had me sitting in on some interrogation that they were doing with a guy from one of the crews."

"Really? Which crew member?" he asks.

"I don't know, I didn't recognize him. Apparently, Lev wanted me to witness what would happen if I caused any more problems." I pray that my words are somewhat reassuring to try and veer him off the scent of my deceit. I'm unsure if he's jealous or if he has noticed something is going on. Maybe both.

"Anyway, I'm just going to get a few hours of sleep," I say.

"Why do I feel like you're lying to me?" He stands up and slowly wanders towards me.

I really want to high-tail it and run. I wasn't prepared for all these questions. Jake is the equivalent of a noose around my neck.

"I wasn't lying, honestly, you can ask Jules yourself."

Rather than pacify him, it seems to annoy him. He pushes me up against the wall, forcefully gripping my chin. The pressure of his hand makes my jaw ache, which is still tender from the last beating. I find myself unable to think or talk as alarm sets in.

My head starts to hurt as my mind starts to become overactive, highlighting memories of what we went through, unable to resist responding to Jake's voice.

Not now.

"Open wide, baby brother."

Don't let him get us.

Go away!

It's okay, do as he says and it will be okay.

The boy is trying to comfort us, he is trying hard to push away all other thoughts. *"Not today... not today,"* I plead with him, fighting to lock him back up in the black hole of my mind.

Breathe in...breathe out.

Finally, I gain some control, managing to remain myself and deal with the predator in front of me.

Slowly perusing my face, I'm shocked at how eerily calm Jake is right now. He is normally so reactive, this side to him is different and unsettling. Can he smell another man on me? I can still feel Lev leaking out of me.

You need to chill, Aaron.

"Okay, baby brother, if you say so, but something doesn't feel right. I think we may need to leave town for a while," he says as he continues to hold me in place.

This feels like six years ago, on my eighteenth birthday. He had me pinned just like this, using that soft tone after he saw me.

"Open wide, baby brother."

I squeeze my eyes shut as if maybe the darkness will take me away. Remove me from the feeling of his body so close to me, his scent that triggers the queasy bile bubbling in my stomach.

"You're mine now, baby brother. I own you."

No!

It's okay, it will be over soon.

"Shut up, shut up!" I repeat over and over. I need strength. As the voices hush, I open my eyes and look into the evil ones staring at me.

"Why do we need to leave?" I ask, not sure if I want the answer.

"I just think it would be best to maybe start over somewhere new. Wouldn't you be happy? You've always complained about living around here, unless you want me to leave you here on your own? Maybe you could move near Daddy dearest, be the good stepson by keeping his fading ass company in that care home?"

Mentioning that asshole is like pouring oil over me before setting it alight and he knows it, especially with that cruel grin he's throwing my way.

"You'd let me stay here?" I ask, stupidly having a moment of hope. Jake laughs as if I'm the dumbest person in the world right now.

"Of course I wouldn't leave you here. Already told you before, you're mine. Where I go you go."

He pulls away. "Go on then, baby brother, get some rest."

I feel thrown off balance by his demeanor, it's too composed, and it scares me. This is not the Jake I know and can predict.

"Aaron, if I find out you've been lying to me, I will kill you, and it won't be quick. Is that clear?"

I turn and see the truth in his face, remaining silent because what can I say to that threat? I just nod my head like the pathetic little boy I am. I go to my room, closing the door behind me, wondering how the fuck everything turned to shit in such a short period of time. I wish I was still with Lev. I wish I was still in that bed feeling safe and protected.

Without undressing, I collapse face first onto my bed, grimacing slightly at the ache in my ass, but I also take comfort in it. It's like he's still with me in some way. I turn onto my back, but my mind won't shut off, trying to work out what I should do next.

Should I leave like Shay said? Should I beg Lev and Dima to help me and take me in? I snort at that idea. Lev would never allow that. *I don't do repeats,* he said. Or should I just do what I want to do and kill Jake in his sleep?

Finding my switchblade that I left on my bed, I play with it between my fingers as I contemplate my next move. Confusion about how to navigate this shitstorm is making my head hurt and I need to sleep, but before I do, I remove my burner phone from my back pocket.

I don't know why I would think there would be a text from Lev, it's wishful thinking, but of course there isn't. I doubt he's even gotten up yet, but fuck. Last night was one of the best nights of my life and it's one thing no one can take away from me. As I settle down into my pillow, I replay my best bits from last night as I drift off.

Another night where Lev is the last thing on my mind.

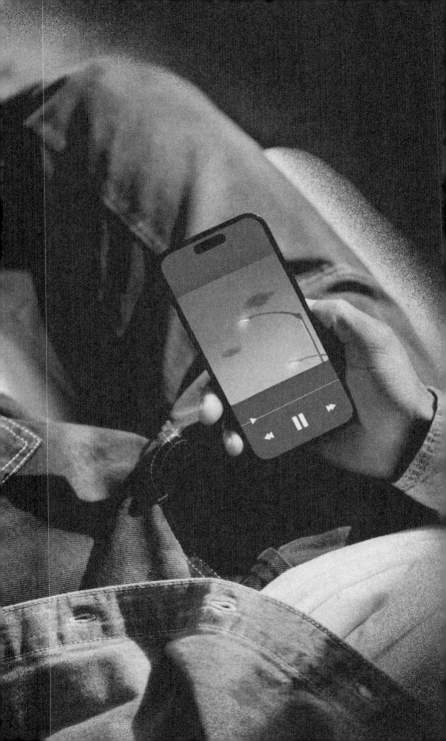

CHAPTER 19
AARON

AARON - 6 YEARS AGO - 18TH BIRTHDAY

This is the first night in a long time I am having fun. No Jake breathing down my neck or my stepdad looking for a reason to beat on me like it's his favorite sport. Sitting under this tree in Spencer's garden is heaven. It's a warm evening, but it's dark and the stars are so bright tonight. I feel an arm around my shoulders and I lean in. Spencer and I have been sort of dating quietly for a couple of months. We go to high school together, and these are moments we cherish. We can be who we want to be. If my stepdad ever found out I was gay, I know he would lose it, and that's not even including my stepbrother's reaction. Although, I suspect he knows from the occasional homo and fag comments he snarls my way.

"Happy birthday, baby," Spencer whispers in my ear and I turn to look at him. Big beautiful blue eyes, hair as dark as night like my own, beautiful porcelain skin. He is gorgeous and I must say, a beefcake for his age. He plays football so he's a lot bigger than me, but he is the best. We both have a lot to lose if this gets out so we treasure our time together.

He leans in to kiss me, gentle at first and it quickly turns passionate and needy, tongues caressing. He runs his hands through my hair and moans into my mouth. I love the feel of him. But it is short lived.

"Get your fucking hands off him."

I know that voice. The fucker followed me. Shit. Spencer pulls back and looks over my shoulder, his eyes wide in fear. It may sound dramatic but I feel like my life has just flashed before my eyes. They will beat me to death for this.

I have to try to convince Jake though, so I stand, and before I get to speak, he grabs my arm.

"Not a fucking word. Get in the truck." He turns to Spencer. "This is your only warning. I see you near him again, I will make sure you say goodbye to your football career and that everyone knows what a disgusting cock sucker you are."

Spencer is frozen in place.

"Spencer..." I try to go to him, but Jake drags me away and Spencer remains where he is. Will anyone ever save me? This is the last time I'll ever see him and it's all because of Jake. I want to kill my stepbrother right now. I hate him and I hate his dad. If I could burn the fuckers alive and get away with it, I would.

Jake forces me into the car and drives us away. The car is deadly silent and I notice we aren't driving home. He turns down some country back road where there is nothing around us, no sign of life and I start to feel cold all over. Is he going to kill me?

He pulls over to the side of the road and cuts the engine and lights. We are only illuminated by the bright moon that reflects down onto the truck and the sounds of wildlife roaming around the woodland on the roadside. He turns to face me and I daren't speak, not wanting to make this worse.

"You are to never see him again, Aaron. You disgust me with

what I witnessed tonight. What do you think Dad would say? That his son who already disappoints him is also a fag?"

I don't respond. He has me backed into a corner. I'm lost for words right now. I take the chance and look at him watching me. I shake under his stare. There's a wicked gleam in his eyes and a small smirk on his lips. He has been waiting to hold something over me. For years, he has been trying to control me, make me heel to his commands, and I have always fought against it even though it frequently cost me a beating.

"Don't worry, baby brother. I won't tell him if you're good to me."

I frown. "What do you mean?"

"I already told you that Dad wanted to whore you out before I convinced him to just use you on drug runs, but once he knows you're gay, he will have guys from all over fucking you for cash. You don't want that, right?"

I can't stop the trembling of my hands as I process what he says. I remember he said this a couple years ago, but I never thought back to it again, thinking it was a way to keep control. Was there some truth to it?

My stomach churns in revolt as he runs his hands into my hair, gently tugging it, but not in a brotherly love way. Oh fuck, no, please no. Tears well in my eyes and he smiles. He recognizes that I've figured out what he wants.

"I'll protect you, Aaron," he whispers as he undoes his jeans and pulls them down until his cock is on full display. I think I'm gonna be sick.

God no.

It will be okay. It will be over soon.

He grabs me tighter by the hair and pushes my head down, level with his dick.

"Open wide, baby brother."

CHAPTER 20
LEV

Waking up, I let out a long yawn as I stretch my hands over my head. My body aches like a bitch this morning. From playing in the pen, to fucking Aaron through last night like a wild beast, I feel like my body has aged a decade.

I turn my head to the side to see the empty space. I'm kinda surprised he didn't stay. He is so random that I was expecting him to be hovering around me, but I'm glad he left. He is a distraction and the most needy and codependent person I have met. I don't need that shit in my life, even if he is the best fuck I have had in years.

Doe. Those innocent-looking wide eyes that hero worship me for whatever reason, but it's a paradox. Last night, I truly saw the real Aaron behind his multiple masks. He craves attention and craves violence to obnoxious levels. It turns him on. It was a fucking rush being with someone that uninhibited, freely displaying the wild unhinged parts of them. But I had my fill of everything I needed last night, and for the first time in weeks, I have slept like a baby. I feel like myself again.

My stomach rumbles loudly. I get up and throw on my shorts and T-shirt, take a piss, and head to the kitchen where I pray our own little Princess Seb has at least made the coffee. Not that I would tell the little fucker, but he is the only one who makes a decent cup.

Walking into the kitchen, shocker, Dima has Seb in his lap. Do they ever fucking stop? Rolling my eyes to myself, I walk towards the table noticing the large pot that has hardly been touched, excellent. Pouring myself a cup, I am aware that they are watching me. Such nosy fuckers.

"What?" I snap. I've been awake five minutes and I'm already irritated.

"Wow, I thought you would be more relaxed after yesterday but clearly not. Did little doe not say goodbye?" Dima chuckles, and I send him a death glare that halts his laughter.

"Don't fucking call him that. I should cut Jules' tongue out for telling you that shit. Yes he has gone, yes we fucked all night long, and yes it was fantastic. Now it's done. So can we move on or do you need some more gossip for your knitting circle later?"

"I met him before he left. He's an interesting guy, Lev," Seb says.

"Interesting is certainly a word you could use. Mentally deranged is another," I say.

"Yeah, I heard about the antics in the pen," Seb jokes.

"Yep. Seems to be some kind of aphrodisiac down there, like when you were finger fucked by D in front of all of us, remember?" Take that you little shit. Seb scowls at me. Hypocrite.

"Watch it brother," Dima warns. Predictable.

"Or what? Just 'cos you are together, does not mean Seb can speak to me how he wants or interfere in my business, so maybe *you* should watch the fuck out, *brother*." I'm not sure why I am defensive or snappy, but I hate people in my business and these two are the worst.

"I get it. Sorry, Lev. I won't mention it again," Seb apologizes while Dima clenches his jaw, trying to hold back whatever bullshit he wants to throw at me. I stare just as hard. They need to back the fuck off, and I'm going to change the subject before we get all physical with each other.

"What are we doing now about Jake and the crew? Are we bringing them in?" I ask.

"Yeah, planning on bringing them in tomorrow. Simon says rumors have been circulating, everyone talking about something happening and being paranoid so don't want to spook them. I wanna do it quietly. We still don't know for sure if any other members from our side are involved. Mario may not have known the full truth."

"Agreed. Okay. I'm gonna work out and then I'll be heading to Starlight. Vince is coming over to look at the books."

Vince is sort of an accountant. He makes sure the books look good and money is filtered through without suspicion.

"Cool, I'm meeting with Carlos later to give him the footage with the extra rat's info that he needs to dispose of. I'll take Jules with me, but I'll try and stop by the bar tonight," Dima says.

"Oh fuck, I forgot about Carlos. You sure you don't want me there?" I say.

"Nah, I can handle him. You go do business and we will catch up later, brother." Happy with his reply, I'm about to leave, but Seb stops me.

"Lev, I think maybe you should check in on Aaron

today. He said he was fine but he seemed worried about going home to his stepbrother," he says.

I pause and think about the implications of all of this on Aaron, but there isn't a lot I can do, so I just grunt my reply and head down the gym to punch the doe-eyed hottie from my mind.

After spending over an hour facing off against the punching bag, I get myself ready in my signature black shirt–leaving the top open–my black trousers, combat boots, and thick woolen black coat. It's decided to snow outside, which is a pain in the ass. I won't be able to take my sports car, so I go for the truck instead. You never know how bad the snow will get around here and you end up being stuck.

It's early afternoon so the club isn't open yet. I walk through to the office where I'm meeting Vince. It's rare for me not to have either Jules or Simon with me as backup, but Dima needs them more, so I have one of our new guys on me today, Kai. He happens to be Jules' nephew so he comes from good stock and is nearly as big as Jules. He looks just like him, only younger.

"Hey, Lev," Kai greets me as I walk into the office.

"Send Vince straight in when he gets here."

"No problem," he says as he leaves.

I start getting all our documents out and ready for Vince, but I'm unfocused today. I keep having flashbacks from last night, which never happens. Fucking Aaron. The little shit sure knows how to worm his way into your thoughts. I can't get out of my head how good his ass felt, how his hole was gaping so wide when I finished with him. You could've fit two cocks in there no problem. I ruined that little ass, and I'm proud of it. I hope I have left a lasting memory of how my dick made him feel. The idea of nobody else being able to please and fill him like I did last night makes me feel smug as fuck. I try to ignore my dick's attempt to fill while I reminisce about last night.

Thankfully, the door opens and in walks Vince who succeeds in deflating it.

"Lev, how's things?" he asks, making small chit chat. Vince always tries to be friendly with me and I wish he would just get on with it. I hate making conversation with people outside my family. Even they push on my patience.

"I'll leave you to it. I'll be out front if you need me."

"Chatty as ever," he mumbles as I walk away.

"Shut the fuck up and do what you're paid to do, Vince." Damn idiot.

Walking out to the main bar area, I see that Jess, our bar manager, is here. "What are you doing here so early?" I ask.

"Nice to see you too, Mr K. Dima asked me to come in early for the liquor delivery with him being in a meeting, so I thought I'd make a start on opening so I'm not rushing around later," she says, which is followed by a pause as she watches me, her forehead frowning probably trying to decipher why I am so moody.

"Is that okay? You look kinda angry, Mr K."

"I'm not angry. That's fine." My phone rings. It's Dima so I move towards one of the booths reserved for Dima and me.

"How'd it go?" I ask.

"Good. Well good as in there are no issues with us and Carlos. Not so good for the fuckers who have betrayed him. I don't think he would have believed me without the video, but he is dealing with it and that's it. Vince turned up?"

173

"That's good news. Yeah, Vince is here now and Jess has just arrived."

"You contacted, Aaron?" he asks.

"Dima, why would I contact Aaron?" Why is everything all Aaron, Aaron fucking Aaron.

"I don't know, check if he is okay?"

"Why'd you care? He is a grown man, so will you stop with the questions about him please?"

Dima sighs down the phone. "Fine, I'll shut up. Seb is working tonight so I may see you later. Are you staying at Starlight?"

"Yeah, I think I'm gonna hang here for a few hours, and find a willing body for the night."

Dima laughs down the phone. "Some things never change. Okay, later."

He ends the call and I sit back in my booth seat. I don't give a fuck about Aaron, only getting his stepbrother and making him suffer. But one more ride of his ass would be nice.

No. No repeats and that's why a hook-up will cut that cord of longing for the needy doe-eyed man.

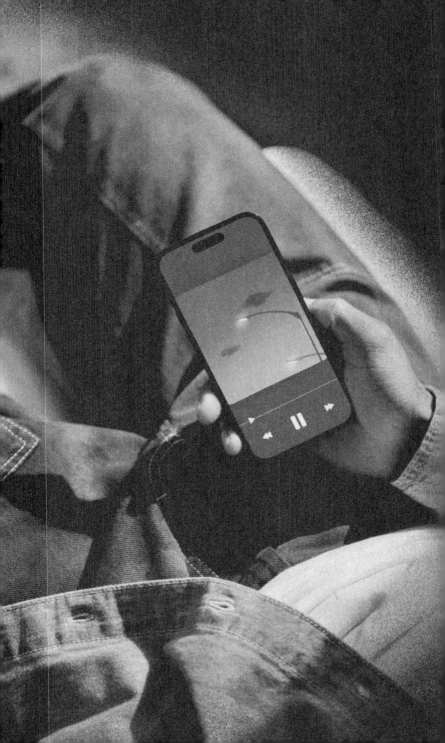

CHAPTER 21
AARON

W hy haven't Lev and Dima come for Jake yet? I'm sitting at the kitchen table, staring at my sandwich. Why haven't I heard anything yet? Are they going to come for the crew tonight? Tomorrow? I need to know what's going on. Everything seems to be falling apart. Jake is more on edge than usual. Tommy is sketchy. Shay's hardly speaking to anybody.

Does … does Jake know that I'm the one that's ratted him out? No, that can't be it. Jake wouldn't be able to contain his anger. But the waiting and the not knowing is killing me. Part of me wants to contact Lev and ask him what to do and the other part … well, I just want to run as far away from here as possible.

I push my sandwich away, officially having lost my appetite. I can't eat, I can't sleep. I hate this.

I get up and just as I'm about to throw my lunch away, Shay walks into the room.

"Are you okay, Aaron?"

I move towards the trashcan to discard the unwanted food and keep my back to him. "Yeah, why?"

"I dunno, you seem quiet, not really present. I mean, to be honest, everyone around here's on edge and Jake won't speak to me. Tommy's hardly here, and I just don't know what the fuck is going on anymore. Did you follow them the other night?" he asks.

Should I be honest? Can I trust him? Hell, I don't think I can trust anybody anymore. I need to do what everyone else is doing. Lie.

"No, I didn't follow him. I ended up wandering around thinking about what you said about leaving. I'm just as in the dark as you are." I am shocked at how convincing I even sound to myself.

He thinks about that, nodding his head slowly. "There's still time for you to leave, Aaron. I can help you before it's too late."

"What do you mean too late? I am so sick and tired of all the secrecy, treating me like some dumb child. If you really gave a shit about me, you would tell me what's going on instead of the riddles that fly outta your mouth. Just be fucking real with me for once. My life is tied up in whatever shit you have going on!" I say. I've had it with Shay. With all of them.

What I don't tell Shay is that it's already too late. With Jake talking about leaving town and him refusing to let me go, what the hell else am I supposed to do? I know what I want to do. But I can't.

Just as Shay is about to speak, Jake and Tommy walk through the door. Tommy with his ever-present frown just for me. Whatever, bitch. I really couldn't give a fuck anymore. Honestly, after last night, for the first time in my life, I'm feeling like my true self. Even though I'm alone without a single person who gives a rat's ass about me. It's a hard fact to swallow, but fuck 'em, I don't need anyone in my life.

"We're heading out tonight, and I'm not sure when we'll be back, but you're not to leave this apartment, Aaron. Do you understand me?" Jake says.

I want to argue with him, but what's the point? I'm fully healed and don't fancy another beating. "Yes, I understand, Jake."

"Good, finally learning your place," he says. "Shay, be ready in ten minutes and we'll head out."

Everyone falls in line like usual.

Shay walks out of the room, leaving me on my own with Tommy and Jake. There's a shift in the air between all of us and I'm not sure what it means. I just know that something is about to happen.

"When will you be back?" I ask because my mouth never knows when to shut up.

His nose wrinkles in my direction like he's smelled something rotten. The vast emotions and feelings he has towards me are so confusing. It's like he hates me with every bone in his body, but wants me under his control. There's uncomfortable silence until Shay returns. "It will be late," Jake says, finally answering my question. "No doubt you'll be in bed like a good little boy. I mean it, Aaron. You will not leave this apartment."

"Sure, have fun or whatever," I grumble.

The three of them leave the apartment and I'm stuck here in the deafening silence with too many thoughts and decisions spinning in my mind. I want to text Lev, but I'm apprehensive in case Jake is secretly watching me. I'm so fucking paranoid and tense. So, I decide to be a completely reckless asshole and do the stupidest thing possible.

I'm going to find Lev in person. The man will be at

either Desire or Starlight tonight. He seems to do nothing else but work. I could text, but I'd prefer to speak to him face-to-face and tell him what's going on with Jake.

Plus, I need to know where I stand. I need to know when he's taking the crew.

Who am I kidding? I'm just pining to see him. Fuck it. I'm going.

A couple of hours later, I'm standing outside Starlight. I hung around the apartment for a bit to make sure Jake and the guys actually left, and it wasn't just a test to see if I'd remained confined to quarters like a good boy.

I look up at the large sign, hesitant to walk in. What have I got to lose at this point? Absolutely fuck all. I push through the double doors, and the sound of the sultry music of the burlesque show that's currently going on sweeps over me, relaxing me instantly.

It's such a great bar to come to. Hidden dark corners, seductive music that hypnotizes you, a place filled with lust and secret desires. A place where you leave all your shit at the door before you walk in here. Nobody cares who you are or how you've sinned, you can melt into the crowd and stay hidden. I love it here.

I survey the room looking for Lev, not sure that I'll actually find him, but it's worth a shot. I notice Seb behind the bar, but I ignore him for now. I don't need any interference tonight. As I scour past the bar, I notice a back in the corner that I would know anywhere.

Those broad shoulders, thick neck, and tattoos dressed all in black. It's a back I only memorized last night with my hands, but what really throws me off, is the guy that he has pushed up against the wall, and not in the violent Lev way, no, it's more like "I'm going to fuck your brains out".

Molten anger turns my blood to hot lava that seeps out of my pores. If anyone touched me now, they would burn to ash.

When my vision returns from the burning haze that clouded it at first, my focus zooms in on Lev as he grabs the guy and pushes him towards the door to the back of the bar that I know leads to his office. Lev tilts his head to Seb who is still behind the bar. Seb shakes his head in return. Okay, apparently, this is a regular occurrence and it ain't fucking happening tonight. He only fucked me last night, how can he possibly want more? No way this prick's ass feels as good as mine

Are you really gonna let another man touch what's yours? Make the fucker bleed.

The rational voice in my head has left, leaving only Crazy, and that guy should stay locked away no matter how often he begs for attention. But he has a good point, I can feel his malicious smile in my head which transfers onto my face as my hand strokes the switchblade in my pocket. No one else in my brain has shown up to stop him, so I'll let my crazy psycho have his fun. He deserves it after being hidden away for so long. Psycho recognizes psycho after all, so Lev can only blame himself for unleashing Crazy's wrath.

Firmly grabbing onto my switchblade, I'm not sure whether to use it on both of them or just Lev. That can be a last-minute decision.

All I know is that another part of me is at the helm. A cunning one. A dangerous one. He's the one who leaves the scared young boy locked in the apartment, doing what Jake says. Crazy, on the other hand, is fearless and takes what he wants. I nearly let him loose in the holding pen when Lev was comforting Mario before killing him.

181

Lev seems to be the trigger to my crazy. Not surprising, really.

With confident strides, I make my way over to the bar. Seb swallows, a tad bug-eyed. The fury coursing through me is palpable and Seb feels it. I like Seb, but even he won't get in my way. "I'm going back there Seb, and you can't stop me."

I expect him to try, but he laughs. "Go get him, Aaron, and make the smug fucker suffer." He pats me on the shoulder and goes back to work.

Okay. I didn't expect it to be that easy, but now I'm back on my cockblock and stab mission, which will involve the switchblade that's firmly gripped in my hand.

With a determined pace, I storm down to Lev's office. I'm surprised Simon or Jules aren't guarding it, but I can't think too much on that right now. As I push the door open, I find the fucking man slut straddling Lev's thighs on his obscene leather chair. I'm not sure why, but I laugh. I don't fucking think so. Lev's eyes startle in alarm when he notices me and the knife I'm holding, but I'm quicker than him. Before he can do anything, I haul the slutty prick who thinks he can touch Lev off his lap and hold the knife to his throat. Nothing more than a little twink I could snap in half.

Lev slowly sits back in his chair taking in the scene with a huge smile that I have never seen before appearing on his irritatingly gorgeous face.

I'll show you, fucker.

CHAPTER 22
LEV

J ust when I think my doe can't surprise me any further, he pulls shit like this. I have to say, I am impressed. The jealous unhinged look suits him and with the addition of the knife, my dick is harder than it was before he interrupted the fuck-a-thon that was about to happen.

Not that I really wanted to screw whoever this guy Aaron is holding. I won't say anything, but it was mainly to distract myself from the possessive little monster that's staring at me like he will tear me apart. God, I would love to see him try.

"You can't fuck him. I won't allow it. No one touches you," Aaron says, pushing the knife a little harder into the currently terrified potential body who looks like he may piss himself.

The sight makes me giddy. This is fun.

"Stop smiling, Lev, it doesn't suit you. Tell this whore to fuck off, or I will hurt him."

I chuckle. "And why would I do that?" I subtly rub my

cock over my pants. This is the kind of foreplay I can get behind.

"I don't like him touching you," Aaron says, voice detached, completely devoid of human emotion. A new mask has slipped in place. This side of him is dark and untamed. Fucking perfection. I have never been interested in possessive lovers, but shit, this is something to behold and it's so arousing, I swear this room is warmer than it was five minutes ago. I want to toy with him a little more though, push him to the precipice of madness.

"That's not your choice, Aaron." Which is technically true, I don't owe him anything, even though he seems to think he has a claim on me because of the fuckfest we shared.

The high-pitched laughter that bursts from Aaron is as manic as it is painful, and slightly terrifying. It's not a humorous laugh, it's a pain that makes my gut ache. I don't know what has made Aaron like this, but it's fucking sad to witness. His frenzied eyes move around the room before he refocuses on me as if waiting for instructions. His hand holding the knife shakes and causes the blade to nick the guy's throat. I should really ask for his name.

"Ok, doe. Let him go and he will leave," I say, trying to bring him back from wherever his mind has gone. It takes a few minutes before he robotically lets his arms fall, releasing the guy and standing back.

"Leave," I say, hoping that the guy picks up that I mean him. I can't force my gaze away from Aaron right now. He looks like he is about to lose it, and while that excites me, this seems a little off. He needs anchoring. Hook-up guy hurries out of the room, mumbling something I can't hear, but I don't care enough to check.

"What the fuck are you doing, Aaron?" I ask as I slowly approach him.

"I needed to speak to you." His eyes are still wide, pupils dilated, and panicked but his breathing calms.

"What about?" I ask, hoping to redirect him onto something else.

"About Jake, he's planning something else and I didn't want to text you. I thought it would be best face-to-face ... although it seems like I have disturbed you," he sneers.

It's so fucking hot and intoxicating. I go to my desk and retrieve one of my cigars. I need it to ease the fucking tension in this room. Bringing it to my lips, I light the end, take a deep inhale, and enjoy the high it adds to my blood. I blow away the smoke, letting it relax my muscles, but the momentary peace is interrupted.

"Who was he?" Aaron asks, giving me conversation whiplash.

"No idea. Just a guy."

He nods, thinking that over. I move a step closer to him and those fucking innocent eyes that draw me in hold so much longing that it nearly knocks me over.

He didn't just come here to tell me about Jake. He is needy and wants attention. His mind needs to be settled and apparently, it's only me that can do that. I grab him behind his neck, which I have noticed makes him focus better.

"You know what you need, doe? You need someone who grounds that crazed mind of yours."

He slackens under my touch. I take another smoke and force Aaron's mouth open, exhaling the deliciousness into his mouth, which he greedily accepts.

"Well this is a new side to you, Aaron. Stabby jealous to needy doe?"

"Why do you call me that?" Another change in his tone. This one is more innocent and honest.

"Because of your eyes, they remind me of Bambi. Big and brown and full of innocence. Although, I know that word would never be used to describe you."

He scoffs at that, a hint of the icy attitude returning. I think he is embarrassed by how much he likes that I have a name for him.

"You know, I like this side of you, stabby-psycho Aaron. I knew you'd be a clinger. It's like having a groupie."

"Yeah, well we can't all be perfect like you," he says. Cheeky little shit.

"True. So tell me why you are here, apart from to block me from getting my dick wet."

His face contorts to a look of irritation.

I'm going to be on the receiving end of that knife, aren't I?

Internally, I grin at how easy he is to twist into knots as I move back to my desk, stubbing out my cigar, saving the rest for later.

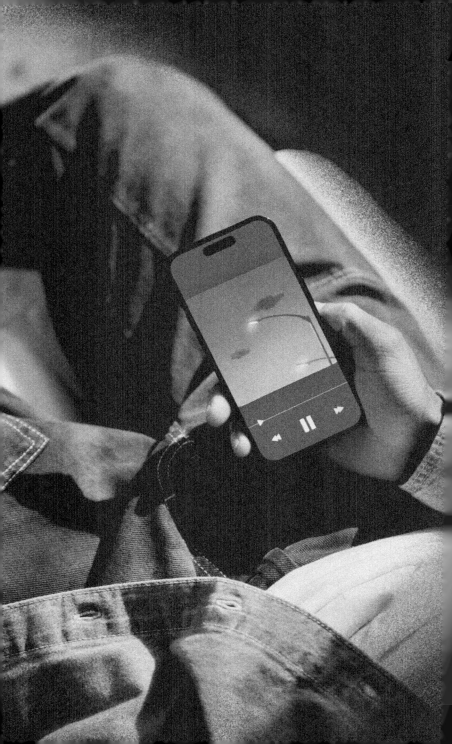

CHAPTER 23
AARON

"Jake is planning on leaving. He told me last night when I got home, and I don't know if he knows something or if he was testing me. They left to go somewhere tonight, he didn't say where but something is happening," I explain, trying to bring the conversation back to why I came here in the first place.

That hysterical outburst frazzled my brain. It just came out of nowhere. It was like when I was younger, how I latched onto anything that made me feel something. It's trickled into adulthood and Lev is taking the brunt. It was like I was having a breakdown, the fear I was losing my grip on him. But he isn't fucking mine. Why can't I get that?

"I knew we should have had the fuckers brought in straight after, but Dima wanted to wait," he says, then pauses in thought. "Okay, I'll call Dima and get the ball rolling."

"And what about me? What happens to me now, Lev?" I ask, and I allow the slight vulnerability in my voice to show.

He looks at me with no emotion, no reaction. It's like nothing has ever happened between us and it's the first time I feel a slight stab of pain in my chest. I can't allow it, he was clear from the start and this is my issue. Considering my behavior tonight, it's something I need to work on. Maybe keeping my distance will help.

"Nothing. I told you if you helped you would be free, and you are."

"And what about the other thing?" I ask and he looks confused, like he is trying to go over every encounter we have had to look for the question I am asking.

"What thing?" he says.

"I want to be in on it. I want to be the one to end Jake. That was the deal." He snorts and it annoys the shit out of me. "Don't fucking laugh at me, Lev. This is my life!" I shout at him.

Instantly, all the humor from his face drains. Before I know it, he has me slammed against the door, locked in a chokehold and fuck, does it feel amazing to have his hands on me again.

"You forget your place, doe. I have killed for less than your current attitude. I made no such deal, you just assumed." He relaxes his hand but with his breath so close to my face, I feel my body go limp, like he is the only thing keeping me upright. I keep my eyes closed. I can't look at him right now. It's too much.

A gravelly chuckle vibrates next to my ear, the smells of his cigar and aftershave fill my nostrils, settling into my core memories as his signature scent. "I get it now, you want some attention, doe, don't you? Hmm? That's why you are really here," he says in a hushed tone into my ear. It's making my brain melt to goo. His voice carries a hypnotic lilt that pulls me under, making it hard to think.

"I came here to tell you what Jake is planning," I say, trying to sound convincing.

"You could have messaged that to me. I know my little monster wants to tear his brother apart. I know that thought gets you off, but you wanted my eyes on you. I've said before that you give yourself to me too easily, doe. You need another fucking? Does your hole need to be pounded until you feel like yourself again?" He licks under my ear, and goosebumps flare on the surface.

How the fuck he knows all this is scary but also such a damn turn on. I open my eyes and gaze into his vivid green ones, refusing to look away as I let the rawness of my need for him come to the surface.

"Yes, I want you to fuck me, but what about '*no repeats?*'" I try to mimic his deeper voice.

Lev doesn't look impressed.

"Watch the attitude, doe," he scolds me before mauling my mouth with that talented tongue. As expected, Lev just forces his way into my mouth, completely dominating it, making me yield to his control, and I eat it up like the ravenous slut I am.

He is the only one who quiets those voices in my head. I feel lighter around him. For the first time in my adult life, I have some awareness of who I really am, who the person buried underneath all this trauma is.

Lev sweeps his tongue with long slides over my own. I groan loudly at the sloppiness and intensity of this kiss. I don't think my mouth could get any wider. The burn of his stubble around my lips sends tendrils of warmth over my skin that travels down to my cock. He kisses like he fucks, hard, unapologetic, and possessive. His large hands grab onto my ass as he forces our covered cocks together, and the contact is exquisite, but I'd prefer to be naked.

I feel a slight wetness at the tip of my cock as it rubs against the monster dick that is hard as rock behind Lev's pants. Pulling away, he grabs the collar of my shirt and turns me around so fast before shoving me over his desk, causing the papers and ashtray to fall onto the ground. This is not what I expected when I came here tonight, but I'm not complaining.

"Gonna ruin your ass now, doe. Hope you are ready. You asked for this." His smoky voice lingers on the back of my neck. He undoes my jeans and aggressively pulls them down my legs along with my underwear. "Fuck yeah, this ass is just begging to be owned isn't it, doe?"

"God yes, own it, fuck me, please, please, Lev." I swallow hard and look back over my shoulder at him. "Destroy me."

His eyes flare, no green to be seen as the black from his pupils has taken over any color.

A glob of what I assume is spit covers my hole before two large fingers penetrate me without hesitation and without care. The burn is welcome, I'm horny for anything he will give me.

"Just do it," I beg.

I need more and I don't want any more prep. I want this to hurt. Unlike most people, Lev does not question it. I hear him spit on his dick before I feel the large wide tip push against my hole, the barbell of his piercing rubbing against my rim.

"Wish granted," he says and thrusts inside me in one hard push.

Holy shit, it feels like all my insides have been rearranged. No sound comes from my mouth as the pain and heat from his monster dick leaves me overcome with extreme fullness.

"Unngghh, so fucking good, doe. This is the tightest hole I have ever fucked," he pants as he fucks me with such force I would consider it a hate fuck.

The piercing on his cock rubs over my prostate with such heavy pressure, it makes my body light up like fireworks. Every part of my body vibrates, mini explosions of heat as he repeatedly hits that spot.

I want more.

The room is filled with the sounds of his hips slapping against my ass. The desk is starting to move with his full weight pounding into me as I grip onto the edges of the desk for life. The shouts of ecstasy leaving my mouth are so loud, I think it may be louder than the music outside in the bar, but I don't care. I'm letting myself go. Lev is no better, grunting and panting with every move.

He slaps my right ass cheek hard. "Fuck, doe, your greedy hole is gonna make me cum. Rub that thick dick of yours."

Grabbing my dick, I move my hand up and down, my precum makes it slide with ease. It's so sensitive to the touch that it doesn't take more than three strokes before I'm yelling out my release that spills over my hand. The shout is not only from pleasure that trumps any other orgasm I have ever had, but it's a shout that releases all the tension and worries that I have going on. It settles me in a way I never thought sex could. My body ripples with contented aftershocks.

"Fuck, fucccck," Lev yells as his cum breeds me until I am filled completely.

I missed that sensation from last night. I loved being wet and sticky, having my body used by him. I feel claimed. For a brief moment, he rests his head on the back of my sweaty neck, trying to compose himself.

His breath on my damp neck makes my sensitive skin shudder. When he pulls his cock out of me, I hiss at the loss. His juices start to drip down the back of my thighs, the filthiness of it makes me preen with pride that I made him cum, that I have his cum in me, and it's all mine. *Mine*. I want more of his juice in me, to have it leaking from me daily, reminding me who I belong to.

I look over my shoulder where Lev is transfixed, staring at my ass while holding my cheeks apart, enjoying watching himself spill out of me.

"Fuck, that's a pretty sight. Hold on," he says as he lets me go and walks around to the desk drawers to grab some tissues that he then hands to me.

I'm thankful. I love his juice in me, but I don't want it on show to others. I'm wearing black after all.

After I clean myself up, I stand and notice Lev is already put back together again. He doesn't even look like he has just fucked me senseless. He looks at me with a heavy hooded gaze as I pull my jeans back up. It makes my hands waver as he watches me, my physical reaction to him has not subsided. It's getting worse and I think I'm getting to a point where I don't want to live without his attention and touch.

"You are doing that weird smile again," he says and I don't give a shit.

I know that others find my quirks unusual, but this is who I truly am, and around Lev I don't fight it. I can't fight it, and I've given up trying. He always comments on my smile with annoyance, but I know he secretly likes it. I think he likes it because it reminds him of the Crazy that lives in my brain. Those parts of ourselves call to one another and that's why the connection between us when we come together is so powerful. Lev needs that in another person as much as I do. It means we don't have to hide, but I remind myself that is not something he wants.

"What do I do Lev?" I ask, needing to change the path of this conversation before I lose it again.

He takes a deep breath. "Let me call Dima. Go sit out at the bar. I'm sure Seb will talk your ear off while we sort this out. I keep my promises, Aaron, you won't be included in this. You are free to go," he assures.

"I want to kill him," I say, unable to keep the icy hatred in my voice away.

Lev walks back over to me and holds me behind the back of my neck, a move that I yearn for. I meet his wild stare. "Then I will make it happen, doe," he says in a rumbling voice that calms me to my core. He guides me towards the door and reaches for the handle.

"Go wait at the bar while I call Dima and don't move."

"Okay," I say, but I don't intend to stay. I need to get back home before Jake does, but I also need to pull away from this family. The longer I spend with them, the more my mind makes up the lie that I am one of them, which I'm not. I have to protect myself on both sides, but I need to keep Jake's suspicion away from me. I should mention it to Lev, but it's not his problem, and I don't think he would give a shit anyway.

Walking towards the bar, I do feel a sense of relief, that I finally may get what I want and the weight on my shoulders lifts, knowing this will come to an end.

I'll officially be able to call my life my own and I'll be rid of all family ties. I am so tired. Between all this fucking emotional back and forth and the amazing sex I just received, my body is exhausted.

My aim was to leave the bar undetected, but I hear a voice from behind me.

"So, is Lev alive back there? I saw the guy he was with run out of here so I daren't go back to check if everything was okay," Seb says, stopping me in my tracks. I can't help the laugh that leaves my mouth as I turn back to him. He really is gorgeous.

"He is alive, for now, and well fucked, too, in case you're interested. Anyway, I gotta get back before my step-brother does. See ya around, Seb," I say before I walk away to the sound of Seb calling out to me. I ignore him and keep moving, increasing the pace of my footsteps. I need to put the Kozlovs in the past.

CHAPTER 24
LEV

As Aaron leaves, I could punch my own face for giving into those big brown eyes and fucking him over my desk. I'm a bad man, so when it's offered so freely I won't say no, but I'm more concerned that Aaron is unlike most hookups. He is more likely to cut off my dick in a jealous rage than he is to listen to reason as to why I can't offer him anything. The need in him is palpable and it calls to me like a moth to a flame. The rush of having someone to share the pain and violence, to feed that bloodthirst along with sexual craving, is hard to ignore. But I can tell it's more for him. I do think he would do whatever I asked, and fuck does that make me a hot mess. To have him as my own little doe-eyed monster. For him to watch me play, and to let me use him as a sex toy when I want, wherever I want, brings forward a possessive side I didn't think I had.

Dima is the possessive one, whereas I have needs, but have never been attached to anyone or anything. It could become a problem if I allow it. I know Aaron sees the true me. We are the same in some ways, and I think that's what makes it different. Even with that truth, he still looks like he wants me.

Grabbing my cell phone, I hit the dial on Dima's name and wait for him to answer. "We've got a problem," I say as soon as he picks up.

"Okay, what's going on?"

"Aaron stopped by the club and said that Jake is planning to leave town. I'm not sure when but it sounds like it will be soon."

A long pause follows.

"I don't know if anyone has tipped them off but we need to bring them in, D," I say.

"Fuck, okay. Meet me back at the house in an hour and bring Aaron with you. We will get to work."

"Fine." I end the call.

The warm sensation that builds in my chest at the idea of playing in the pen, sends me into a giddy state with a half-hard cock bulging in my pants to match. It also helps that the idea of Aaron watching me work again has me nearly fully erect. He fucking loved watching me last time, and while it was distracting, it made it so much more enjoyable, knowing that every cut I made, every drop of blood lost, was turning him on as much as it was me. Sharing that hunger with another was a special experience, like some spiritual shit where I'm walking on air with nothing but power driving me. This should put a smile on doe's face.

I head out of the office, expecting to see Aaron at the bar talking to Seb, but he isn't there. I walk over to Seb who is making some weird-looking green cocktail.

"Where'd he go?" I ask.

"You mean Aaron, I assume?" he snarks.

He lifts the side of his mouth upwards, trying to annoy

me on purpose. I think Dima needs to work on his punishments better. Actually, maybe it should be a family event, putting the cocky shit in his place.

"Yes, you bratty little fuck."

He shakes his head smiling, like he of course knew I would take the bait. Prick.

"He said he had to get home before his stepbrother gets back."

"I'm gonna kill the little shit. I'm heading back to the house, so I'll call him on the way. Just so you know, we may all be busy in the pen when you get back later."

"I know. D already called."

"Of course he did. Can you take a piss without telling each other?"

"Yes, we do have some boundaries, Lev. Now fuck off. I'm working and your face is scaring the customers."

"I'm having a word with Dima about you. He clearly doesn't spank that ass enough."

His mouth gapes, and he is unusually quiet. A self-satisfied grin beams across my face. He didn't know that I am aware of exactly what my brother does to him. And I don't blame him. "I might suggest that we all take part, help Dima out."

"Ha. Yeah, right. Dima would kill you," he says.

"Well, we could find out … he does put family first. I'll let you know what he says." I turn to walk out before he can say anything. I wouldn't ever suggest such a thing, but it feels good to have pissed Seb off.

Leaving Starlight, I am thankful that it has stopped snowing. I head towards my truck and call Aaron. The little shit can't have gotten far. He answers right away.

"Lev," he says.

I love the way he says my name into the phone.

"I thought I told you to wait at the bar? Get over to my house. Dima wants you to be there for an update."

"I can't, Jake will wonder where I am and I don't want another beating, Lev," he says.

"Aaron, get the Uber to bring you to mine now. Otherwise I will come over to yours, tie you up and carry you over my shoulder whether your stepbrother is home or not. I am your boss. So you do as you are told," I say, making it very clear who is in charge.

"Ugh, fine." A momentary silence is then followed by, "If I stay will you fuck me again?"

Talking to Aaron is hard work when he shifts so quickly with his train of thought. It's fucking exhausting. But, hell am I tempted to fuck him again, even though that side of our relationship needs to end. I have already done more than I usually do, plus his jealousy is beyond the realm of normal, not that anything he does is normal.

"Aaron, you know there is no more fucking. No more anything. It's done. Now get over to the house."

"Fuck you, Lev," he snaps and my fury rises further when he hangs up on me.

He needs some fucking discipline, but that's not my problem. It has to be this way now. Plus, after we bring Jake in, he will be free to do as he wants, get away from this town, and start anew. I try to ignore the slight ache that pinches in my stomach at the thought of not seeing Aaron again, but this is for the best. My family comes first and there is no room for anyone else. I don't need the hassle.

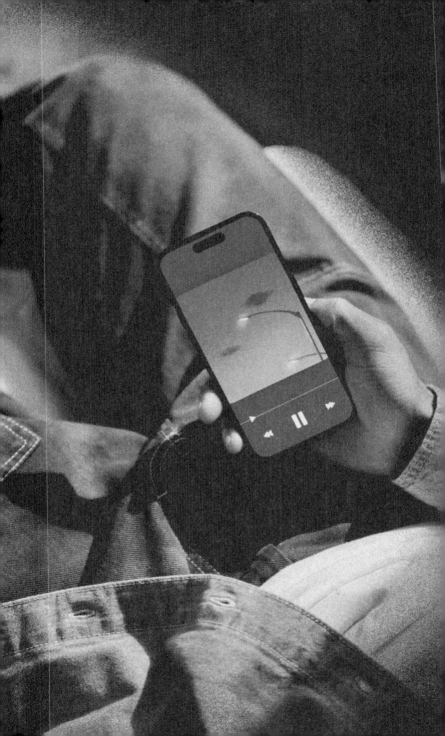

CHAPTER 25
AARON

I am seething to the core when I arrive at Lev's. How dare he dismiss me on the phone? The bastard. I seem to be in a constant unhinged mode when around him. At least it keeps my flitty brain on track for a change.

A guy I don't recognize opens the door as I approach. Wow, he is fine as hell. He looks like Jules, but younger. Is it his son? Doesn't matter. I walk up to him and I am surprised he knows my name.

"Hey, Aaron. Dima is in the office waiting ... is Lev not with you?" He peers over my shoulder.

"No, hopefully the asshole got stuck in the snow somewhere."

He grins at that which only makes him even more handsome. This house is a gay man's fantasy with all these hot alpha males. "Giving you a hard time?" he teases.

"Just being a dick. What's your name?" I ask

"Oh sorry, it's Kai. I'm Jules' nephew."

Ahh nephew, now it makes sense.

Hearing a car approach, the hair on my skin prickles. I just know it's Lev. Even his truck sounds moody.

Like a lightbulb moment, an idea hits me. Kai gives me the perfect opportunity to test my theory that Lev does want me. I'll see if he gets as jealous as I do.

You know, the mature approach.

Loud footsteps that sound like they are on a mission, approach the door. I lean into Kai's space, knowing that Lev can now see us as he enters the foyer. Excitement boils inside me in anticipation of pissing him off.

"That explains it. You look just like him, but a hotter version." I try to flirt but I have never done it before, so I'm not sure if it sounds right or if the fake grin on my face is flirty or murderous.

"This isn't a good idea, he looks ready to kill us," Kai whispers.

I smile again. "Good."

He shakes his head with an uncomfortable smile, and I lean in a little closer. Kai stiffens. I know I shouldn't do this because he'll also be on the receiving end of Lev's anger, but I can't stop myself. Besides, Lev doesn't give a shit, right?

Moving closer to his ear I whisper, "Just go with it." For a second I get distracted by the encapsulating spicy smell from Kai. Damn, he smells good.

Before I have a chance to pull away, a large familiar hand grabs the back of my neck, making me wince. It's fucking painful.

"Fuck off, Kai," Lev says and the flame of passion that has been ignited makes my body sing in delight. I knew it.

Keeping a punishing grip on my neck, he guides me roughly down the hallway, which I remember is the direction of his room. *Oh fuck*. This is so hot. My cock is begging to be played with right now. It's impossible to keep the victorious smile off my face as he shoves me into his room and then aggressively hurls me onto his bed, like I am weightless maiden, not a grown man.

Turning me over onto my back, he grabs my throat. Shit, I love that move. I want to beg him to grip me harder, but by the wicked squint in his eyes and the menacing line that his mouth is set in, he may actually kill me.

"This what you wanted, doe? You are such a fucking attention whore."

I whine in response, trying to connect my cock with his, but he keeps himself above me, only touching my throat.

"What was the plan exactly, fuck Kai to make me jealous?"

"Yes, and it worked," I say.

"I'm not jealous," he says mockingly, but his actions say otherwise.

"Yeah, looks like you are completely in control, Lev. You fucking want this too so just take me and stop being a pussy," I taunt, lifting my leg to rub it in between his thighs, feeling the hardness of that beautiful dick. I need it in my mouth right now, or ass, I don't really care as long as I can have it filling me somehow.

He slaps my face and holds it in his grip. I groan as the warm sting lingers and spreads over my cheek. "You should be careful trying to taunt me, doe. You will never win."

"I think this situation says otherwise." I smile knowing my weird grin is present. It's only for him.

He smirks back at me knowingly, like he can read my mind. "You are so beyond fucked up, you know that?"

"Yeah, and what are you gonna do about it?" I ask,

putting all my dirty intentions of that question behind it with my softer voice.

"I'm gonna fuck you up, doe. Destroy you piece by piece. You wanted my attention and now you fucking have it. You'll regret it," he says. His voice sounds like a deadly combination of silk and untamed growls.

"Never, as long as your eyes are on me you can do whatever the fuck you want." I realize I'm panting in shallow breaths. I'm on the precipice of him finally giving me what I need. What I want.

"As I keep saying, you give yourself to me too easily," he says.

Lev leans into me and connects our mouths in a violent joining of tongues and teeth that bleed with anger and pure fucking desire. It makes the room feel like it has been set alight. I have come to realize that I am the oil to his flame and nothing but explosive heat exists between us. We need a warning attached to our toxic nature. I don't know what the fuck it is about him, but the pull is too strong to walk away from. Lev overwhelms my mind and it has decided we are claiming him for our own. One taste was never going to be enough. He may kill me, he may control me, but I will not think twice about making his life fucking miserable if he even thinks of leaving me. He is mine now as much as I am his, and I will fuck up the world to keep this little piece of happiness and feeling of belonging, no matter how toxic it seems to others.

Lev moves back and his hand squeezes my cock hard through my pants. Just as I think he is about to get me off, he rises from the bed and walks over to his full-length mirror, putting himself back together.

"Come on, doe, we got work to do," he says in a neutral tone like we weren't about to devour each other.

I sit up on the bed. I know my hair looks a mess but I'm pissed that he has stopped. I want to get off.

"What about my dick? You can't leave me like this!"

"You wanted this, doe. I told you I would destroy you and this is part of it. You will have to wait, we need to meet with D."

I stand up and roughly mess with my hair to make it look like I haven't just been slammed into a bed and teased. Bastard.

"Fuck you, Lev. Don't think you're getting any ass later."

My moment of smugness fades as I am pushed face first into the door I was about to walk through. He grinds his hard dick up against my crack. Okay, maybe he can fuck me.

"Oh I will, doe. I will take that ass when I want, in whatever way I want." He places his hand to the front of my jeans again and starts to squeeze, the pressure is between perfect and painful.

"You are not allowed to make yourself cum from now on. You can only cum when you are with me and when I say. You need to learn some fucking manners and control."

Oh fuck, this is so swoonworthy. I think I will explode in my jeans. I never realized how much I needed this. "And what if I don't follow your rules?" I say, trying to push his limits.

"Don't follow my rules and you will become very well acquainted with the holding pen, where I will leave you bound, and your dick locked in a cock cage until you have learned your place." I hum in joy at that idea. "I will make you watch me play in there too. Imagine watching me work, doe, and not being able to touch yourself, being denied my attention," he teases.

That sounds amazing … and like my idea of hell. I am going to be a handful, and I know being with him will make it worse. I will need his attention twenty-four seven.

"I'll do whatever you want, just don't ignore me, please," I beg and sulk in defeat as he removes the pressure from my cock. This meeting with Dima is going to be a test in restraint. Turning me around to face him, he grabs my throat and takes my mouth, sucking on my tongue. Fuck I want to eat him up.

"Come on, doe. I'm not in the mood for an annoyed Dima," he says, taking his heat with him, leaving me pouting as I follow behind him.

CHAPTER 26
LEV

I am so fucking stupid. What the hell have I signed up for? I'm such an idiot for giving in, but seeing him all over Kai, it completely blindsided me. I have never experienced possessiveness like that over anyone, and the thought of someone else touching Aaron made me see red.

It took all I had not to cut Kai's throat, but I knew what Aaron was doing. The wild little shit. He may be hot, the best fuck I have had, and kinky, but he is completely unstable, weird, and beyond needy for attention. I think he needs help, but it also makes him perfect for someone like me. I could never do normal. *We* are not normal and that makes it feel normal, normal for us anyway. For fucks sake, I need to stop rambling to myself and just accept the fact that I have a clingy fucker who wants me and if triggered may kill others or cut me up in a jealous rage.

I smile to myself. That thought turns me on like nothing else. Fucking doe. Dima won't let me hear the end of this ... oh god, Seb will love it, the little prick. May be best to keep it quiet. I don't have to confirm anything. We aren't in a relationship, we are just fucking together and playing. But only with each other.

Aaron is such a complex guy, but I have started to notice that the more time he spends around me in my surroundings, he is less erratic and more present. There is an openness, and he revels in what's around him. The handful of times where he was quiet and vulnerable haven't happened for a while. He appears more confident, he isn't afraid to show that he wants me to himself, or demand for my eyes to be on him.

It's kind of refreshing getting what you see without the bullshit filters, pretending to be someone you are not. It actually makes me feel like I can be myself too. Dima is the only one who knows the real me, but I think Aaron compliments my needs and makes whatever lives in me come to the surface. Is that a good thing? I don't know, but it's thrilling.

We walk into Dima's office where he is texting on his phone, sitting behind his desk. I push Aaron down into the chair and he sits without complaint.

I stand behind him. There's only one chair in the room —and subconsciously put my hand around the back of his neck, squeezing. Aaron leans into my grip, his shoulders relaxing, less tense than when we walked in. Dima doesn't miss anything, losing interest in his phone, taking note of where my hand is. He looks up at me and whatever expression is on my face, he doesn't say anything, doesn't even smirk or make a smartass comment. But I have no doubt he will be fishing for information later.

"Aaron, Lev said that Jake mentioned he is leaving?" Dima asks.

I let go of him, but he grabs my wrist, stopping me from pulling away, so I grasp back onto his neck. Just like I thought, my touch grounds him, and it's a fucking buzz knowing I have that much dominance over him. I clamp down the acute feeling of wanting to lift him up and take him against the wall, rut into him and claim him.

"Yeah, well he wants me to go. He has been erratic for days and he's getting more controlling. I shouldn't be here. If I'm not home when he gets back, he promised to hurt me, and it'll be worse than before," Aaron says too casually, like this is standard sibling behavior.

Dima watches him quietly. "Well, we are bringing them in tonight, Aaron. Simon and Jules are on it now, trying to track them down, so I wouldn't worry."

"You didn't say anything before?" I growl. I hate being left out of the loop.

"I'm telling you now. It was a last minute decision. I want this to be finished as much as you do, Lev. Makes me antsy knowing we may have more traitors around us," he says.

Aaron turns in his seat to look up at me, those big innocent brown eyes begging. I'm not sure what for until he opens his mouth.

"You promised I could kill him." His eyes flash from begging to cold murder. Fuck. I am so turned on at the thought of watching Aaron hurt and kill his stepbrother. I never would have thought that would be a thing, but I'm finding out a lot about myself with doe around.

"I promise," I say. I won't go against my word.

He gives a curt nod, and faces back to Dima.

"Fine. I'll let you know when they are back. Why don't you both go relax or whatever? It's gonna be a long night if Lev has his way." He laughs but he is not wrong.

I have been waiting for what feels like years to have

Jake and his boys in my pen. And I will savor every moment of it. I might actually film it.

"I need to go back to the apartment to get some of my stuff, Lev, I don't want to risk leaving any shit there in case they go back," Aaron says.

"I don't think that's a good idea, Aaron," Dima says, and I agree.

"I wasn't asking. There are some things I need," he insists. Brave little Aaron. Dima won't appreciate that tone, but he doesn't say anything to Aaron.

"Like what?" I ask. "What could be so important?"

CHAPTER 27
AARON

I let out a snort of irritation. "You wouldn't understand, and it's private."

It's the best response I can come up with. I need my music, but it sounds strange when I think of saying those words out loud. I need my own phone and earbuds. It will sound silly to others, but if Jake is coming here tonight and if things don't go as planned, I need my coping strategies. They don't know that's what kept me going through my younger years, hell, even to this day. I promised myself I would never let anyone see me like that, and don't want to give that information freely.

"Look, I won't be long. Like you said, Jules and Simon are out looking for them so they probably already know where they are. If it makes it better, let Kai take me," I suggest.

I'm pulled from my chair and swung around to face Lev. Holy shit he looks angry, the vein I have never noticed before on his forehead looks like it's about to burst.

"Kai isn't taking you anywhere, doe." Ah the jealous and possessive Lev is out to play. I barely contain the small moan that rises from my throat. This is the most romantic way I have ever been treated.

"Oh for fucks sake, I'm outta here. Don't fuck on my desk. I'll text you when the guys show," Dima says before slamming the door behind him. The air in here is like being in a sauna. Perspiration forms on my hairline, and my clothes feel too tight. I want him to tell me what he wants, to do to me as he pleases.

"Slutty doe, will you ever stop wanting my dick?" he says.

So arrogant but I can't deny that I do.

"No, I won't. I want it to live inside me and I don't give a fuck how." Wow, I really am a disgusting slut and I actually don't care. "You know I'm yours, Lev, only yours and you better only be fucking me, by the way. We never clarified that before, but we are now."

"Thinking you can give orders again, doe? Do you need to be on a cumming ban until tomorrow instead? Do you know what? I might just do that. Maybe you should get me off and if you behave I may let you cum tomorrow," he says, choking my throat as he loves to do. He rubs his mouth like a whisper over my lips. I mewl like a little bitch.

"I've told you, do whatever you want," I say, meaning it with every part of my soul. He studies me for a second and he must see the honesty in my words.

"Okay, doe, I'm convinced. Go on, get Kai to take you. You are to be back here within the hour. I mean it, unless you want me to make that ass bleed later from my hand," he says, and the threat makes me vibrate with need.

I lick my lips before I start drooling from his words alone. "You are so sexy," I say, and I give him one more kiss.

Lev releases his grip on my throat, and entangles both his hands into the back of my hair, gripping it to the point I think he will pull it out, deepening the kiss and holding me closer. We moan into each other, forgetting the world around us. But as usual, Lev has more control than me and pushes me away.

"Go on, before I change my mind," he says.

I head out into the foyer. "Hey Kai, can you take me to my apartment, please? I need to collect a couple of things. Lev said it was cool."

"Sure, let's go," he says.

I can't wait to get back here already.

Leaving Kai in the car, I dash up to my apartment to collect my stuff. I'm relieved that this could be all over tonight, but I'm uneasy. Where will this leave me? No matter what I think of Jake, it will be the end of any family ties that linked me to my mom. It's so damn sad. I thought it was so exciting to be a part of a whole family when Mom got with his dad. I was beside myself with excitement at the idea of having a big brother, someone on my side. Then after my mom's passing, the ugliness and cruelty that they held towards me hurt. Fuck, it really tore me apart. I lost my entire family the day she died and exposed the lie that surrounded us for years. We were never the wholesome unit I thought we were.

On entering the apartment, my senses are on high alert, something feels different. It's quiet, but I don't know what it is that's making the hair on my arms prickle with awareness. Everything is telling me to leave, but of course like the stupid idiots in those horror films, I decide to investigate. I need to get my shit anyway.

Nothing looks out of place, but when I get to my room I freeze on the spot. It's been completely destroyed. Fuck,

Jake was back here and this must be my punishment for leaving when he told me not to.

I walk over all my smashed up bottles of aftershave, my bedside lamps smashed, my clothes strewn across the room. The closet door is wide open and the carpet has been torn up, exposing the floorboard that has been removed from where I usually keep the burner phone. Thank god I had it on me tonight. Uneasiness settles over me. I need to get the fuck out of here, so I grab my earbuds that I always leave stashed under my pillow and pick up my actual phone that is under the array of clothes. Luckily it isn't broken. Snagging a bag, I stuff a few pieces into it. As I turn to leave, I nearly jump through the ceiling. Tommy is standing right in front of me with a wide grin on his face. Oh shit.

"What the fuck happened to my room?" I ask, trying to distract him from noticing the bag in my hand. He doesn't say anything and before I know it, he's in front of me. A sharp pain radiates in my head, followed by a blow to my gut. Feeling off balance, my vision blurs as I black out before collapsing on the floor.

"Now I get to watch you die, fuckface," is the last thing I hear before everything turns to black.

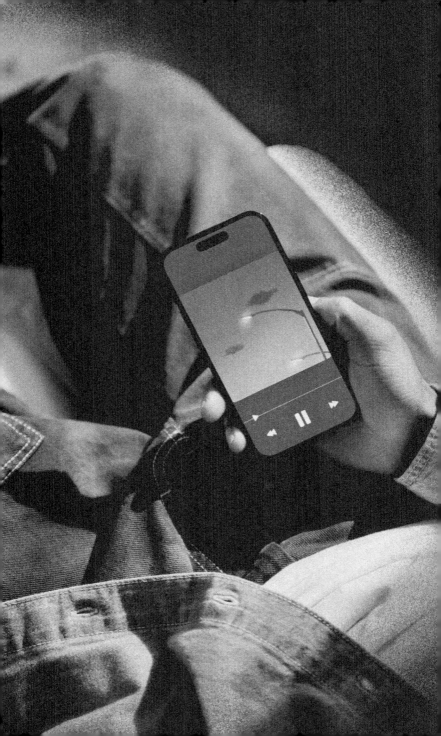

CHAPTER 28
AARON

The pain in my head as I open my eyes makes me feel nauseous. For a second, I try to remember what happened, but the more I come to, the more I become aware that I can't move my arms. I am sitting on the ground and my arms are tied behind me to some kind of wooden post, which is rubbing into my back.

As everything becomes clearer, I remember Tommy hitting me. It takes me a while to realize I am in a room I don't recognize. I must have a concussion. Everything is hazy around the edges and my head feels like it's stuffed with cotton wool. The stench of damp and mildew is enough to make my eyes water. There is nobody here and all I can hear is the faint sound of dripping water. It looks like I am in some kind of basement or outbuilding, I can't quite tell. It's fucking cold, too. The harsh light hanging from the ceiling makes my head throb more. What the hell do I do?

Kai…shit. Did he notice I was taken, or did they hurt him? Was he part of it?

A heavy-sounding metal door opens to my right and of

course, in walks my fucking stepbrother, Tommy, and Shay. Shay is the only one who looks like he wants to be anywhere else but here. I feel the same, but I know there's no point getting my hopes up that he will help me. I don't know why it happens but the frenzied laugh that leaves my lips is uncontrollable. This situation has stripped me bare. Then the realization hits me so hard that I have nothing to lose now. I don't mean shit to anybody and I might as well leave this world with a bang. If anything, I will not allow my last moments to be under the psychological torment of Jake.

"What the fuck is so funny, you freak?" Tommy says, standing over me so I have to lean my head back against the post to see him.

"You. All of you." I continue to laugh, like a deranged witch. I don't sound human, shit, I don't feel human. All the voices in my head have created a war against one another, fighting for dominance to be heard. It hurts, it physically hurts and I want to scream to drown them all out. Focusing back on Tommy, his jaw ticks. He wants to hit me, fuck that, he would love to kill me. Well bring it the fuck on.

"Considering it's you that's tied up, I'd say you should be directing that laughter to yourself," Tommy says.

My laughter is now dying down. I just shrug.

Make the fucker bleed.

It's okay, we will be okay.

Someone help me.

Open wide, baby brother.

All the voices intermingle, and I start rocking my body...*shut up shut up!*

Instead of the dulcet tones, each voice has a different

cadence. Shrill, soothing, and angry. It's so loud I wouldn't be surprised if others can hear them.

Please, please go away, please be quiet.

"Looks like the little freak has finally lost it," Tommy comments, and I have to agree.

Closing my eyes and breathing deeply, I try to regain control of my mind and body.

Breathe in…breathe out.

As everything in my head starts to quiet, I try to focus. I focus on the hard floor beneath me, I focus on the three men in this room, I focus on the ties around my wrists, I focus on the hard post against my back. Slowly bringing myself back to Earth from the imminent panic attack, I grab onto reality and resist drifting away in my head.

Opening my eyes, Tommy is still holding himself over me like he thinks he is the big man, that all his wishes have come true. He's so tragic that I can't be bothered to interact with the dumbfuck. My eyes drift over to Jake, whose stare is locked on me. He's contemplating what to do and I know it won't be good.

"Stand him up," Jake orders and Tommy roughly grabs me under the arms forcing me to stand.

I feel a sway of lightheadedness as soon as I am upright, and I take big gulps of air, trying to control the spinning room. Sickness stirs in my gut from the blow to my head.

"Now, baby brother, you wanna tell me how long you have been spying on me for the Kozlovs?"

I am about to deny knowing what he's talking about until he holds his hand up, showing me the burner phone that Lev gave me, waving it in my face. Well, that's me screwed. He must have gotten it from my pocket when I was unconscious.

I struggle with a response. Mainly because I don't feel so hot, but also, I have no idea what to say. He already knows I have been lying, he is holding the proof.

"I don't remember," I say which is followed by a punch to the stomach, making me bow over towards Jake. Grabbing my shoulders, he pushes me back up. Drool dribbles down my chin from being winded. He's lucky I didn't throw up all over him.

It's okay, it will be over soon. It's okay.

Shut up!

"You know, I've never liked this, it makes you look too girly," he says as he holds onto my eyebrow piercing. "Tommy," he says before Tommy walks over, Jake holds my face as Tommy grips my piercing with a pair of pliers that I never noticed in his hand. Without any hesitancy, he attaches the pliers to the piercing, pulling hard until it rips from my skin.

"Fuck!" I shout. My body shakes, the ties holding my hands behind my back dig into my skin, burning my wrists. Blood drips into my eye, it fucking hurts, and I'm unable to control the sobs racking my body. It feels like someone has taken a hot blade and sliced my skin. Jake smiles, cupping my face in his hands and a triumphant Tommy moves behind him. The fuckers had planned this.

"Now, I'll ask again, baby brother. How long?" he asks, his voice detached like he didn't just tear my skin open. Like I am not his younger brother who he used to care for.

He's not the brother I loved.

You're mine now, baby brother. I own you.

Hold on, it'll be over soon.

Help me.

"The night he called me in to see him after that Santini

shit went down," I say, fear quickly creeping in. My mind is full of how painful the skin around my eye is right now.

"You fucking rat. Kill him, Jake, and let's just leave," Tommy says.

That makes me laugh. I'm starting to lose the plot altogether. Nothing about this is remotely amusing. The hysteria overshadows the fear as the psycho in my mind shamelessly throws itself to the front of the queue, pushing the young boy to the side, which makes my mouth run away from me. I'm surprised the boy remains quiet.

"Aww, are you getting jealous, Tommy? Jake still won't wanna fuck you." I cackle as Tommy pales and moves towards me, no doubt to hit me, but Jake holds him back, blocking him from stepping towards me with his arm.

"He's mine, Tommy, and I have a better plan to teach my baby brother a lesson."

That comment halts the laughter, like I have been hypnotized. I grind my teeth hard, trying to push that term to the back of my head so I don't start to crack.

Open wide, baby brother.

It's okay, it'll be okay. Hold on.

No!

"I'm not your fucking brother." Spit flies from my mouth as I hiss out those words, hoping the venom behind them will rid their effect on me.

Jake gently strokes the side of my cheek and this, this terrifies me more than any beating or torture he could inflict on me. I try to pull back but there is nowhere to go, the post behind me keeping me in place.

"Yes I am, I looked after you. We are as good as brothers, and it's my job to keep you in line," he whispers softly, continuing to stroke my cheek. I would consider it affec-

231

tionate if it wasn't for the fact that it's Jake. My body tremors at the horror of him touching me, my skin feels dirty. He moves back and does an assessing look over my body, it's a perusal that I don't want.

"Shay, guard the door. Tommy, untie him and hold him down," he says and my heart starts beating so fast that I pray a heart attack takes me before I ever have to experience his hands on me.

"Jake, I don't think you should do this, let's just go," Shay begs. He knows what he's planning.

"Shut the fuck up, Shay, before I put a bullet in your head, then what will your sister do?" he threatens.

Shay wavers for a moment before looking at me with an expression full of pity and leaves the room, shoulders slumped. I knew Shay was being blackmailed, now I know it's to do with his sister. I didn't even know he had a sister. It just adds to the never-ending list of Jake's fucked up governance.

Tommy undoes my ties and I can't help the flare of panic. I knew it, I knew it was coming but now it's here. I just want to die.

"I'm gonna make you mine, baby brother," he says.

He's said them. The words that make me shrink, the ones that set my nerves quaking in fear and conjure fat tears that roll hot rivers down my face.

Where is Crazy when I need him? He's nowhere. The scared young boy is the only thing left on offer. Left for dead, just like I was. He seeps into every part of me until I'm paralyzed. If only Jake knew he didn't even need any restraints. The boy only submits to Jake, he doesn't know how to fight him. He's a lonely presence in the darkness of my mind, begging for someone to help him. Pull him out of hell.

"P-Please, Jake," I beg, but it's too faint of a whisper to be heard in this world, only echoing through the place in my mind where the voices live, never reaching them.

Doesn't matter. Even if Jake could hear me, he wouldn't give a fuck. I don't know why I bother except ... there was a time when he was my brother. Was it only pretend? Or did he mean it when he put his arm around me and promised to protect me?

Whatever it was, there's nothing left of that guy.

I try again to call forth the dangerous version of me, the one who could fuck Jake up without a second thought. But it's like grappling with thin air. I can't gain purchase.

"You're gonna know your place. I'll remind you as often as you need it."

Nooooo, the young boy begs through the gloom. But there's no one to hear him and there's nothing I can do to help him.

All hope is lost.

CHAPTER 29
LEV

It's been over an hour and my gut is telling me that something is wrong. Fuck it. I get my phone out and call Kai, he answers on the second ring.

"What's up, Lev?"

"Where the fuck are you?" I demand.

"What do you mean? You told me to take Aaron home," he says, like a confused puppy.

"Yes, an hour ago. It shouldn't take this long for him to get his shit." Something feels wrong.

"Sorry, Lev, he hasn't come back down yet. You want me to go check?"

"What a fucking good idea. Keep me on the phone."

"Okay, hold on." I hear him close the car door and complain how cold it is. I then hear Kai walking up some stairs and knocking on a door.

"Aaron, you ready to go?" he shouts.

"Kai, just go in," I say. I pace up and down the foyer, anger building under my skin, causing the murderous part of me wanting to break free.

"Alright," he says. I hear the door open. "He isn't here.

Aaron! Aaron you here?" Kai calls out, worry lacing his voice.

"Check all the rooms." Some foreign feeling pokes at me and I think it's fear. Fear mixed with a heavy dose of anger. If anyone has touched him, I am gonna torch down this fucking city until I find them. I already know before Kai comes back on the phone that Jake has got to him.

"Oh shit, Lev, there's blood on the floor in what I think is his room. It looks like his bag of stuff has been left."

"Fuck!" I roar. I'm gonna tear that Jake fucker apart. I'm salivating already. I'll remove all his skin slowly until he bleeds dry.

"Get back here now, Kai, and bring the bag." I end the call before Dima comes storming into the foyer.

"You okay? I heard shouting."

"Jake has Aaron and I have no idea where they are. Call Jules now."

He nods and gets straight on the phone. Seb wanders in and instantly picks up on the stressed atmosphere. I have been angry and desperate for blood before, but this feeling of rage is like nothing I have ever experienced in my life.

Irrationality has taken over, I have to get him back. Protect him. I don't feel myself in this moment, the scarlet mist fogging my brain is telling me to kill everyone on sight, to paint this fucking city red until I get doe back.

His brother and his crew will regret this. I will make sure to make their pain last for as long as humanly possible. I plan to live for days in the holding pen with them, making them beg to die, making their screams heard on the other side of town. I silently make a promise to Aaron. I will kill them all for him.

"What's happened?" Seb asks. Before I snap at him I

notice he does look concerned so I withhold the asshole response.

"Jake has taken him. I don't know where they are."

Dima is talking on the phone with Jules, discussing what to do, but standing here is not helping my unbalanced mind settle.

"Your phone," Seb says and I don't know what the fuck he is talking about.

"What?" I ask tersely.

He rolls his eyes at me. "The phone you gave him, did you have it synced with 'find my phone'?"

How the hell did he know about the phone? It clicks, of course it was Dima. D tells him everything.

I pause in place. Dima, hearing this conversation, looks back at us.

"You are a fucking genius, Seb, a first," I add.

"Fuck you, Lev," he grumbles and Dima gathers him in for a hug like he has been a good boy. Ridiculous.

"D, is Jules still on the line?" I ask

"Yep, he's still here. I'll put him on speakerphone."

I bring up the app on my phone and thankfully it hasn't been disconnected. Luckily either Jake hasn't found his burner, or he is too fucking dumb to have checked.

"Got him. Looks like he's in an abandoned house at Lakeshore Woods just on the edge of town. It's around twenty minutes away. Let's go."

"On our way," Jules confirms before ending the call.

I rush to my car, Dima following me along with Seb.

"You need to stay here, beautiful, it's too dangerous and I want you here with Kai in case Aaron gets back here on his own," Dima tells him.

Seb, I'm shocked to say, doesn't argue just as Kai walks in. I walk over to him and he steps back, clearly

237

my intent is written on my face. I punch him across the jaw.

"Do your job properly next time, Kai, or you won't be alive to tell the story. I don't give a shit if you are Jules' nephew. Do we understand each other?" I say.

He stands there holding onto his jaw, wiggling it to make sure it's not broken.

"Sorry, Lev. I'm so sorry," he says, and I believe him.

"Stay here with Seb. We found him so we are going in."

"Okay," he responds, and I head for the door not looking back, knowing my brother is with me as always.

Speeding down the roads, I can feel Dima's eyes on me. I'm in the driver's seat. I didn't have the patience for him to drive so as usual I took control.

"We will get them brother, but you need to control yourself. We don't know what state Aaron will be in so leave all the wanting to kill for when we get back to the pen, yeah?"

"I'm not fucking stupid, D. I know," I shout at him.

I wish he would stop trying to tell me how to feel or behave because I am struggling to work that out myself. I have been thrown off kilter from this. Never given a shit about anything or anyone apart from D.

Obviously the little fucker has gotten under my skin if I'm in this state, but I'm not good at showing it like D is with Seb. I can never be sweet or gentle and who the fuck would want that. Then again, Aaron isn't like anyone else so maybe that's why I'm in this shit, trying to navigate fucking emotions. Christ, the idea of it makes me want to stab my own eyes out.

I hit the dial on the hands free to Simon.

"Hey Lev, we just pulled in. Where are you?" he asks.

"Just at the end of the road, be there in a couple of minutes. Don't go in without us," I say.

"Got it," he says, and ends the call. I let out a long breath I've been holding in since I felt something was wrong. We pull up to the end of the track where the house sits. I look over at my brother.

"Let's do this."

He nods and we get out, removing our guns from our hidden holsters. Jules and Simon appear from the shadows, both armed too.

"You see how many?" I ask in case there are more involved than just Jake.

"Just one van and it looks like it's only Jake's crew with Aaron. No movement in the rooms, not sure if there is a basement," Simon says.

"What's the plan, Lev?" Jules asks.

"Simon, you stay out here and guard the exits. D and Jules, come with me. Anyone tries to leave, kill them, but do not kill Jake. If needed, injure him enough so he can't move, but nothing fatal. You don't wanna deal with me if you kill him. Is that clear?"

They all nod.

"Okay, let's end this," Dima says and we creep along the edge of the treeline towards the house. If you can call it a house. It looks one windy day away from blowing over. Simon stays behind as we approach the front door, no movement or light appears around the windows so they are definitely below ground.

"Try the back," I whisper and we crouch down, slowly moving around the property edge until we reach the back where again, there are no signs of movement or life.

Just as we are about to go through the door, I hear a spine chilling scream that has my blood on fire. That's

Aaron. The anger in me is enough to shake the earth under my feet. I am not Lev anymore, I am fucking death and destruction that nobody would want to be on the end of.

I push through the back door and the sounds become clearer, which leads us to another door that's open at the end of the hall. Stairs lead down to another door, which is closed. It's the entrance to what must be the basement.

Dima grabs my arm. "Be careful, brother."

I nod my head and we make our way, armed, down the stairs. I open the door and all hell breaks loose.

I'm here, doe. Your demon is here to kill for you.

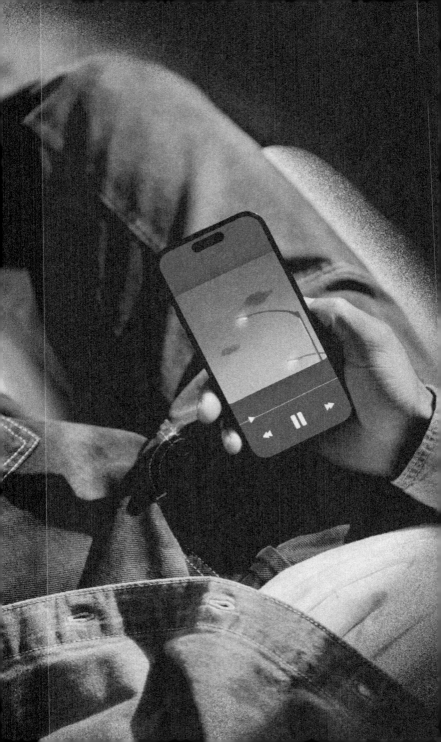

CHAPTER 30
AARON

My body is going into shock, spasming at every touch as Jake rips off my shirt and starts to undo my pants. My mind is trying to fight against Tommy's hold but my body just won't move, it's heavy as lead. It's as if I am watching this happen to someone else, like I am floating above my body, witnessing the horror that I am enduring.

It's okay, it's okay, the boy in me whispers and I don't fight him, choosing to listen to that familiar sound, self-soothing mode kicking in, putting me in an almost cata-tonic state.

"Look at you, finally submitting to me, baby brother. This is what I wanted all along."

He rubs his hand over my chest and I can't respond, my voice has disappeared, the words I want to say don't connect with my mouth. As he removes my pants, all I feel is the streaming wetness of tears down my face. I wish I could drown myself in them. Cold air hits my naked lower body and it faintly registers that I'm lying on a funky floor, beneath my sick stepbrother, who is certainly about to rape me.

Repulsion vibrates through me as a clammy hand holds onto my limp dick. My heart nearly flat lines and I wish to god it would. I feel dirty, tainted. The nausea rouses in my stomach, convulsing at his poisonous touch as it absorbs into my skin.

It's okay, it's okay, the boy whispers on repeat in my head and I try to focus on it this time rather than shutting it out, zoning in on his comfort. Please god, just let it be over, because even if he doesn't kill me after this, there is no way I would want to live. I couldn't do it. The idea of living through a day after he takes my body makes me want to hurt myself, tear my skin off, burn myself until I am nothing but flames. I wouldn't be able to erase his touch off my flesh.

"Look at me, Aaron."

Robotically, I move my head so that I'm staring at this fucking monster. Did my mom know? Did she know before she died what hell I was going to be left with as a family? Jake's eyes look at me determined and wanton, the vile cunt is excited, happy he's getting this. As I sink further into the ground, I feel numb. The cold feeling of the floor on my skin has faded, the pain in my eyes and stomach no longer an issue. My body is shutting down. I don't think I even hate him right now. That would require me to have the energy to care.

"You behave and I'll make it good for you," he says gently, undoing his jeans and moving them down his thighs. Then he parts my legs and I can't control how hard they're shaking. A wet cry tears out of my mouth when the final push of adrenaline encourages me to give it one last shot.

"Please don't do this, Jake, please," I beg him. "Please don't!" I can't stop the wails racking through me. A weighty hand covers my mouth, it smells of oil, and I recognize it's Tommy.

"Shut up, you little bitch," he says.

The feeling of being buried alive assaults me. I can't breathe, everything is closing in on me. Maybe if I stop fighting, he'll kill me, let him smother me with his hand until I've gone from this fucking evil world. My legs are pushed back, and Jake keeps a bruising grip on my thighs. I stare into space above me, detaching myself from this death. I am vaguely aware of the familiar sensation of a wet cockhead against my most intimate part, but it's not Lev's. This is it. End of my life as I know it.

It's okay, it's okay.

Grabbing onto the comforting boy, I let him shield me from terror.

"What the fuck!" Tommy shouts suddenly letting me go.

A gunshot outside the door echoes around the room. Just as I turn my head, I see the door fly open. Unless my mind is playing a mean trick on me, it looks like Lev, Dima, and Jules have just appeared. My legs are dropped to the ground, which hurts as my heel hits the concrete floor, hard, but I'm too far gone from this world to acknowledge the pain. I try to move, but my body won't cooperate.

It's okay, he's here, it's okay.

I drift further towards the boy's lulling words, wishing he would lock us away somewhere safe and quiet, holding us together, protecting us like he has always tried to do. He has never left my side in times of fear even though he is as scared as I am. I just want to protect him too, to set him free by ridding us of what keeps us chained to this hell. Jake. But I can't do that for him, I'm not strong enough to fight Jake off, to kill him and let the young boy rest. So I hold onto the young boy instead, letting him guide me further into his arms.

I'm here. We're safe. Don't let me go, hold onto my hand.

I move further to his voice. It feels like a warm hug.

Barely able to keep my eyes open, Dima storms towards us and gets a punch into Jake who was about to get up. Dima knocks him flat out as Jules rushes over to cuff him. It's hard to keep my eyes focused as I drift further away. I'm so tired.

"Aaron, Aaron can you hear me?" My vision clears as I look up to see the most handsome face ever. Lev. My Lev. "Doe, can you hear me?" he asks and I swear he's pissed off, even now.

Yes, we are safe now. He will look after us.

I smile. "Yes. Get me out of here please," I say barely above a whisper.

A damp smelling blanket is thrown over me before I'm enveloped in Lev's arms. His scent of cigars and aftershave hits my nose and I try to relax into that now familiar scent.

You are safe, we are safe.

"Yes," I whisper before darkness takes me under where nobody can find me.

CHAPTER 31
LEV

A aron has been passed out in my bed for the last two hours. I can't get the image of his step-brother standing over him out of my head. I'm not sure if we got there in time but it looked like the cunt was about rape him, and it takes everything I have not to go down to the pen right now and cut the fucker's dick off with a blunt knife.

I keep my composure, though. I don't want to do anything with Jake and Tommy, who are thankfully secure in the holding pen right now. I always keep my promises. I want to see if Aaron still wants to be fully involved in their demise.

Shay is dead. We shot him on sight when he pulled a gun on us as we got into the basement. All things considered, it went smoothly. Simon stayed back to sort the clean-up, dispose of Shay's body, and to clear the scene of any trace of activity. I know Aaron considered him a friend, but I question that word when he was fine to let Aaron be abused by that sick fuck.

A light knock on the door grabs my attention, and I walk over to see Dima standing on the other side.

"How is he?" he asks. Concern is etched on his face, which is a rare thing to see on D.

"Still asleep. Think it's the shock."

Aaron is completely out of it. Dark circles color the delicate skin under his eyes and steri strips cover where his brow piercing used to be. Seb kindly fixed him up when we got back, but Aaron remained asleep throughout the whole thing.

"Yeah, can't imagine. Listen, it's late, Lev. Just sleep. Those two fuckers aren't going anywhere so it's best to rest up before we start. Then, at least Aaron will be able to make a decision as to what he wants done once he's awake," he says and pats me on the shoulder.

I am dying to get down there, but he is right. I don't think Aaron will wake up anytime soon and I am emotionally exhausted from this. I agree and we say our goodnights. Moving to my bathroom, I wash up quickly. I don't want to leave him on his own. I have no idea how Aaron will react when he wakes up. He is unpredictable at the best of times, but this is something else.

As I make my way back into the bedroom, I see he is moving in the bed. Tossing and turning, quiet sniffles that make my chest hurt. I am so lost on how to help him.

"Aaron, it's ok. It's Lev, you are in my bed." I try to reassure him in as soothing a tone as I can manage.

"Earbuds," he whispers, and I have no idea what he is talking about.

"What earbuds?"

"Need my earbuds ... my music." His sniffles are harsher as he tries to hold back the tears, his hands fumble with mild tremors, and then I remember, the bag that Kai brought back had earbuds in them when I searched it earlier. I retrieve the bag from the corner of the room and grab his Earbuds and his phone. The shaking of his hands is painful to watch as he puts them in and rolls onto his side.

"Do you want me to go?" I ask, unsure how the fuck to deal with this.

He shakes his head, so I get into bed behind him, pulling his back towards my chest. I can see and hear his soft sobs. It kills me. I don't know what music he is listening to, but this looks like a way of coping that he must have used before. After a few minutes, his breathing becomes slower, and I find myself drifting off alongside him.

WHEN I WAKE UP, I have no idea how long I have been asleep but the light of day filters through the windows. Moving my head to the side, I see those beautiful doe eyes watching me, his fingers slowly making their way up and down the center of my chest. I don't think anyone has touched me this gently before. I try to think of something to say that a normal person would, so I go for the standard.

"How are you feeling?" I ask.

Aaron continues to watch me, his eyes look dead, like there is nothing there.

He doesn't break eye contact. "I want you to fuck me, Lev."

His hands slowly peruse my torso in a firmer touch,

which wakes my dick up, but I am not sure this is a good idea.

"Aaron, you have been traumatized, I don't–"

"Don't tell me what the fuck to think and feel, Lev!" he shouts but doesn't pull away.

A tear escapes his left eye, but his stare remains cold and lifeless. He is grasping for control and is determined to get what he thinks he needs.

"Please, Lev, *please*. I need you to erase his touch from my skin before I cut it off. I need to feel safe. I am fucking begging you, make it stop. Only you can make it stop," he cries.

I am not sure what to do. I am inclined to give him what he wants, but is it what he needs?

"Please, Lev. Do this for me, *please*." He closes his eyes on that final plea, swallowing hard.

I finally give in to the heart that I never knew I had.

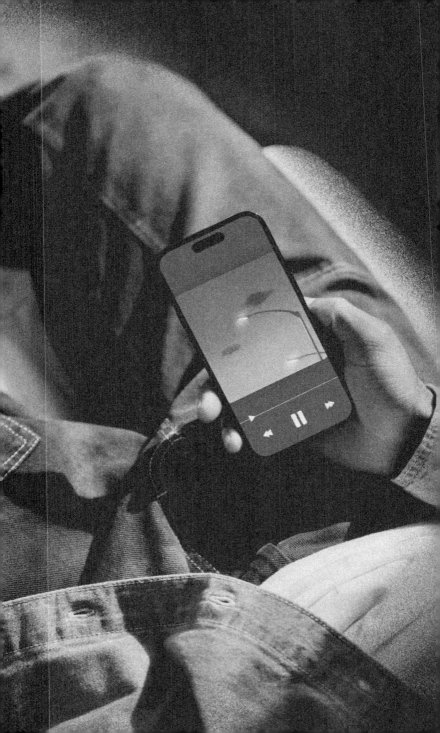

CHAPTER 32
AARON

L ev is looking at me right now like he is not sure if I am in the right frame of mind to make this choice. His lips are set in a thin line and his brows furrow as he mulls over what I have just asked.

But I mean it. I'm desperate for a bath or shower to get that place off me, but I need his touch more. I am beyond thankful that they got to me in time. No idea how he found me, but he saved my life. As relieved as I am, I can still feel Jake's slimy fingers on my skin and his breath on my face. It's like being covered in insects and no matter how many times I try to brush them off, more appear, nipping at my skin, and making me want to rip out of my own body. The only thing that will calm my thoughts and finally erase Jake from my psyche, will be Lev's cock and his bruising touch. Then I can reset. I know I can, I just don't know how to convince him, and it pisses me off that he thinks I'm made of glass.

"Lev, I promise I need this. I want this. Don't let that bastard have any more hold over me than he has already," I say.

That comment seems to do the trick. Lev moves in a flash over the top of me.

"What do you need, doe?" he says. The sincerity in his tone makes me feel exposed, but I allow it, hoping this will repair the damaged pieces of my soul. And I am confident it will. Lev is the only one in this world that can help me, stabilize me, and be with me the way that I need. He owns me.

"I want you to fuck me, hard, I want you to mark my skin with bruises and give me a taste of pain. I want you to let go and use me. No hard limits, no safe words, just us. No boundaries, just be who we are."

"You fucking asked for this, remember that."

He gets up and walks to the end of the bed and pulls away the sheets covering my body. The cool air makes me shiver, goosebumps rise over my flesh. That move alone has already pulled me out of the hell I've been in. His attention will always be my undoing, a cure to anything that's wrong in my life. I will always want his eyes on me and only me. Lev grabs my ankles in a painful grip and pulls me like a rag doll to the edge of the bed, his big hands yank down my underwear and he drops them to the floor.

"Knees to your chest. Now," he orders.

That commanding voice booms through me, making me yield. I grab my legs behind the knees and pull them to my chest, showing him the most sacred part of my body, a part that only I decide who can touch. I can't help the clenching of my ass as he watches my hole as he removes his pants, leaving him beautifully naked and hard. His dick faces up against his belly and his piercing looks delicious as I see the glistening of his precum surrounding the barbell. I lick my lips, remembering how good he tastes in my mouth.

"Do. Not. Move," he says.

Fuck yes.

Lev goes out of view and comes back with a bottle of lube. My horny asshole tenses again.

"Clench all you want, doe, but my dick is going in there. I'm going to rip your greedy hole apart until you can't take anymore. Then, I will breed your ass so good that you will feel my cum sloshing in you for days. Smelling like me for days. You ready for that, my little psycho?"

Yes, this is what I need. "If you keep talking to me like that then this will be over, now hurry the fuck up and get in me." I spread my legs a little wider to the point of pain in my thighs from the stretch. My brain has stopped focusing on what happened before, Lev has managed to pull me out of that misery and make him my entire world. All other voices are offline, leaving just me, plain old Aaron, completely raw and unapologetic.

He slaps my face and grips it tightly, making me moan. *Yes*, more of this, I want more.

"Remember who is boss here, doe. I don't take orders from anyone."

Collapsing on top of me, he leans over and our lips connect as his tongue caresses my mouth in a sensual mating kiss. I cry into him as my body relaxes, welcoming the feeling of safety and his protectiveness.

His kiss is like a massage that soothes my body and soul, taking all the bad away. My brain is starting to get back online as he fills me with the strength that has been absent. Lev saved me, and he has locked those bastards up for me, no, for us to play with. My heart swells at that.

They are locked up in this very house, most probably scared and confused, while I'm about to get the fucking of my life. They didn't break me, I'm still here and worthy.

Lev kisses me for what feels like an eternity before two of his thick fingers breach me, moving in and out at a slow and teasing pace. He curls his fingers, knowing where to hit my pleasure button and I raise my ass further off the bed, searching for more of it. Every nerve is alert, and my nipples harden as if they are attached to my prostate.

I don't know if Lev hears my thoughts, but he starts to kiss down to my neck where he sucks in the skin, hard, forcing a loud cry from my mouth as the pain settles over the tender mark. It feels oh so fucking good. He licks down to my chest then covers my nipple with his mouth, and sucks on it like a hoover, biting, nibbling, licking then sucking again. I make tormented sounds as I writhe under him, but he still takes his time, continuing to finger me while he moves on to my other nipple, giving it the same treatment. The trail of burn from his stubble lights me up, leaving an extra layer of tenderness where he has marked me.

After teasing me to the point of nearly sending me into a coma, he stands back upright and I keep hold of my legs, spread apart like the whore I become around him. He then pushes a third finger into my ass as he grabs my dick, stroking it in a tight hold that borders on painful, making my cock stiffen some more as the tip starts streaming pre cum like a fountain. He removes his fingers and lets go of my dick. Before I know what is happening, he bends over in between my legs and sucks my entire cock into his mouth in one move.

"Oh fuck, Lev! Oh fuck, yesssss."

Holy shit, the wet heat from his mouth brings me to the

edge, and my cock repeatedly hits the back of his throat. To my glee, he doesn't appear to have a gag reflex.

"Lev, stop, I'm gonna cum," I pant and he pulls off.

Slicking that huge cock of his with more lube, he leans back over me and guides the head of his dick to my hole, giving me one final look. I know it's to double check I'm good, so I push my ass towards him, giving him the hint to take me, which he does.

One deep shove and his piercing hits my button like it was made for me to take. Lev doesn't allow me to adjust, he just pounds into me like a beast mating his prey in the wild. No sweetness, no love, just the bone-deep possessive need of claiming and I love it. I needed this. Every thrust heals a bit more of me.

"You feel so fucking good, doe. So good. Ahhh."

The sweat beading on his brow drips down his face. I lean up and lick it away, enjoying the salty taste of it. I can tell from the way his face contorts he is about to cum so I grab my dick and start pumping, the groan of relief leaving my throat as I let myself fall into absolute bliss. "So close, Lev, harder, fuck me harder!" I snarl, and he picks up the pace. We are now bouncing off the bed in motion, the headboard banging against the wall. The noises we make are as intense as the feel of his dick inside me.

His grip on my thighs turns painful. I'm grateful there will be marks, knowing that he has re-claimed me, destroying any evidence that Jake ever touched me.

"Fuck yeah, doe, gonna breed you good, gonna fill you up."

I cum as his warmth fills me. I have lost my ability to breathe with the power of this orgasm. My mouth falls open on a silent cry as my body jerks to the climax, and my back arches off the bed as I cum. He's destroyed me inside and out and I feel clean again. I've been reborn.

Lev collapses over me and I could just fall asleep again right now. He has never hugged me like this, so while it is new, it's nice.

"I really need a shower," I say.

He laughs. "Yeah, you do. Come on. Then we need to talk."

CHAPTER 33
LEV

A fter we wash away our post-sex high, we head to the seating area of my bedroom. It feels like there is a distance that's formed and I'm not sure if it's my fault. I'm uncomfortable as hell when it comes to emotions and comforting anyone, but I don't want to get this wrong with Aaron. I want him to trust me as much as he can trust in the fact that I will kill all the demons that haunt him.

He sits on the other side of the couch. Considering what happened yesterday, I give him his space in case he needs it. I can't help but be blunt, it's all I know so I go for it. I need to know what happened.

"Did he rape you?" I ask, keeping my eyes locked on him.

He stares at his hands and is back to the quiet Aaron I have only seen a handful of times. I hate it. This isn't the real him.

"No, he was going to do it, but you busted into the room just before he was about to...to.."

I put my hand up so he doesn't have to finish that sentence, I know what he means.

"What did they do? I noticed some bruising on your stomach and your eyebrow piercing has been ripped out."

"The usual Jake and Tommy shit. Punched me in the stomach. They had me tied up, and when I woke up Tommy ripped out the piercing."

"What happened in the apartment?" I ask.

"Should have followed my gut. I knew something was off when I walked in, but I ignored it. Just wanted to get in and get out with my stuff. As I went to leave my room, Tommy appeared and hit me over the head with something. It knocked me out and I don't remember anything until I woke up in that basement."

I keep quiet, trying to stay calm, but I am bursting with blood hunger to get down there to make them sing.

"He knew I'd been watching him for you. They took the burner when they knocked me out, and saw everything on there." He shrugs. He seems defeated whereas I am getting more riled up with every word.

"What do you want to do, Aaron? As you know, aside from what they did to you, I have to enforce for our family. They need to pay and I plan to do it in the worst way possible."

"I know, Lev. You have your job to do," he says.

"Shay is dead isn't he?" he asks and his eyes glisten.

I'd forgotten about Shay, to be honest.

"Yes. He was manning the door to the basement. We shot him before he shot us," I say.

"He had a sister," he says, mind distracted as he looks over to the window, lost in thought. "I don't know who or where she is."

"Does it matter?" I ask.

"Jake was using her as blackmail to keep Shay in line. What if she's in danger?"

"She won't be in danger now, but we can find her. I'll get Simon on it," I say. Personally, I don't give a shit, but Aaron deserves some peace from this.

"Okay, thanks," he says and starts to fidget with his hands, rubbing them back and forth over each other, making his palms red. I need his answer and I know he needs the distraction.

"So? Do you still want to watch? Do you still want to kill Jake and have your revenge? You don't have to do anything, you know, I can do it for you. You can watch or stay in this room. But I need an answer because we have to finish this today. I need to make an example of them to keep our other crews in line."

I am trying to be empathetic, if that's what it's called, but I also have to do my job and protect our family. Plus, Carlos wants proof after we have finished.

His eyes are wide and unblinking as he stares at the wall, face blank. Shit, is he going into shock again? "Aaron. You okay?"

When he looks at me, it's like another person has taken over his body. Doe is back with that fire in his eyes, his cold persona radiates off him. I already know the answer and I must admit, I'm fucking ecstatic.

"Oh, I wanna watch, but I also want to join in. My face will be the last thing he sees before he burns in hell," he snarls, and fuck it's hot.

He grins his creepy smile that would unnerve a lot of people, but I find it a damn turn on. I know it means my feral doe is out for revenge and I'm excited for our playdate.

"Come on, coffee, then playtime." I grab his hand and pull him up.

"Wait, Lev? I need to tell you something."

The wariness in his voice has me now thinking all kinds of shit. Did his brother really do something?

"What?" I ask.

"I don't want you to say anything, but I need to get this off my chest and I don't need it back from you. But…" A little color blooms his cheeks, and I just want him to hurry the fuck up and spit it out.

"Go on," I encourage.

"I like you, Lev, and I think I'm falling for you or maybe I'm addicted to you? I know you don't do feelings, and this is probably your worst nightmare, but after everything that's happened, and before we go down there, I wanted to tell you I'm yours. You can do what you want to me, and I will do anything you ask. But, to be clear, you are mine too, and I won't let go. Is that weird?" he says, sounding oddly adorable.

I'm glued to the spot. Those words are not computing in my brain. What the fuck is going on? Aaron is looking at me like I'm his world, but also in a way that reads "you will be with me, whether you like it or not".

It's a glimpse of possessive Aaron. What is love anyway? I mean, I love my brother but I was raised with him and he is my blood, my purpose. With Aaron, he makes me ache in places I have never ached. I would kill any fucker that looked at him or touched him, and I feel like his ass is mine as if he's some kind of real estate.

I like having him near me. I know I like him too, but these feelings and emotions are hard for me to acknowledge right now. I don't know what to say back, so I just go with what I know to be true.

266

I grab his neck firmly and give him a brief hard kiss. "I would kill for you."

I wasn't sure what response I was going to get but the big cheesy grin wasn't it. Shit, why am I so surprised? Aaron knows me, he knows what I mean and he won't push for different words. Like one soul combined of two crazed messes, he accepts that my love language is different.

"That's a contract you have just signed, by the way. Fine print says that you don't touch anyone else, Lev, I mean it. I'll cut your dick off in your sleep," he says.

So fucking romantic.

"And if I see you near anyone else, doe, I will skin them alive in front of you, beat your ass raw and then ignore you," I say, knowing that the worst part for him would be no attention, and from the pout on his lips, I am right.

After getting a quick coffee, we both head to Dima's office where I assume he is. Without knocking I walk in, greeted by Seb straddled across my brother's lap. "I'm surprised you two have any cum left in your bodies. Don't you have a room?"

Seb scrambles off Dima's lap, nearly falling over. I've seen him fingered and jerked off by my brother, but *this* makes him shy.

"Shut it, Lev. This is my office, remember? You should knock before you come in if you don't like seeing me with my husband."

"What's the point in knocking? You fuck on nearly every surface in this house anyway. You need house training."

"Jealous?" Dima asks.

"No, got my own piece of ass and that's more than satisfying," I say.

"I know, we heard that satisfaction earlier. Maybe we need soundproof walls?" Dima says.

I shrug, I don't give a shit who hears us.

"Aaron is still in. We are ready when you are," I say.

Dima looks over to Aaron, like he will see something I don't. "Okay, let's go."

He grabs Seb for a kiss as we walk out, and Seb says goodbye.

The three of us head down to the holding pen. I look over at Aaron, expecting that he may be feeling unsure, but he looks determined, a grin on his face, walking with confidence. After today it will be a new chapter for him. Actually, it will be a new chapter for us both.

As Dima leads us down to the holding pen, he opens the large black door where Jules and Simon greet us. The two pieces of shit wait in the center of the room. It smells of piss in here. It's almost overwhelming but there is another smell, a pleasant one.

Fear.

It gives me a high like no other. Looking at Aaron's face, I think he feels it too. He's still sporting a huge grin and is zeroing in on his stepbrother. I sense that he is imagining what will happen down here, so maybe it's time to get started and provide my doe with a private show.

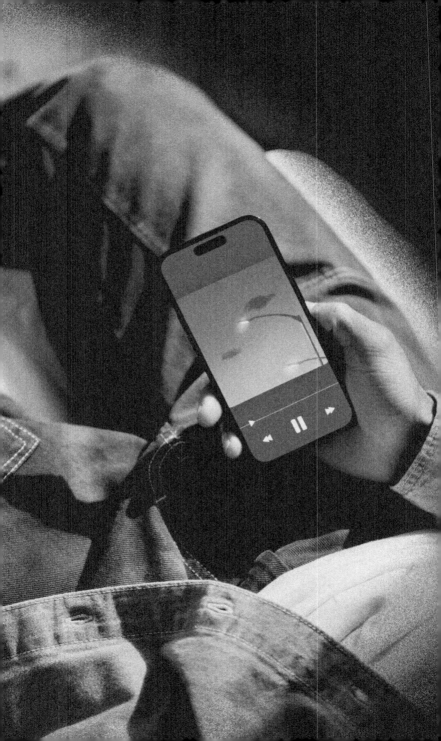

CHAPTER 34
AARON

This moment is so surreal. When you dream of something and imagine it in such detail, it eventually becomes an idea that you know deep down will never be a reality. So walking into Lev's holding pen and seeing Jake helpless, is a real pinch-me moment.

Jake. My abuser, and my manipulator who destroyed all the happiness and good in me all those years ago. Granted, his dad was involved too and I still hate him, but Jake went that extra mile, and last night he was prepared to hammer that final nail into my coffin.

What he planned to do was no different than ending my life. Distaste fills my mouth just thinking about it.

A strong hand grabs the back of my neck and instantly I am centered again and calm. Lev. Fucking Lev has now become the air I need to survive this life and while he laughs at my possessive comments, I won't let the fucker be without me. I refuse to be without him.

I close my eyes and inhale the stale oxygen that fills the room, before focusing on Tommy and Jake who are on the floor in front of me. They are back-to-back, chained together. It looks like they had an uncomfortable night, and from the smell of piss, I would say they don't feel at their best.

Jake is zeroed in on Lev's hand on my neck, and his jaw tenses like he's grinding his teeth in anger. Even on the doorstep of death, the jealous controlling monster in him refuses to die.

"Have a comfortable night, boys?" Dima asks, but they don't respond. Jake is still staring at Lev's hand on my neck while Tommy is looking at me like everything bad in his life is my fault. Nice to see nothing changes.

"Wanna watch or play, doe?" Lev whispers into my ear.

I know I shouldn't, but my cock starts to perk up from his question. Watching him play is the same as watching porn is for others, only this time, it's more intense. I know the victims, and I know I'll enjoy it. For now though, I think I'll watch. I'm not experienced in torturing people, but I want to be part of the end for Jake. I think I'm the type who would enjoy messing with my food more.

"I'll watch. For now." I don't intend for that to come out all sultry and breathy, but it results in a quick deep kiss. I wonder if we could sew our skin together so I never leave his side? I ponder that thought but think Lev would not agree.

"Go sit." Lev shirks his head over to a chair that I hadn't noticed before, which has been placed at the side of the room, with a full view of everything that will happen. It makes my heart skip an extra beat that he would do something so thoughtful and romantic. I take my seat and prepare for the show.

Lev walks to the back of the room and I nearly swallow my tongue as he removes his shirt. Part of me wants to leave the pen and go back to bed with him. I have yet to dine on that meaty muscle ass that looks so delicious in his gray sweatpants. His back is so strong and wide, I want to kiss it all over, rub my naked body over it. I've already memorized his tattoos but I want to do it all over again. Dima pulls me out of my thoughts as his voice booms across the blindingly white walls in this room of terror.

"So was it worth it, boys? Betraying your family? Thinking you pussies would be able to take over our turf?" he asks as he walks around them in a slow circle. Tommy tries to follow his movements, nervous with what may happen. But Jake is as cool as a cucumber. Silent and still watching me. Normally, I would be wilting like a flower in the corner, avoiding his direct gaze, but I feel strong down here, I feel untouchable wherever Lev is. Yes, I know that's stupid because nobody is untouchable, but I don't give a shit. I bask in that feeling. I've never had it before.

Lev starts as fast as lightning and moves towards Jake where he backhands him across the face. "Dont fucking look at him, you sick cunt. You wanna look at something, look at me," he says.

Swoon.

"Why the hell would I wanna look at you?" Jake sneers, still arrogant even in his current position.

"Because I am the gatekeeper to your life and I decide when it ends. Answer back again and I'll cut that fucking tongue out," Lev says.

Jake's nostrils flare as he uses everything possible to keep a retort in. Deep down, he knows Lev will do it. It's what the brothers are known for, yet he still challenged them.

Movement at the door grabs my attention as Kai walks in. Jules does a double take as he sees him and stomps over to him, touching his face where there's now a bruise forming.

"What the fuck happened?" Jules asks.

Kai looks to the ground, uneasy as he shifts from foot to foot. Of course, Lev answers for him.

"I did it. He was supposed to watch Aaron and didn't notice he had been taken by these pricks," Lev says, raising an eyebrow to Jules whose face is now red as if he is about to explode.

"Careful Jules, remember you recommended him and if you have a problem with how I deal with my men, you are welcome to sit down and join these two," Lev says, pointing between Jake and Tommy.

Jules remains quiet and mutters what sounds like a "sorry" under his breath, but he still looks pissed. I know Kai is his nephew, but I didn't realize he was so protective of him. Kai is still looking at the ground and it's making the atmosphere between him and Jules palpable. Interesting.

"What are you doing down here?" Jules whisper yells at him. But again, Lev answers for him.

"I fucking told him to come down here, now if you have both finished your family catch up and questioning your boss, it's time to move this shit along." Lev is pissed. He has been looking forward to this moment and Jules is ruining it for him.

"Sorry, Lev," Jules says and Lev ignores him, preferring to just get on with it.

"Kai, get over here now," Lev orders and Kai obeys.

"You stand here and observe, when I ask you to do something you do it. Understand?"

"Yes. I understand," Kai says with more confidence, the awkwardness now gone. Dima moves over near me and stands next to me. I am all but on the edge of my seat. I don't know what Lev has planned.

"Jules, you and Kai untie them. Jules, hook Jake to the wall. Kai, you help me get Tommy strapped to the table," Lev says.

Fuck, he is so hot and alpha-like.

Tommy starts to lose it and it's a fantastic sight to see. Always knew he was just a little bitch who acted as a bully.

"No, *no!* Get off me, get off me! Please!" Tommy cries.

Nobody cares about his pleas as they manage to untie him from Jake. Jules drags Jake up by the chains that are still attached to his wrists and hooks it to the wall at the side where there are bolted attachments, firmly locking him in place. Kai and Lev lift a kicking and screaming Tommy onto the metal table. Kai lays a punch to Tommy's stomach as he kicks out, briefly immobilizing his movements. They spread him on the bed, locking him in place by his arms and feet with the leather straps that are fixed to the corners.

I didn't realize the table was on wheels until I see Lev unclip the brakes and roll the bed to the center of the room. I briefly glance at Jake who still looks emotionless and unaffected by what's happening, staring at where Tommy has been placed. Is he scared? Or is he hiding it well? Does he really not have an emotional bone in his vile body? I suppose it doesn't really matter; the end result will be the same.

"Not nice being held down, is it Tommy? Like you did to Aaron," Lev says.

Tommy is full on going into hysteria and I don't really blame him. This has to be stressful.

"You fuckers…I'll kill you! I will kill Aaron and destroy you!" Tommy shouts and the full guttural laughs from Lev and Dima fills the room sending an icy chill down my spine.

"Of course you will, Tommy, let us know when that will happen, yeah?" Dima teases. Dima looks so much like Lev right now, his eyes are hard and focused, and you can see the darkness in him build like I do in Lev. They seem like one person in this room and while it's creepy, it's also fucking hot.

"Aaron, keep looking at my brother like that and I'll beat your ass raw."

I bolt back at the stormy warning. Lev is laser focused on me right now and I really wasn't staring at Dima in any way other than curious. Shit. Lev looks like he is about to walk over here and teach me a lesson. I'll admit, part of me is intrigued to see how far he would go.

Dima chuckles beside me. "Now you know how it feels, brother," Dima casually comments.

"Fuck off, D. And that's your final warning, doe," Lev says.

Oh hell yes. Tiny jabs of mini orgasms flare up around my cock at the sound of his warning. I won't lie, I'm liking the possessively potent way he has started treating me. I will only crave more.

"Kai, remove the fucker's clothes. Best to use the hunting knife over there. He won't be wearing them again anyway," Lev instructs as Tommy's whimpers start up again.

The wet gurgling sounds in his throat make him sound like a wounded animal and so far, apart from the sound of Lev cumming, it's my new favorite noise.

Kai makes quick work of removing Tommy's piss-covered clothes, discarding them in a pile in the corner of the room. Tommy lays on the table, pale and soft. I never realized he had pierced nipples, but then again, I have never had the misfortune of seeing him without clothes. His small limp dick is wilted and hanging to the side of his thigh. He is not enjoying this as much as my cock is, which keeps twitching the more Lev works.

Holding a pair of pliers, Lev grabs the nipple piercings and rips each one out in one swift move, no preamble, so I am momentarily shocked but pleased by the screams that now create a perfect backdrop to today's entertainment. Poor Dima starts rubbing his head.

"Always fucking scream," he mumbles. Dima hates the noise, which is fair I guess, but I love it.

"That should make it even for what you did to Aaron's brow. It's only fair, and I am always fair," Lev says, cocking his head to the side, looking directly over Tommy who is convulsing so badly that the metal table rattles against his restraints. I quickly sneak a look over at Jake who still looks indifferent to what is going on, completely unaffected. Maybe he is more sociopathic than I thought.

The blood from where Tommy's piercings used to be, starts to glide down the sides of his chest and under his arms, creating little puddles of sticky red underneath him. It's like a piece of art, the bright red against his pale skin and shiny metal of the table. It truly is a pretty sight.

"Jules, come here and hold his head," Lev says, and moves to the back to pick up a very sharp knife. It's a little smaller than the hunting knife but looks like it could cause just as much damage.

"Kai, put your hands on either side of his jaw and push hard until his mouth opens," Lev says.

"Wait … No. No! Please!" Tommy struggles against Jules' strength who holds his head firm at the top of the table.

Kai stands to the left, leaning over to grip his mouth open while pressing firmly on his jaw. Excitement builds in me. I can see where this is going.

Lev looks like a god. His torso is making me thirsty with the slight sheen to his skin. He looks so fucking edible right now. I want to mold myself to his body as he plays, rub myself up and down his thigh. My cock is hard as steel now as Lev reaches into Tommy's mouth. Lev has a pair of metal tongs which he uses to grab a hold of Tommy's tongue. He pulls the tongue as far out of his mouth as possible and with quick precision, he slices the knife through the muscle, so quickly I almost don't see it happen.

Kai and Jules move away and the screams have quieted to wet breaths. Blood is streaming like a current from Tommy's mouth. He looks like he is drowning in it and fighting to stay alive. Lev holds up the severed tongue and parades it in front of Tommy's face before throwing it on the floor.

"Consider this payment for turning on the Kozlovs and for all the bullshit that has ever left your pathetic little mouth. You will die here, where nobody gives a shit, choking on your own blood. Should I still wait for you to fight back?" Lev says as he grins down at Tommy who has gone ghostly pale. The gurgling sounds become less, drowning in his own blood as it overflows his mouth. He remains strapped to the metal table, flat on his back. After what feels like a few minutes there is just...silence...a still but eerie silence. It's like a soothing balm that's been rubbed all over me. He's gone, and the relief makes my heart settle and the cracks in my skin are filled in a little bit more.

Lev drops the bloodied knife to the ground where it clatters against the black tile, and rolls his head trying to loosen some tension that I would be more than eager to help with. I need to get off so badly right now, but I need to control it. I have been waiting for this moment for years and I refuse to miss a second of it.

"Put Jake on the hook," Lev tells Kai and Jules.

They walk over to the vacant-looking human that appears to be Jake. I don't trust him though, Jake would never go down without some kind of fight, it's not him. He has to have control, especially when it comes to me.

The guys lift him and unhook the chain off the wall. It's a longer chain than I thought, which they then attach to the meat-hook extending from the ceiling in the middle of the room.

Tommy's table has been pushed to the side, so that Jake is standing in the small pool of Tommy's blood that collected on the floor. His arms are hooked above his head so he's suspended from the ceiling, his feet just about lay flat on the ground. When they move away, his eyes are on me. I may feel stronger, but I still have to stop myself from shrinking back. He's barely even blinking at me. His blue eyes look dull and are slanted in anger that's aimed at me. His mouth holds no expression, and to be honest, he looks relaxed. It's freaking me out a little.

"We can take this one from here, you guys can wait outside. Dima you can go," Lev says.

"You sure?" Dima asks.

"Yeah, this is just for us. Anyway, I can tell you have already reached your limit for noise and are on the verge of one of your headaches," he says mockingly.

"I can't help it if their screaming hurts my head. Fucker."

"Jules, wait outside the door," Lev says.

"You got it," he acknowledges and before I know it, the door closes and it's just me, Lev and Jake.

It feels weird, and the atmosphere has changed. I don't feel fear from Jake, only angry tension, from both him and Lev. In some ways they are so similar. Have to be in control. Know no limits.

"What oh what should we do with you?" Lev fake contemplates, looking at Jake with a superior expression.

Jake, however, doesn't seem to notice. He still hasn't taken his eyes off me, I think he forgot Lev's warning earlier, that's why I'm not shocked when Lev punches him across the face. Jake's head jerks to the side, a low groan leaves his throat as a small amount of blood drips out of his mouth.

"I told you not to look at him," Lev warns.

Jake laughs like he isn't here chained up and about to be tortured to death.

"You can't tell me to do anything, Kozlov. Aaron is mine and always has been. I worked hard to get him in line and no amount of pain will make that less true." He smirks.

"I was never yours," suddenly leaves my mouth. I wasn't intending on speaking, but it looks like I'm just going with it.

"You forced me, bullied me, fucking abused me for

years, Jake. I was never yours. I was scared of what your dad would do."

That elicits another laugh from Jake, which annoys the fuck out of me.

I take a step closer to him. "What's so funny?" I ask.

"Dad was never gonna do shit, baby brother," he giggles, like a child telling a joke.

"Don't call me that," I hiss.

"Why? You seem to like me calling you that, always made you more...submissive. *Baby brother.*" His grin is predatory and even though he's tied up, the words have their intended effect.

I grip my hair, pulling on the strands until the pain is unbearable.

"It's okay, it's okay..." the young boy whispers.

Fuck!

"Get out of my head!" I shout and look up.

Lev comes to my side. "Breathe, doe. Fucking breathe. I'm here. Remember, I'll fight your demons."

I try to control my breathing and focus on Lev who is looking at me like he wants to hurt me, but that's his normal face. I know he is worried, as worried as Lev can be, anyway.

A couple of minutes pass before I am in control of my emotions.

"What do you mean he wasn't gonna do shit?" I ask, trying to get back on track. *Breathe in...and breathe out. Get a hold of yourself, Aaron.*

"I made it up. Dad just wanted you on the drug run. He was never gonna sell you for that gay stuff, he hated all that shit," he says.

I'm floored. How did I not see the lie? Oh god, he manipulated the whole situation. Stupid fucking Aaron!

As the penny drops, Jake continues to smile at me. He can't keep his fucking mouth shut, though.

"I seized the opportunity to take you. Protect you. You were always going to be mine, but then when you got all weird and we joined the crew, I bided my time. As soon as we took over our own territory, I was going to make it official," he says.

Like this makes all the fucking sense in the world.

Stunned, I am fucking stunned. What the hell does "make it official" mean? "Do you know how deranged you sound? I was never yours, never gonna be yours and never will be yours!" I yell before I stride forward and punch him across the face. Shit, my hand hurts but it was worth it.

"Look who's all tough now. Being fucked by this dickhead finally made you a man, baby brother," he says as he spits the blood from his mouth to the floor.

Lev punches him in the stomach, which finally stops him talking, he heaves from the blow, trying to regain his footing.

"He is all mine now, fuckface. And he loves my dick, he rides it so well," Lev says and moves to the back of the room.

"Time for talk is over. Doe, come here." He wiggles his finger at me in a come hither motion.

I sidestep around Jake to walk over to Lev. He pulls me in close and I bury my nose hard into his neck and inhale that intoxicating scent. It brings me back down, grounding me and I look into those evil green eyes of his. I feel like I am being charged with courage and strength in his presence. He is magnificent.

"So, you wanna play or watch?" he asks.

"I want to do both," I whisper against his lips.

He smiles against them, "Well, pick your weapon of choice and let's finish this. I want you riding me hard in my bed after this, doe."

I groan. "Anything you want," I say and he snickers.

"So easy for me," he says. I nod as he gently grabs my throat. "Only. Me."

My breath hitches at the possessive tone.

"Only. You," I say. My head is starting to hurt from this mental gymnastics that's going on with me right now, too many emotions happening at once.

Lev lets me go as I look along the wall, and I know what I want to do to Jake. After what he tried to do to me yesterday, it's the only appropriate justice that will help me sleep better. That will put those voices to bed for good.

I pick up a scalpel and Lev raises his brow. "Interesting choice. I'm gonna go for something a little different," he says. He picks up a cordless drill then attaches a large drill head to it. Now that will hurt.

"You wanna go first, doe?" he asks as we walk back over to face Jake who has finally gotten over the stomach punch. Fucking pussy. I feel disconnected, like I am floating, waiting for something to happen that wakes me up, telling me this was a dream and I am still in the nightmare. But nothing happens. This is real.

Lev stands still, cool and composed, waiting for me to take the lead. I know what I need to do.

"Lev, can you take off his pants, please? I don't want to touch him more than I need to," I say.

Lev places the drill on the ground and unbuckles the belt on Jake's jeans. Pulling them down, he looks over his shoulder at me. "Underwear?" he asks.

I nod and he removes all his lower clothing. His dick hangs and memories flood back to me like a camera reel.

The night of my eighteenth, followed by the horror of last night. My gut twists, giving me the urge to heave. He was going to rape me and the fucker didn't care, never cared. In this moment I feel cleansed, all my sins are about to be washed away. He branded them onto my body, and they've been burning me ever since.

I have nothing left to say, nothing left to prove or shout or cry. Forcing myself to keep my eyes on his, I lift his disgusting flaccid cock. I swallow hard, forcing the acid back down my throat. Aiming the scalpel at his dick slit, I use all my strength and push it until it won't go any further. As his screams and cries fill the room, my pain and agony lift off me like a spirit has come down and removed them from my soul. Will I always be traumatized by what happened to me? Yes. But I'll be damned if I let this fucker tarnish and have a hold of my life any longer. My hand starts to feel wet and when I look down, it's covered in blood from the hole now gaping open at the end of his cock. It almost looks like it's split in two. I close my eyes and breathe in…and out.

"He can't hurt us anymore," I whisper to the boy hiding in my head. He's not as talkative as he usually is when we're this close to Jake, he's more at ease. Opening my eyes, Lev's hand grabs my neck, knowing that I need anchoring, and I pull the scalpel away, letting it fall from my hands. It's enough. It's over.

"Finish it. Please," I say with a timid voice.

Lev picks up his drill from the floor.

Moving to stand behind Lev, I put my arms around his waist, resting my chin on his shoulder, taking in his smell. It gives me the strength and comfort I need right now.

"Tell me, tell me you want me," I murmur at the shell of his ear.

284

Under my fingertips, goosebumps cover his skin as I rub my palms up and down his hard stomach. He feels so good, I will remember this exact second for the rest of my life as I say fuck you to my past and welcome my future.

He aims the drill at Jake's temple. "I would kill for you, doe."

The sound of the drill whirrs with the screams of my tormentor and the shattering of bone. I've found peace.

CHAPTER 35
LEV

The silence in the room is deafening. Aaron is still clinging to my back as we stare at the body hanging from my ceiling, brain and splintered bone covering the end of my drill, blood and gunk pouring from the large hole in Jake's head.

Witnessing Aaron's reaction to Jake cleared up a lot of questions I had. It certainly explains Aaron's erratic behavior changes. He folded in on himself.

To say I didn't like it is an understatement. I have accepted that this thing between us won't be going away any time soon. He is part of my blood now and the thought of anyone touching him makes me want to tear someone's throat out and lock Aaron in my room for my access only.

This is not how I expected this to go, though. I thought we would spend hours down here, ripping Jake apart piece by piece, but the more the fucker opened his mouth, the less right it began to feel.

Jake's been given enough of everyone's time and attention. I'll bet that seeing Aaron with me, so strong and

287

committed, was the worst torture for Jake. He loved control, loved affecting Aaron in any way possible, as long as he had a reaction.

The mood shifts. I expected a crying and emotional Aaron. Not him rubbing his hard dick on me and licking the back of my neck. He is a horny little shit.

Aaron moves his hands, and grips my ass in a tight hold, making my dick perk up. "Can we go now, Lev? You've teased me enough. I want to eat your ass."

He starts to massage my cheeks and the kisses on my neck make me shiver.

"You are the only person who thinks torturing people is foreplay, doe. But I'm down." I drop the drill onto the floor, and we leave without bothering to look back at the carnage in our wake. It's finally fucking done and I haven't felt this much like myself since all this Santini shit started.

Leaving the pen, I see Jules, who is talking quietly to Kai. I didn't like his little display earlier, trying to question me, especially in front of others. I will not let it fly.

"You can start clean up, we are done for the day. But Jules, tomorrow we are going to talk about your little outburst earlier," I say.

"I figured," he says, resigned to what he knew would happen. Kai looks like he wants to say something, but he must see something on my face that warns him to keep his mouth shut.

"Let's get this shit washed off," I say to Aaron as we walk through the house to my room. The house is very still, like some curse has been lifted and given us life again. Dima is nowhere to be seen, no doubt fucking his husband. Blood to him is like viagra.

We remain quiet as we wash down in the steamy shower, scrubbing off the blood and sweat. Aaron watches the carnage wash down the drain. He looks up at me under those long lashes, his big brown eyes dilated, nothing but sex is written in his expression. "I want my reward now."

"Reward? Why, did you do something?" I smirk.

I get a scowl in return. He's like a feral kitten when he looks like that, as if he is about to use his claws to scratch the shit out of me.

"Yes. I got you Jake and the boys. Now I want to eat your ass."

"You didn't get me Jake and the boys, you got kidnapped and I found you. That's totally different."

"Hands on the fucking wall, Lev, before I stab you."

"Kinky fucker," I say as I turn around and put my hands against the shower tiles and part my legs. I've never done foreplay, always eager to get to the act. I expect Aaron to take his time, but no. With unnerving speed, I feel his thick tongue push forward into my hole while he holds my cheeks apart.

"Holy shit." My breath hitches. I've never played with my ass or had it touched like this by anyone. I certainly won't say no to this, but he better not get any ideas. I am never going to be a bottom, but I don't think I need to worry. Judging from the hot as fuck sex we have, Aaron loves the attention from getting pounded. He is a slut for it.

My dick is at full mast and I immediately grab it, rubbing hard from shaft to tip at a speedy pace. His tongue pushes in and out of me in fast stabs. I can feel him lick the walls inside me and it won't take me long to cum.

He licks and sucks around the puckered entrance, teasing me, before plowing back in.

"Fuck, Lev, you taste amazing," he groans into me, and then gets back to work.

My balls begin to tighten, and he reaches between my legs, holding them in a firm grip that sends me gloriously over the edge.

"Oh shit, oh shit…hnngh." Long spurts of cum coat the shower wall as I allow the orgasm to wash over me in ripples. Aaron lets out a long moan behind me and I feel his warm release on my calves.

"We are so doing that again." He sighs as he stands under the shower head with me as we wash off our cum. I lean in and kiss him long and deep. He sags towards me as I hold him. "Give me twenty, and then I wanna ride that cock, baby," he purrs.

I pull back. "Don't call me baby," I say. Not happening.

"Why?" he asks, barely containing his laughter.

"Because I don't do pet names, it's fucking cheesy." I think I'm pouting. I *don't* do pet names.

"But you call me, doe. That's a pet name."

Ok, he has me there.

"I'll only do it when we are like this," he croons.

It's still a no.

"Don't do it at all, Aaron," I warn.

He grabs my dick. "Shall I call you monster cock instead?" he snarks.

I give him a flat look. I think the more I protest, the more he will do it, so I choose to be mature and ignore him.

He cackles behind me as I leave the bathroom, little shit. It's late afternoon now and I'm starving.

"Want some food?" I ask.

Aaron has collapsed on my bed, wearing nothing but a towel around his waist. Water droplets run through the lines of his defined abs and his skin glistens. He's my addiction and I'm desperate to bury myself in him. But if I don't eat soon, I'll pass out.

"Hmm, I'm tired." He exhales, eyes closed.

"You want me to bring you something? You gotta eat, Aaron."

He opens one eye. "You looking after me, Lev?" he teases.

"No, just want you fueled for when I fuck you later," I protest. He hasn't eaten since yesterday. Not that I care. But I do. Fuck! I'm turning into a caring asshole.

"Yeah, okay, I'm not really in the mood for company right now so if it's okay with you, I'd prefer to eat in here."

I nod as I pull on some jeans and a T-shirt. "Don't fall asleep." I point at him in warning. "You eat then you can sleep."

"Yes, sir." He mock salutes.

"Don't be a smartass," I say as I leave the room and head off to find some food. My stomach growls as loud as thunder at the smells that hit me when I approach the foyer. Following the deliciousness, I walk into the kitchen to see Kai...yes Kai, in an apron, dishing up what looks like ... lasagna?

"What the fuck you doing?" I ask. This is weird. A guard who kills, cooking in an apron.

"Flying a plane, what the fuck does it look like he's doing, brother?" Dima says as he walks in behind me. How someone as large as him can move so stealthily I have no idea.

"Look, I know I fucked up, Lev, but it's the first and last time. I swear. This is just to make peace," Kai says.

"It better be 'cos if anything happens to Aaron again, I will chop you into little pieces," I say.

"Okay," he says.

I grunt. "I'll take a couple of plates to eat in my room."

"Is he okay?" Dima asks as I wait for Kai to plate up our meals. It looks so good, not that I'll tell him.

"Yeah, he's fine, just tired and doesn't want company," I say.

Dima looks at me carefully. I know he is dying to ask questions, but I'm not doing it. What goes on between Aaron and me is private. Jules walks in, breaking the tension.

"You left quite a mess down there, Lev." He chuckles.

"Nothing less than they deserved," I say, eager to get back to my room away from these busybodies.

"Damn straight," Dima agrees. "I've informed Carlos and sent pictures of the bodies so we are all even now. Hopefully things can go back to normal."

"Make sure Simon spreads the word to the other crews, they need to learn from this," I remind Dima.

He nods. "Already done. Now, can we stop talking about work? My stomach is about to shrivel up and die if I don't get some food in me."

I grab my two plates and head back to my room. Aaron better be awake, otherwise I will beat his sexy ass until he can't sit. I walk to where he is sitting on the corner chair, he has put on a pair of shorts and is looking through his phone.

I hand him a plate. "Who cooked this?" he asks before piling a forkful of steaming lasagna into his mouth.

"Kai. It's an apology, I think."

"It wasn't his fault, Lev," he says.

I level him with a stern look. "Yes it was and leave the dealing of my men to me, Aaron. I'm not Dima who can be swayed by sex."

"Is that what I'm doing?" He snorts.

"I don't know what you're doing, but I'm telling you it won't be like that. Just because we are together doesn't mean you get a soft hand with me. When it comes to our work, I make the decisions."

"You're so hot when you're angry," he hums at me.

"I'm not angry, I'm stating facts. For fuck sake Aaron, are you turned on?"

He's just moved his hand onto his now bulging crotch.

"And people think I'm the crazy one," I mutter, stuffing my face with more food.

"You are and I'm your plus one crazy addition." He smiles before taking another mouthful. I roll my eyes and continue to eat. Damn, Kai knows how to cook. Considering what a shit guard he is, maybe we should make him house chef. Before long, we put the empty plates onto the coffee table in front of us.

"Will you be able to take me back today, or should I call a ride?" he says.

It takes a second to register what he is saying. "Take you where?"

His confused brows scrunch together. "Back to my apartment. I'll need to get it sorted before I leave."

"What the fuck do you mean leave?" I bellow, unable to hold in the panic. It comes out as aggression instead. Of course, he isn't bothered by this.

"Well, I'm gonna have to find somewhere else to live, Lev. I can't stay in that apartment. Apart from the obvious, I couldn't afford to live there on my own anyway. Why are you so mad?"

I sag a little in relief. He means finding a new apartment, not leaving here, not leaving me. *Oh fuck off, pussy.*

My meaning must register with Aaron. "Oh, you

thought I meant leaving Grinston. Do you not listen to anything I say? I told you earlier, you are not getting rid of me. I'm here to stay whether you like it or not." He grins and moves over to me, climbing onto my lap. I'm unable to resist grabbing his juicy ass, kneading the perfect mounds in my hands. The perfect stress relief.

"You can stay here," I say without thinking. Why the fuck did I say that? Are feelings contagious?

His eyes are as wide as saucers. "You want me to move in here, with you and your brother?" he asks.

"Why not? Be easier access, and then I can fuck you when I want."

"Huh. I suppose I could move in."

"I wasn't asking, doe." I start sucking on his neck, adding extra bruises to the ones I left yesterday, his skin looks perfect with my marks. Owned by Lev Kozlov. May have to get that tattooed on his neck so it's clear to others.

"Okay," he says, as easy as that. "But I do need to go get my stuff. I can't keep wearing the same pants, plus I need to clear out the guys' stuff."

"You ain't touching shit. I'll get the boys to deal with that, burn it if we have to. Just get your own stuff," I say.

"I need to find a job too," he murmurs.

"Are you trying to piss me off?"

He barks out a laugh. "Why the fuck would me working piss you off, Lev? I told you that I wanted out of the crew."

"You will work with me, and for me," I confirm, ideas running through my head, mainly of him sucking me off under my desk.

"Doing what exactly, dancing at the club?" he sasses, and I spank him hard on the ass. "Ouch, I was kidding."

"Watch the attitude, doe," I warn and his eyes glaze

over, so needy. "You can work as an enforcer alongside me and help out at the clubs when needed. You can also be my cockwarmer."

"Cockwarmer? Are you asking me to be your on-call whore?" I get the impression he wouldn't mind that job.

"I'm not asking, I'm telling you that you will work alongside us and we will find you a place, but you won't be working in the clubs behind the bar or waiting. I don't care that Seb does it. I won't have anyone look at you or touch you."

"Fuck, Lev, I love it when you talk to me like that." He rolls his hips into my lap.

"You'll be happy here then. I don't plan on changing."

"I wouldn't want you to." He presses a kiss on my lips that has me pushing my groin up into his, holding onto that tight ass while I rut against that gorgeous body.

Mine. He is all mine.

CHAPTER 36
AARON

As much as I wanted to stay in bed with Lev, I need to get my stuff and get this part over with. I didn't want to prolong going back to the apartment, I just want this day to be full of closure, so I can shut that door forever. It's the only way I know I can move forward.

Lev walks me into the apartment, hand gripping my neck, which he seems to prefer over holding hands, and I actually prefer it too. I like him guiding me and showing ownership. His touch gives me clarity of mind, and I'm less chaotic.

"Don't look at anything, just lead us to your room," he says.

Lev encourages me to move toward the hallway to my room. A moment of sadness washes over me when I see Shay's bedroom door. I really wish it would have turned out different for him, and I get why he chose his sister over me. We found out that Jake was threatening to expose her and her child's whereabouts to her abusive ex who also wanted custody of the child. He used it as a way to keep Shay around.

Simon found her and told her what had happened, giving her some money to move on along with a subtle threat to keep her mouth shut. I can sympathize, but I can't forgive him for allowing Jake to do what he did that day. Clearly, he was willing to die for it.

Cutting off the sad trail of thoughts, I move to my door, which is partially open. It looks like a tornado stormed through here. There is blood on the carpet, which I know is mine from when I was hit on the head. I'm not sure how I thought I would feel, but standing here now, I don't feel anything. This place feels like it belongs to a stranger. It's weird. It's like I have no memory of my life in these walls. I'm not sure if my coping mechanism has shut off that part of my life because of the trauma, or if I have truly been cleansed of all feelings of that time, but I'm indifferent to it now. I just want to get back to Lev's place, my place of comfort and safety.

"Get your stuff and I'll wait in the living room," he says and walks off. The cigar smoke wafts into my room, reminding me of sex, leather and old library books. A smell I associate with Lev. He wanted a quick smoke. I think the idea of me freaking out stresses Lev out. He doesn't know how to respond in those situations and I don't need him to. I love how we are together. It's real and that's all that matters.

I grab my clothes, underwear and a few other items, and put them in the extra duffle that was in my closet. Quickly, I collect my items from the bathroom and try not to linger too long in any one area.

When I return to Lev, he is standing facing the apartment window that looks out onto the street below, inhaling his cigar. He resembles the king that I'll always believe he is. He looks so damn majestic standing there like nothing can touch him. He must sense my approach. He turns to face me.

"You done?" he asks on an exhale. The smoke trails into the air. Looks so sexy.

I lift my bag. "Yeah, ready to go."

He stubs out the cigar on the window and grabs the back of my neck, leading me out of this place for the last time.

We head home together.

CHAPTER 37
LEV

T he further we get into winter, the darker the nights are getting, so as we drive through the streets, the sun has started to set. It's been a long-ass day. My phone starts to ring on my bluetooth and Camila's name flashes on the dash screen. Shit. Camila is a Colombian goddess who I met a few years back. She manages a famous Latino singer and we hook-up whenever she is in town, which only tends to be a handful of times a year.

"Who is Camila?" Aaron asks curiously.

"Just an old hook-up," I say. I don't need to hide it and also don't plan on seeing her again, so I let the call go to voicemail. Until it starts ringing again. Fucking hell. I can see stabby Aaron start to manifest next to me. He looks like he is sucking on a lemon right now, a telltale sign that he's jealous.

"Well, she clearly is a fan of your cock. I thought you didn't do repeats? You not gonna answer?" he asks and I don't miss the bitchiness in his tone.

"She lives overseas so it doesn't count. I'll call her later and explain," I say, hoping that's the end of this conversation.

"No, do it now," he demands. The phone continues to ring. Aaron has now officially come to the end of his tolerance. "Answer it, or I'll fucking do it for you, Lev. End it with her. *Now*."

I am going to have to rectify that attitude later.

"Hey," I say, answering the call. Her sultry voice fills the car. It's full on sex and it's clear what she is after. I smile to myself. I find it amusing as Aaron starts to lose his shit. I'm grateful she is on the phone after his last performance when he got into his jealousy and nearly slit that guy's throat.

"Hola bebé. I'm in town for two nights, want to meet up?" she purrs into the phone. Camila is sexy as hell, but I wanna keep my dick.

Before I get to answer, the fireball next to me explodes. "Bebé? Fucking bebé! I thought you didn't do pet names?" he admonishes me.

Taking my eyes off the road, I look at him, and I think he may draw blood with the burning hate he throws my way. I don't answer, just shrug. I don't think it's a big deal.

"Err, who is this?" she asks, sounding a little annoyed. That's not good.

"I'm Aaron, Lev's boyfriend and you ain't fucking touching him again unless you want to feel my knife in your throat. You get me, *bebé*?" He sounds so bitchy and I want to laugh, but I'm more unnerved by the boyfriend comment.

"Boyfriend? I'm not your boyfriend," I say with distaste in my words, forgetting Camila is on the phone.

"We live together and we're exclusively fucking, what else should I call it? Lifelong companionship?" His sarcasm game is strong today. Murder obviously agrees with him.

"Hello? Lev, have I interrupted something?" she asks and just as I start to talk, Aaron grabs my dick over my jeans, where he has his switchblade pointing at the tip of my cock.

Hint taken, doe. I shake my head. This is ridiculous, but also does wonders for my ego.

"Yes, I am with Aaron. I was going to call later to tell you our little arrangement has come to an end now, Camila. Sorry. It was fun though." I know I sound awkward, but we were hardly in a committed relationship.

"Oh, well that's a shame." She sighs into the phone, disappointment lacing her words. But I don't care. It was only a regular hook-up. She knew the deal.

"Adios, *bebé*," Aaron says in a high-pitched mocking tone before ending the call.

"Bebé my ass," he mutters beside me as I pull into our driveway.

"Can you let go of my dick now?" I ask and he removes his hand and knife, slipping it back into his pocket.

"Stop sulking. I fucked others before you. It's over now, you made sure of it," I say. It's not worth being bothered about. He will be bumping into plenty of other ex-lovers around town, so he should get used to it. I don't think now would be a wise time to bring that up though.

"Fine, but if I want to call you baby from now on, I will." He gets out of the car and slams the door, which spikes my temper. What the hell have I gotten myself into with him?

"Of course you will," I mutter under my breath to follow him inside. Time for a lesson, little monster.

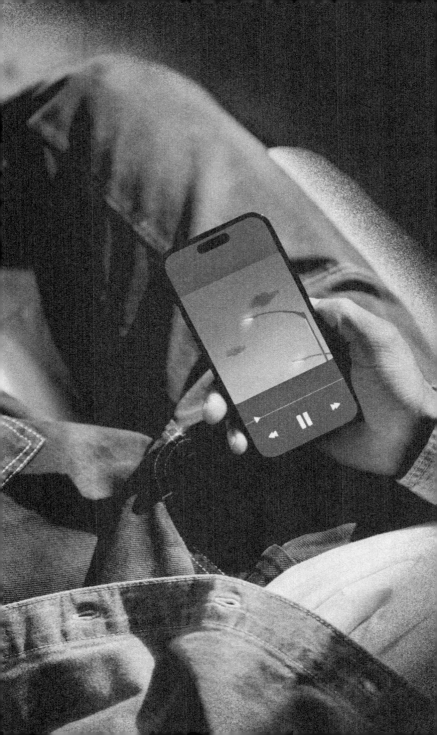

CHAPTER 38
AARON

I am filled with jealousy, and I want to punch something, preferably that stuck up bitch with her sexy exotic accent. And he allowed her to call him baby!

Storming down to the bedroom, I can't help my theatrical behavior. This is the most fucked up day ever. I have had traumatic breakdowns, murdered and tortured my stepbrother, eaten Lev's ass, and gotten jealous to the point of violence. And it's not even nine pm yet. My head hurts.

Entering the bedroom, I'm about to collapse on the bed in a dramatic fashion when I hear thundering footsteps approaching rapidly behind me.

I turn just in time for Lev to slam the door and grab me by the throat, pushing his face into mine. His green eyes are vivid, he looks satanic like this with his hawk-shaped eyes making his squint more intimidating. I don't care though. As I've said, I want his eyes on me and that's why I'm being a jealous bitch. If I could kill off all his past partners, I would.

"You think that little attitude in the car is gonna fly with me, doe? You think you can threaten me?" His voice sounds like gravel on the road, smoky from the cigars mixed with his perfect fucking scent.

"Yes, you're mine, Lev," I say. Fucking duh.

He forces me down to my knees by holding tight on my throat in one hand and pulling the hair on the back of my head with the other.

"And you are mine, doe. But you need to remember who's the boss. Now open that bratty fucking mouth." I moan as he pulls his jeans down, no underwear. Shit. This isn't a punishment like he seems to think it is. But, I speak too soon. He slaps my face, which forces me to look up. "Oh and you don't get to cum."

"Fucker," I complain before swallowing him whole.

He groans in delight and the thickness of his length fills my mouth beyond comfort, that damn piercing hitting the back of my throat.

I pull his dick away and gently nibble and suck around the barbell. I lock my gaze with his. He looks stunning, panting, the look of pure need on his face.

I tease the barbell with my tongue, making him hiss, punching his hips forward before I engulf his length. I bob up and down, letting my saliva drip freely over his cock, slurping, tasting, and licking this magnificent piece of meat. I rub my hands up his thighs, loving the feel of his soft hairs. Lev is pure man, pure sin, and pure evil. I am willing to live in hell for eternity to have him everyday.

I continue to suck him deep like a pro, my jaw is aching and tears are streaming down my face. This feeling is magic ... sucking Lev. I always feel like I'm levitating above him. The overwhelming need for him to fill me somewhere takes over my soul. As weird as I know it sounds, I feel the doors in my head start to fully close. Lev starts to stutter his movements above me, close to cumming.

"I'm so close, fuck I'm gonna cum."

I then feel a lock turn on in my brain.

Hot cum spurts in my mouth. Like the flick of a switch, it feels like he is gone. That boy is gone, he is safe and locked away, protected, and all that is left is…me. Crazy, weird, and authentic me.

Holy shit, I can't believe he is gone.

"Shit, Aaron. Damn, you know how to milk a cock." He groans softly, stroking my hair.

Not to let him have the last word, I remove my switchblade from my back pocket and aim it at the base of his now softening cock. He looks down but doesn't seem surprised. "I know you are the boss, and I will do anything for you, Lev, but I promise you this. Touch another, or let them touch you, and this gorgeous dick will feel my blade," I warn.

Lev sniggers at me and pulls my head back by my hair. "I think it's time for bed, little psycho."

And he lets me go. He removes his shirt leaving him fully nude as he gets into bed. I put my knife away, happy that my point has been made, and I join him wearing nothing. Perfect for waking him with the morning dick riding I have planned.

"Night, baby," I say to him as sweetly as possible.

He covers his face with his arm. "Fuck off, doe," he says with an irritated sigh before we drift off.

CHAPTER 39
LEV

Soft moans make me stir.

I'm in between sleep and being awake, but I become aware of a hot sensation around my cock, wet and tight. I then hear another moan, which feels like it came from me. Confusion stirs me awake, and before I open my eyes, I feel a weight on me and my dick. It triggers my fight or flight—no surprise, I'm fight—and I sit upright, ready to attack. As I am about to lash out, my eyes open and I realize it's Aaron on top of me, his creepy grin present on his pretty face. A rocking motion on my cock makes my eyes roll to the back of my head as I flop back down onto my pillow. I grab his hips and watch as he fucks himself on me.

"How long have you been riding my dick?" I ask, gasping at the pressure his ass is creating around my shaft as he clenches. He rubs and tweaks his nipples, happily groaning softly as he grinds and grinds on me.

"Not long, only a couple of minutes," he pants.

"Fuck, yes, you feel so damn good," I say, rubbing my palms up and down his chest making him whine. He leans back, making my dick go deeper. "Oh fuck yeah, ride my dick."

His tight hole sucks me in, refusing to let me go.

He rests his hands on my knees and starts bouncing up and down. I admire the lines and muscles of his gorgeous body that are on full display for me. His hard cock bounces against his belly as he moves, alternating from bouncing to grinding. The sound of the lube squelching is so fucking dirty, he must have prepped himself well before this. He is fucking me like a champ. Shit, I'm gonna cum already.

"Fuck, Lev, you feel so big. Feels so good, I want you to fill me, make me leak all day, baby," he says.

"Aaron, don't call me that," I say, grinding my teeth.

"Would you prefer bebé?" he says, slamming down on me in a savage move. I grab his throat and throw him onto his back.

"Gonna destroy you now," I say, and he grins. The little psycho loves this shit. I start to thrust in and out of him in an almost violent rhythm, the noises he makes spur me on as it feels so fucking amazing, and he feels so goddamn tight. Always willing to please me.

I grip onto his hard as granite cock which pulses in my hand. He cries out. After only two tugs he cums and his orgasm seems to go on forever as it explodes all over his chest and stomach. Aftershocks make his body quiver as I continue to hit his sweet spot.

"Ready to be filled up?" I ask, feeling the tingle in my balls intensify.

"Fuck yes, give it to me."

I roar out my orgasm, completely giving over to it, and my ass clenches as I unload inside him. It's so intense that little white specks of light flash in my vision. I have never unloaded this much cum. He will definitely be dripping with me today, my smell clinging to him. I feel huge satisfaction at the idea of others smelling me on him, knowing he is full of me. My doe-eyed monster.

Collapsing over him, I raise myself up, my elbows on either side of his head. I lean down and kiss those pouty lips. He tastes delicious everywhere I touch, tasting of temptation and sin. It's making me an addict. Who am I kidding? I am already addicted. After a long and slow kiss that helps bring us back down to real life, Aaron chooses to try and kill me.

"I think I love you," he says.

I frown and I'm not sure why. Is it because he said it, or is it because he doesn't sound sure? He mentioned he was falling for me before, but this time it feels more "official". Thinking it and feeling it are two very different things.

"You think?" I ask. Surprised there isn't a Lev-shaped hole in the door.

"Well, I want to be around you all the time, I want your attention all the time, and I'm murderous at the thought of you being with anyone else, so that's love, right?" he asks.

"Fuck if I know, doe," I say.

He smiles softly, it's so pure and real. He has so many expressions that I can decipher now. This one feels like it's only for me, and shit, that makes my heart skip a beat.

"Yeah, it's love. I do love you," he says like the decision has been made.

I put my head into his neck, breathing him in. Do I have to say it back? I know how I feel about him but it sounds more aggressive than what I would think love would mean.

"Well...do you love me?" he asks but he doesn't seem upset.

I raise my head and let my eyes roam over his hopeful face.

"I know I want you here every night in my bed, I know I'd burn the world down if anyone touched you, I know I will never let you leave ... not sure if that's love though," I say.

He watches me, silently, and nods.

"Well, I love you, Lev," he says with more conviction.

I smile. It feels nice hearing him say that, although I don't want him to say it outside this room. I have my reputation to uphold.

Clasping his face in my hands, I say what I feel, knowing that this is my version of love and I will never feel for another. "And I would kill for you, doe."

He beams beneath me, a slight sheen to his eyes. "You fucking romantic, you. Promise to kill for me forever?" he says.

"I'd kill for you after death, Aaron, and I will always find you, even then," I say.

Am I perfect? Fuck no, but neither is Aaron. We both have our reasons for being as we are, but I make no apologies for it. The way I feel for him is beyond lovey emotions, it's dangerous and toxic. But we are made for each other, and nothing will tear us apart. I fucking dare anyone to try.

EPILOGUE

4 MONTHS LATER

"Your new piercing looks good," Seb says to me from across the table. I decided to get my other eyebrow pierced, the one that hasn't been ripped. It was like my fuck you to Jake in hell. Fortunately, the small scar on my damaged brow is barely visible. Luckily, my eyebrow has grown back enough to cover it, so I don't have to see the reminder everyday.

"Yeah, I like it." I smile as I take a sip of my whiskey sour. Seb started making them for me when I moved in and it's my new favorite drink. Beers don't quite cut it anymore.

It feels so good to be out of the house, relaxing with a few drinks. Seb has a night off tonight so we decided to enjoy ourselves at Starlight, because god forbid we went somewhere else. The brothers nearly lost their shit when we mentioned it. I don't mind though. It's nice to kick back and enjoy the show instead of only glimpses as we work. Well, Seb still works at the bar. Lev is not keen on me

313

doing that, so I tend to help out with office stuff and basically follow Lev around. It would drive others mad being so attached at the hip with their significant other, but we're happy, and we don't care what others think.

Seb and I are sitting back in the booth that is reserved at Starlight for Dima and Lev, enjoying a full cabaret show tonight. Not my kind of thing, but it's fun to experience a free life, to be young and smile for a change. To embrace who I am, no hiding, no fear, and to have family on my side. Because that's what the Kozlovs are to me now, the family I always wanted. I would rather cut my arm off than betray them.

Things are a lot better for me too. Mentally I am coming to terms with who I am, and I accept my quirks, psycho voices and all. I've had a couple of nightmares where Jake tries to pry back into my brain, but as soon as I wake and see Lev next to me, it calms me straight away. As time goes on, hopefully the nightmares will stop altogether. There was bound to be damage left from what he did to me, but Lev and his family have glued me back together. There are still cracks, but those cracks fill more everyday.

Seb has become a good friend since I moved into the Kozlov mansion. He's like the brother I always wanted and it's nice to have someone who understands the brothers and what it can be like to be their obsessions. Seb struggles more than I do. More often than not I'll do something to prod Lev into going full deranged on my ass.

As Seb and I are enjoying a general chit-chat, movement casts a shadow over the little lamp on our table. I assume it's the brothers but when I look up it's two burly guys. I can tell straight away they are gonna be a problem, especially with how the blond is leering at me. His redhead friend tries to sit next to Seb.

"What the fuck do you think you're doing?" Seb challenges as creepy red moves into the booth next to him.

"What? Don't want the company? I heard you two like men and you're hot. Thought you'd be up for a good time," redhead says.

Ick.

"Fuck off, man. We ain't interested," I snap.

But that doesn't seem to do anything but encourage them. I move to grab my switchblade in my pocket, which Seb sees and subtly shakes his head and nods, cocking his head to the side. I follow where he's pointing to. Lev and Dima are storming over here. Oh shit, this will be fun. I'm already starting to get hard, watching the look of murder that's written across Lev's stern face. I'm so damn lucky. He's so fucking hot. I want him to fuck me right here in front of everyone.

Arriving at the booth, Dima strikes first, grabbing the head of red hair from beside Seb, pulling the big guy out of the booth and onto the floor. He kicks him in the stomach. Jules storms over with Simon and Kai. Jules helps grab the redhead.

"Do you have a death wish, touching my man, fuckhead?" Dima shouts at the redhead on the floor.

Meanwhile, Lev stealthily moves over and punches the blond who is still standing above me. He falls back into the wall next to the booth. Lev holds the guy's head low and knees him in the face, making him fall flat to the ground. Fuck yes!

"Do you know who we are?" Dima asks the redhead who is shooting daggers at Dima. Oh boy, I don't think he does.

"I don't give a shit who you are," he says.

Lev and Dima laugh, and it sounds like the belly of evil as it rumbles from their mouths.

"Well, let us introduce ourselves. I am Lev Kozlov, and this is my brother Dima. These are our guys, does that help?" Lev snarls. He sounds like a lion. I want him to mate me.

The redhead's face pales. Ah, so he does know who they are.

"Oh shit. I thought you owned the strip joint, not this place," he says, floundering, but it's too late.

"Well, now you know, and I think you need to be taught a lesson in not touching other people's things without permission," Lev says, the excitement written all over his face.

"Wait!" the blond shouts, holding onto what looks like a broken nose. "It's not like we knew. We ain't from round here," he pleads.

"Oh shucks, but you will learn for the future. Boys, take them out back, we will be there in a minute," Lev orders, his eyes now focused on me.

I rub my cock under the table. I can't help it. I can already see the preview in my head. Lev glances down to my lap with an appreciative smile on his face. He leans over the table. "Wanna watch me play, doe?" he asks.

That voice. Goddamn.

"Fuck yeah, then I want you to fuck me after," I demand.

"Aaron, seriously? I didn't need to know that," Seb bemoans beside me. I forgot he was there.

"Stop being a prude, Seb," Lev teases and grabs my neck. I love the way he holds me.

"You coming, Seb?" I ask

"To the violence orgy? No thanks, I'm good. I'll wait here for D," he says and continues to sip on his drink.

Dima bends down to whisper something to him before kissing him. We walk out, all eyes on our movements, but nobody says anything.

"Time to play," Lev whispers in my ear.

"Love you, baby," I say, just to piss him off. He growls and grabs my ass.

"I'd kill for you, you little shit," he says.

I cuddle up in his arms, which is a new thing, and bask in the attention and safety I feel with him here.

That feeling of utter contentment. That feeling of home.

AFTERWORD

I am so sad Lev and Aaron's journey has finished as I could've continued their story forever. This book was a definite labor of love, especially when it came to Aaron. He was a challenge to write but I think he was the perfect person for Lev. His mixture of crazy and vulnerable really balanced Lev and gave him more focus. Certainly kept Lev on his toes.

Lev is such a great character, I love his non-empathetic attitude to life. His inability to say "I love you" I think made him more endearing. It showed the broken sides to him that Aaron somehow filled, but on terms that made Lev feel comfortable himself.

I always want to stay true to the darkness in dark romances as its nice to just keep the rawness without softening it into a mushy romance. The Kozlov men are huge red flags, but they are devoted to family and their men, and I hope that comes across that this screwed up family are never going to conform to the normal social standards.

WHAT'S NEXT

At some point I may come back to the Kozlov brothers, but to do a spin-off as I feel Jules and Kai may need a story and also Simon, but that will be something for the future as I am currently in the middle of two books that I hope to release early next year.

They are both MM and I am unsure which will come out first as I keep switching between them. One is the dark stalker book that I have mentioned before, and the other is another dark romance, but with a different vibe when it comes to the 'dark'. Keep an eye out in my newsletter or Instagram for updates on those as I do have titles and blurbs already done.

ACKNOWLEDGMENTS

This has been an interesting journey so far, highs and lows, haters and fans, but there are a few people who have really kept me going and motivated me.

The person at the top of that list is Christy. Thank you for being my mentor and sanity whilst writing this story. Aaron caused a lot of headaches but you helped me through, and again I could not have done this without you. You are my soul sister and one of the best people I know. Thank you for taking the time to edit this labor of love. I appreciate you more than you know.

A huge thank you to my BETAs, Stacy, Julia, Amy, Jordan and Sadie. You are the best and I am beyond grateful for your input and time reading over this story.

Jordan at Euphoric Promotions, thank you for all the amazing edits you have made for me and being so freakin amazing.

Hannah at HC Graphics, I love the cover so much and I am astounded how quickly you turned it around and helped me.

Ayanna – monstrous_brutes. You are one of the kindest people ever. Your messages and support really pushed me through when writing this. I always look forward to our chats about all things horror and torture! LOL. You are a gem and thank you for being there for me.

Have to give a shoutout to my girls, Dee, Stefka, Lola, Tina and Gena.

To all my ARC readers, thank you for taking the time to read and review. You are the best group and I am thankful to you all.

To everyone who has cheerleaded and supported me, made edits or shared promos, it hasn't gone unnoticed and I hope you will continue to stick around for more depravity!

ALSO BY

If you want to read about Dima & Seb, Tied To You is available on Amazon Now!

Tied To You Link:http://amzn.to/3PyBS85

For updates sign up here:

Newsletter:https://tr.ee/Fj-zoIuG7v

ABOUT THE AUTHOR

Syn lives in the UK countryside and is a lover of all things dark in books, movies and music. She also has a book addiction and is slowly running out of places to store them in her home, but they make her happy.

She is sarcastic, has dark humor, cannot read anything without spice, and would not survive without coffee!!

Find me on Amazon!

instagram.com/syn_blackrose_author

goodreads.com/Syn_Blackrose